FINDING YOUR FEET

Cass Lennox

RIPTIDE PUBLISHING

Riptide Publishing
PO Box 1537
Burnsville, NC 28714
www.riptidepublishing.com

Finding Your Feet

Cover art: L.C. Chase, lcchase.com/design.htm
Editor: Chris Muldoon
Layout: L.C. Chase, lcchase.com/design.htm

ISBN: 978-1-62649-488-6

First edition
January, 2017

Also available in ebook:
ISBN: 978-1-62649-487-9

FINDING YOUR FEET

Cass Lennox

RIPTIDE
PUBLISHING

For Woodcrow, who knew first.

TABLE OF CONTENTS

CHAPTER ONE

This was potentially the most stupid thing Evie had ever done. She looked at the status board above the baggage carousel and sighed. *Delayed.* Of course. She was overcaffeinated, underslept, in a city very far from home, and somewhat uncertain about her accommodation arrangements, so of course the airline was sending her luggage the long route to the carousel. One more thing between her and a bed.

She stretched her arms out to ease the stiffness from the flight and caught a whiff of ten hours' sweat and three mugs of airline tea. Delightful. So she could add a shower to the list of things between her and rest. Evie closed her eyes. *I must be mad. How did I end up here?*

A whim. That was how she had ended up in a Canadian airport at nine o'clock in the morning instead of looking for work at home in rain-ridden Blighty. A whim suggested by Sarah, sure, but Evie had made the decision to indulge it.

Thing was, she'd forgotten she didn't *do* whims. When she did, she planned. She liked plans. She'd had a great plan, actually. One that had started out wonderfully about two months ago: an acceptance into the master's course she wanted at the University of Toronto. Superb. The logical next steps had been quitting her job in a few months' time, allowing for the notice period and the couple of weeks necessary to pack her things, cancel her lease, and say good-bye to her friends, family, and country. *Then* she'd start her degree in Canada, arrange a few internships, perhaps do the touristy stuff, and see what the new qualification would bring. That had been The Plan.

But then The Plan had gone to shit. Her company had gone into receivership and kicked everyone to the curb. Evie had found herself facing four months of summer in York waiting for the settlement payout because she couldn't formally move to Toronto while her student visa was still processing. Her parents had called her every other day asking for updates. Her brother, Richard, had teased her about being an unemployed bum. Her options, she'd been told, were hanging around at home living off her savings, travelling for a while (on those savings), or working a scummy retail job to *build up* her savings.

Or moving back in with her mother and stepfather for the summer and not touching her savings. Not even an option.

So here she was. Only for two weeks, because of visa issues, but at least she was out of York and away from her family's questions and fuss. Two whole weeks of getting away from life. Two whole weeks to see if Toronto was all she hoped it would be.

Evie scowled at the empty carousel. Sarah would be waiting for a while. *If* she was waiting.

It felt weird calling her *Sarah*. They were Tumblr friends, and Evie knew her better as her username, *gaybeard-the-great*, or simply *Gaybeard*. Despite having emailed each other for a few years now, it was dawning on Evie that while she knew Sarah's favourite food, and the actors she'd bang if she was at all interested in doing so, and her personal journey to queerdom, Evie didn't know that much real-life stuff about Sarah. She did something vague for a law firm, lived with Bailey, her long-term queerplatonic artist partner, was originally from some "asshole hick town in the asshole hick wild," liked bad movies, and her last name was Delaney.

Sarah had also been super supportive; she'd gushed her sympathies about the job and suggested Evie come over early for Pride, because Toronto did Pride amazingly well and they could finally meet in person and Evie could totally stay with Sarah, who'd introduce her to the city. Yes, all very well and good, but now that Evie was thinking about it, agreeing to stay with someone from the internet whom she didn't know *that* much about was pretty dumb.

Oh God, this *was* a mistake.

Evie felt light-headed. She sank down on her heels and hugged her backpack tightly. Working scummy retail for a summer suddenly looked quite sensible, despite the teasing she'd have received from Rich. Save a bit more money before she moved to Canada properly, keep herself busy, do the adult and responsible thing. She was twenty-six for Christ's sake. Why hadn't she done that? What was she doing? How was this a good idea? What the *hell* had she been thinking? How was she sitting on an airport floor in bloody Toronto at the age of twenty-six without a job or a plan or her luggage or a definite place to stay?

She needed a cup of fucking tea.

The carousel alarm sounded. The belt started moving. Bags emerged.

Evie stood.

Right. She could do this. New plan: she was going to collect her suitcase, walk out, and see what happened. If Sarah was there, great. If not, she had the address of a hostel written in her diary. There. Things would be fine. Just fine. She would deal. Because *that* was what adults did. They dealt. They didn't sit on the floor and bemoan a lack of tea.

She collected her suitcase and turned towards the exit, hoping that . . . that . . . well, that whatever happened, there would at least be a café selling tea in Arrivals.

Coming out of Arrivals, she discovered there was no café. There *was*, however, someone standing in an oddly wide gap in the crowd with a massive, glittery purple and black sign screaming *WELCOME QUEEN EVAZILLA* over a stencil of Godzilla. *Queen-evazilla* was Evie's Tumblr name. The dark-haired woman holding it bounced up and down at the sight of her, waving furiously. *Aha.* That would be Sarah. The dapper person standing a few feet away from Sarah—a stuffed Godzilla toy in hand and a stoically blank expression on their face—had to be Bailey.

No one had ever met her at an airport like *this*. Not with glitter.

A small thrill ran through her. Sarah and Bailey were real. Evie waved and headed towards them.

"Oh my God," Sarah shrieked as Evie reached them. "I can't believe you're here!"

"Hey, Gaybeard." Evie extended her hand, only to find herself engulfed in a massive hug. Sarah was tall, her long arms crushing Evie to her. "Pleasure to meet you," Evie choked into Sarah's shoulder.

"You too! Oh *wow*, it's so great to finally see you in person!" Sarah released her and turned to Bailey. "This is Bailey."

Sarah had described Bailey Girelli as "sweet and wonderful and a good dresser." Obvious bias aside, Evie had dutifully followed Bailey on Tumblr but hadn't ever emailed or seen pictures of them, so she wasn't sure what to expect. They'd certainly delivered on the outfit score: a dandy pinstripe suit; shiny brogues; half-shaved, gel-slicked do of violet curls visible under the brim of a derby hat; and purple eyeliner. Evie felt like a grubby mess next to them.

Bailey raised one hand. "Hey."

"Hello." They held out the toy, and Evie took it, smiling at the asexual flag badge on Godzilla's chest. "Thank you."

"I saw it in a shop and I *had* to get it for you." Sarah waved the glittery sign. "Bailey did the sign."

"Yeah," Bailey said. They ducked their head so their face was hidden by their hat brim; whether out of shyness or embarrassment wasn't clear to Evie. "It was fun."

"I love the sign. Very, uh, distinctive." It was certainly growing on her.

"Listen to that accent!" Sarah's eyes were wide. "You sound so polite. 'I love the sign,'" she mimicked. "'Very distinctive.' Oh my God. You sound like the Queen."

Evie had to laugh. She lived in York now but had been born and raised in Devon. Her accent was an unholy mongrel of two very different English counties with the odd London twist tossed in. "I assure you, I sound nothing like the Queen."

"I can't wait for you to meet everyone." Sarah took Evie's suitcase in hand, and they turned towards the exit. "They're going to *love* you. This is going to be the best Pride ever. I've talked to some of the other Tumblr aces and we're doing a meet-up next week and you're totally, like, the British representative. Plus I can't wait to take you around your *new city*. Oh my God, I can't believe you're gonna live here." She skipped, giddy as a little girl. "We have so much planned for you. Wow, I am *so excited* you're here!"

Evie could well believe it.

"You look so fresh! Did you sleep on the plane?"

"Not really—"

"That's a shame. Oh hey, we can take you to Timmies!"

"Timmies?"

Sarah looked at her, aghast. "You don't know Tim Hortons?"

"They sell coffee," Bailey supplied.

"And doughnuts," Sarah added.

"And Timbits," Bailey said excitedly.

"They're the doughnut holes." Sarah said it as if that explained something.

Evie's head was spinning already, and it was only nine—she checked—thirty. "Coffee would be wonderful." She wondered if this Tim place also served tea and if that was an acceptable alternative to coffee in Canada. They stepped out of the terminal into the tepid morning air, and Evie took a deep breath. Toronto tasted damp and urban and new.

"This is your first time in Canada, right?" Sarah asked as they walked to the slab of a car park towering next to the terminal building.

"Yes." Evie scanned the area. Apart from the currency denomination and the word choice, everything around the terminal looked fairly . . . familiar, actually. Airports were the same everywhere.

Sarah paid for the parking, took the slip, and walked out into the darkness of the concrete slab, chattering the entire way. In the middle of promises to visit Niagara Falls and eat poutine, "Hungry Eyes" chimed thinly from Sarah's purse, and she reached in with one hand. She cut the call and glanced at Bailey. "Tyler."

"Ah."

"I'll call him back later. So, Evie, you vegetarian or vegan?"

"Neither, but flexible."

Sarah laughed at that for some reason. "You're in good company."

They reached a two-door hatchback that had seen better days, perhaps back in the early nineties. Sarah put her suitcase in the boot of the car while Bailey opened the car door and pushed the seat forward.

"Now," Sarah said, rounding the car and pointing at what Evie assumed was the backseat under a pile of jumpers and discarded chocolate wrappers, "sit your tush down and we'll get this show on the road."

Evie squeezed in and gingerly sat in a clearish space. Things rustled. Something squeaked. Sarah and Bailey settled into the car and turned on the radio. The melodious notes of Tom Waits drifted through the car as Sarah screeched into reverse.

Evie made more space among the jumpers as they left the car park, and tried to relax. So far so good. When Sarah took a corner sharply, Evie excavated the seatbelt, hugged Godzilla tight, and allowed herself to feel optimistic. It was, at the very least, an improvement on uncertain.

Tyler shifted in his chair and took another sip of coffee. Just after nine o'clock, which meant Derek was officially late to his own meeting. Again. The other dancers and instructors milled around the studio, stretching and showing off—those that weren't still waking up in their seats like Tyler. Gigi was trying to out-fouetté Eddie in the corner, which was never a good start to any day. Carmen sat next to him, looking as awake as Tyler wasn't. He shrank deeper into his hoodie and curled his hands around his coffee cup.

Derek's wife, Jean, checked her watch and pulled out her phone, then strode out the door. Carmen leaned over to Tyler. "He's in trouble now."

Like Tyler had any sympathy for the guy. "It's my day off. Jean's not the only one who's going to ream Derek's ass if he's not here soon."

"Ohhh, who's a grumpy baby?" she cooed, pinching his cheek.

He jerked his head away from her hands. "Knock it off."

"Watch your fingers, Carmen, he bites." Gigi plunked himself into the chair next to Tyler. He looked annoyed, which meant Eddie had pulled off a ridiculous number of fouettés again.

"How many this time?" Tyler asked.

"Ten doubles from a *grande plié.*" His lip curled. "I don't understand why Monster Thighs Eddie can do it and I can't."

"She's got more leg muscle than you and me combined, that's why," Carmen said.

"She's actually good," Tyler said.

Gigi glared at him. "Oooh, someone woke up on the asshole side of the bed this morning."

Couldn't anyone give him a break? Weren't these clowns meant to be his *friends*? He slouched further into the chair. "It's my day off. I'm not supposed to be awake, man."

"I *am* good." Eddie leaned on the back of Gigi's chair, her red hair dark with sweat. "So, anyone know why Derek called this meeting?"

"Maybe he ordered more classy merchandise." Gigi held up his key ring, which said *QS Dance* in gaudy rainbow letters.

Those keyrings had proved to be an epic marketing disaster. Derek and Jean had set Queer Space Dance up as an integrative, diverse, and LGBTQ-friendly dance company and school, but as it turned out, that didn't necessarily mean their dancers and students wanted that friendliness screamed from their keys.

"I saw five boxes of those in the stationery cupboard," Carmen said.

"I'm supposed to be rehearsing," Eddie moaned.

"I'm supposed to be *in bed*," Tyler said.

Gigi's glare turned into a concerned frown. "You know, you really don't look so great. I don't know why I'm even asking, but were you out last night?"

Tyler shook his head. "Stayed in."

Maybe that was the problem. He stayed in too much now. He hadn't been out as much since breaking up with his girlfriend, Lucette, a year ago. At first it had felt necessary to keep to himself and focus on work, but maybe he was too used to it now. The thought of barhopping with friends was starting to have its appeal again, but those same friends were adamant he meet someone new. His stomach turned at the thought. Friends from his transgender artists group understood, but Gigi and Sarah, friends from college, alas, did not.

Gigi scowled and opened his mouth, but whatever he was going to say was interrupted by the studio door opening. The buzz died as Jean and Derek came into the room, Derek carrying his own cup of coffee and Jean looking pissed. She sat down immediately, arms crossed and back absolutely straight.

Derek waved for attention. "Sorry I'm late, everyone!" The dancers stretching along the barre at the back of the studio eased up.

He grinned at them all. "Thanks for coming to this meeting on such short notice."

"Thanks for showing up," someone muttered audibly in the back.

"I just wanted to tell you I've put QS Dance forward for a new, very last-minute event. It's really exciting, and I wanted you all to have a chance to participate." Derek paused, building anticipation.

Someone coughed.

He threw out his hands, coffee sloshing in his cup. "QS Dance, in direct competition with Cherry Studios, is having a dance-off at this year's Pride!"

Tyler sank down further in his chair. Oh Lord, no. No way in *hell* was he competing against dancers from the biggest dance school on this side of Toronto. Around him, he could see others reaching the same conclusion and avoiding eye contact with Derek.

"But there's a twist!" Derek continued. "The dance-off is partnered. Three instructors will each be paired with a member of the public, teach them a routine the week before Pride, i.e., next week, then perform at the dance-off. The couple with the best moves wins. Three dancers from each school. You get to showcase your moves *and* your teaching skills!"

Everyone looked aghast. Tyler pulled his hood over his face. Teach some random yahoo to dance? In a *week*? Against, never forget, one of the *biggest dance schools in Toronto*? Normally Tyler was all for dance competitions, but this was a mistake waiting to happen. What was Derek thinking?

"Public auditions are being held the day after tomorrow, so you need to decide now if you want to join in," Derek said. "Anyone can do this. Anyone at all. Given it's for Pride, it's going to feature LGBT people; that's literally the only condition for the couples. You can dance any style you like." He glanced around the room, taking in the reaction. An eyebrow quirked. "You will, of course, be paid one and a half your going rate for your time."

Tyler noticed a few people nearby instantly looking more thoughtful.

"It's a great opportunity to show Toronto what our little school can do," Derek said, apparently moving on to the inspirational part of his speech. "We're progressive! We're forward-thinking! We're diverse and dedicated! Not even Cherry Studios offers the focused classes and talent that we have. Frankly, we can win this. I have no doubt that we can. So," he scanned the room, "volunteers?"

Next to Tyler, Gigi's hand shot up.

Tyler stared at him as Derek gave a one-handed fist-pump. "Gigi, awesome! Who else?"

"Are you kidding me?" Tyler hissed at Gigi.

Gigi's eyes went big and innocent. "What do you mean?"

"Cherry Studios. *Cherry Studios.* They're going to cream us."

Gigi leered. "Not if I cream them first."

Carmen also volunteered, and Jean wrote down her name. Tyler was sitting between Carmen and Gigi, and Derek's eyes almost naturally latched on to his. Almost. Tyler's stomach plummeted. Derek grinned wolfishly. "Tyler! Good man!"

"Huh?"

Everyone was looking at him. Tyler stared back at Derek. "You can't be serious."

"Write his name down, Jean," Derek said, ignoring him. Jean's pen flickered.

Tyler turned to Eddie. "He can't be serious."

Eddie's expression said she was reluctantly impressed. "Oh, he is."

"Fantastic, everyone! Thank you so much!" Derek beamed at the crowd, and Tyler felt like throwing his coffee into the guy's face. "Time to rock on with our day. Gigi, Carmen, Tyler, stay after, please."

Tyler closed his eyes and leaned his head back. "This is supposed to be my day off," he groaned as people gathered their things and left.

"Quit whining," Eddie said, patting his shoulder. "It'll be fun."

"For you."

"And for me," Gigi said dreamily. "Maybe I can teach some scruffy bear cub how to tango."

Carmen snorted. "And you wonder why you're still single."

Tyler opened his eyes and watched the other dancers leave. A few of them smirked at him, and he glared back.

Eddie poked Gigi on her way out. "Take this seriously."

Gigi gasped with mock outrage. "Since when *don't* I?"

"Since always, Gigi," Derek said, approaching them.

Carmen stood, elegant in her bun and favourite red flamenco skirt. Noticing her poise and easy femininity, Tyler felt a bite of old conflicted feelings that eased into gentle reassurance and admiration. She caught him staring and smiled. He smiled back and turned to Derek as Jean closed the door and joined them.

"I'm so glad you three volunteered," Derek began.

"Hey." Tyler leaned forward. "I didn't—"

"It's a *crazy* good opportunity," Derek continued, "for you and for QS. The publicity alone is going to be worth it. I'm so excited it's you three, honestly."

Jean passed out three sheets of paper. "This is more information from Pride about the event and this year's theme. It should help you with the choreography."

"Remember," Derek said, "you'll be working with people who've never danced before. It's between you and them how much time you devote to this, but you only have a week to learn a routine."

Gigi's hand shot up. "What about our classes and other jobs?"

Jean pulled out another set of sheets. "Completely up to you. As long as the classes at QS are covered, I don't care how you manage your time. You will be paid for your rehearsals, though, if that helps you prioritize things. I will expect a log sheet from each of you." She handed those out too.

"These auditions," Carmen asked, "do we get to choose who we're teaching?"

Derek shook his head. "You get input, but no, Justine from Cherry Studios and I will be overseeing the auditions. You need to be there to meet and organize schedules with your partners, but we'll have final say over who's chosen. You might end up with someone completely different than you or," he eyed Gigi, "someone very similar to you. Pride said they want to see queer people on the stage. They want representation and diversity."

Tyler figured they'd certainly have that. Gigi was white but had never seen the inside of the closet, Tyler was half black *and* transgender, and Carmen was Spanish Canadian. Tyler wasn't sure of her orientation and was fairly certain she was cisgender, but she was a nice person who would work with anyone and everyone.

Unlike him.

Time to pin Derek to the wall. "Derek?" he asked. "A word? Outside?"

In the corridor, Derek crossed his arms and leaned against the door. Tyler took a moment to calm his anger and nerves. He opened his mouth to tell Derek that this wasn't a good time for him, that partnering was a bad idea, that this was going over a line, that he just wasn't ready—

"I'm sorry, Tyler," Derek said, taking the wind out of Tyler's sails.

Goddamn it. The worst thing about Derek, far worse than his lack of punctuality or misunderstanding of the word *volunteer*, was how genuinely nice a person he could be.

"That was a shit thing to do, man."

"Yeah. But I mean it—you're perfect for this. You're exactly what this competition needs. And it would be an excellent opportunity for you."

Tyler was unconvinced. "If it was any other school, maybe. Cherry Studios? I say this with total respect, but are you high?"

Derek grinned. "It's a challenge, but you and Carmen are up for it." He glanced at the door to the studio. "Gigi would be too if he could stop flitting around for five minutes and focus."

Tyler drew himself up and stared Derek straight in the eye. "I don't want to do it."

Derek leaned towards him. "I get it, Tyler. You know Lucette's no longer with Cherry? Justine said she found work with another dance company in Vancouver. So, no worries, she won't be one of the Cherry dancers, and oooh, wait, before you get that look on your face—"

What look? What fresh bullshit is this?

"—yes, *that* look, I'm certain this will be a great thing for you." Derek put a reassuring hand on Tyler's shoulder. "You have talent, Tyler. You need to put yourself out there and show everyone else that. Put Lucette behind you. I know it's been a rough year for you, but I think this could help."

Fuck. Trust Derek to deliver the solid emotional goods. He *knew* the mere potential of Luce's presence would be an issue. Damn him for thinking of everything. Tyler was almost convinced this was an okay idea now.

Derek's hazel eyes burrowed into his. "I know you can win this thing. I know it. And here's the thing Tyler: I think you know it too. So how about it?"

Tyler's mouth twisted. Derek maybe had some reasonable points. And it *would* be a fun challenge, provided he got the right person. *Oh, fuck it.* "Fine."

The guy actually victory-punched the air. "Yes!"

"On one condition: no girls."

Derek's eyebrows flew up towards what was left of his hairline. "Huh?"

Tyler meant it. "No girls. I want to teach a guy."

"Not sure I can promise that, Tyler. Can't discriminate like that."

"But it's not—" His brain caught up with his mouth. "Fuck, I mean, not *like that*, no, just not—"

Derek nodded, uncharacteristically serious. "I know what you meant. I can't guarantee anything, because honestly? I think what you need *is* another female partner. You need to get over Lucette and whatever she did to you. Get back on the horse, as the saying goes."

Tyler knew that, but it was somewhat humiliating to hear it from his *boss* of all people.

"Sorry, buddy, but you can't control this. Just roll with it. Read the sheet." He tapped the papers in Tyler's hands. "Get some choreography down ahead of time. And none of that interpretive shit you like—do something for the crowd."

Derek smiled encouragingly at him, then went back into the studio. Tyler stared down at the information sheet in front him. *Auditions: 9 a.m.–1 p.m., University of Toronto St. George Campus, Front Campus (King's College Circuit). Dance styles: any suitable for performance in public with a partner. Please keep the abilities of your partner in mind. PrideTO hopes to raise awareness during the event for the PrideTO charity fund for homeless LGBTQA2S teens. Theme: Fierce.*

What the hell? Would anyone actually go for this? His heart sank. *Fuck.* He was going to end up with a fifteen-year-old who was more flexible than him and would flake after two sessions. Or a creeper. Or a fortysomething in the middle of a life crisis. Like hell he'd let himself be paired with someone like that. There were only so many crises a guy could handle at once.

He pulled out his phone—venting was needed. He scrolled through his list and went straight to Sarah. The woman was made of sunshine and empathy, and she hated Lucette more than he did. He dialled, but she didn't answer. A memory wormed into place from the last time they'd spoken. Something about a friend? Going to the airport? She was picking someone up. *Damn it.*

Derek opened the door. "Get back in here. I'm not done talking."

Tyler bit his tongue and silently made peace with the fact that the next two weeks of his life were going to be crappier than normal. At least it couldn't get worse.

He re-entered the studio, only to be presented with another form from Jean. "What's this for?" he asked, scanning it. *Personal Release Form? What does that mean?*

Jean said blandly, "Katie asked that I distribute these to you."

"Who?"

"The director of the documentary team."

Documentary team? Tyler looked over at Gigi, who was scribbling his name on the form while Carmen read hers carefully. "People will be filming us?"

"Yup," Derek said. "Katie is Justine's daughter. She's doing a film degree at U of T and wants to document the practice sessions and performances for a project."

Tyler stared at the form. He wanted nothing more than to shred all the paper in his hand and throw it over Jean and Derek.

"Remember, one-and-a-half times your going rate," Jean murmured to him, holding out a pen.

He looked into her sympathetic eyes.

"This ridiculousness will be over by next Saturday. That's what I'm telling myself. I'll let you take the following week off from teaching. Paid."

Okay, now he just wanted to throw everything over Derek. He sighed, took the pen, and signed.

CHAPTER TWO

Evie had heard all the stories of Canadian weather: the perpetual cold and snow and apparently inadequate summer. Thus far she'd found that the summer part at least was completely wrong. She and Bailey were having late-morning coffee in the greenery near the University of Toronto, basking in the sun and enjoying a small, warm breeze. She was wearing fewer layers than she ever had in the UK, while Bailey had made a deference to the warmth by wearing tailored, cuffed shorts and rolling up their sleeves. Hardly inadequate at all.

In fact, nothing she'd seen so far could be described like that. Here in the greenery was downright pleasant. There was a small market at one edge of the park, with pastry stands, farm groups offering vegetable deliveries, and one stall offering a free go on a dance machine. She could see the banner asking passersby, *So You Think You Can Dance?*

Bailey tipped their coffee at the stall. "Not sure how legal that is."

"It's not the official dancing show?"

"No."

Wait, hadn't Sarah mentioned something about this? Evie's jet lag was minimal, but the last two days had been an absolute whirl of activity. Sarah and Bailey couldn't be better hosts, and Evie wanted to smack her paranoid airport self for doubting them.

The first day had been a feat in keeping Evie awake long enough to offset the jet lag. After dumping Evie's luggage at Sarah's flat, Sarah and Bailey had delivered her to the promised Tim Hortons—which turned out to be a coffee shop chain selling okay coffee and amazing doughnuts—then walked her around the centre of Toronto.

Yesterday they'd toured more of the city, and Evie was all walked out now. They'd visited Casa Loma, various art galleries, strolled down Church Street and eyed all the rainbows, passed through Yonge-Dundas Square into the largest, most decadent shopping centre Evie had ever seen outside of London, through the financial district, dipped by the waterfront, walked along Queen Street (which apparently had the longest streetcar—*not tram*, she had to remember that—route in the world, a fact Evie intended to google), up through Chinatown and Kensington Market.

She liked Toronto very much.

The city horizon ranged beyond the boundaries of the university park. Evie pulled her camera and Godzilla from her backpack to take a picture of him with the Toronto skyline. The toy had become something of a mascot for her trip pictures. Bailey snuffled in amusement as she took the photo and reviewed it. The buildings were huge, shiny things that reminded her of the City in London. Like London, the architecture varied dramatically from neighbourhood to neighbourhood, getting smaller and more residential the farther one travelled from the city centre. Unlike London (and pretty much anywhere in the UK) the roads were huge and so were the pavements. Evie was used to tiny roads modernized from carriage paths; here there was just so much *space*. Everything about this new, big city demanded similarly brave, shiny things from her. Things like moving away to a new country to try a different, maybe better life in a place she could barely take in, and being independent and positive about it despite being an ocean away from nearly everyone she knew. She could do it. Maybe. She had to, because this was a promise to herself to try for brighter things.

The dance stall still nagged at her. Why? What *was* it?

Yesterday, while staring at the art car in Kensington Market, Sarah's phone had rung: "Hungry Eyes" again. She'd turned away to answer. "Hey, Tyler."

Evie had briefly wondered who Tyler was, because he—or she, because wasn't Tyler a girl's name too now?—seemed close to Sarah and kept calling her. Perhaps he or she was another Tumblr ace.

"Jeez, honey, that's rough," Sarah said sympathetically. "I know, I know, days off are like super rare for you. Wait, what? A documentary crew?"

Evie's attention had been caught by the window display of a nearby souvenir shop. For some reason, it had a few shelves dedicated to British goods, stocking things like Twinings and *Doctor Who* placemats and, to her delight and Bailey's wry amusement, Jelly Babies. They'd gone in. Sarah had followed them in, still on the phone, and found them crouching before a *Downton Abbey* board game.

"What the hell are you doing?" Sarah had asked, before turning back to the phone. "No, not you, Ty, my crazy British friend and Bay."

Evie hadn't really had an answer for her. She'd just left England. Perhaps it had been the novelty of seeing standard brands from home available here as strange imported goods; it had thrown her a little. It'd emphasized how *not* home she was.

"Audition? Well, okay, sure," Sarah had said. "I'll see you then. Bye, honey."

And *that* was it. An audition. Evie frowned at the stall. Was this why Sarah had asked to meet them here? She'd left for work early this morning without saying much more than to meet her at the campus green. Bailey had made Evie pancakes and maple syrup and they'd walked here, enjoying the sunshine.

"When's Sarah meeting us?" Evie asked them.

Bailey checked their watch. "Soon."

She lay back, tucking Godzilla into her arms, and stared up at the sky. The late-morning sunlight fell warm on her skin, and the sky was clear and deep blue. When had she last seen a sky that blue? This was what life should be about. Coffee and warm weather and good people and new experiences. Why had it taken losing her job and flying across the Atlantic to remember that?

"Bay! Evazilla!"

Evie sat up to see Sarah, red-faced and breathless, plunk herself next to Bailey. She pecked them on the cheek.

"Sorry I'm late, honey. Work is killing me right now." She turned to Evie. "The sushi place is just around the corner, but do you mind if I say hi to a friend of mine first?"

"Not at all."

"'Not at all.' Jesus, you *crack me up*."

They stood and ambled over to the dance machine stall. Two people were currently on the machine, stomping in time to the instructions on the screen, while four people with weary expressions sat watching. Two students—judging by the U of T cap one of them was wearing—with a camera filmed the guys on the machine from the edge of the crowd. Sarah went up to three lithe-looking people waiting at a table at the front of the stall. Other lithe-looking people chatted at the back of the stall, but Sarah ignored them.

Evie and Bailey hung back to watch the guys on the machine. One of them was doing well, but the second one lagged woefully behind, messing up further in his haste to catch up.

"You ever do this?" Evie asked Bailey.

"No way." They even wrinkled their nose; clearly the idea didn't impress.

"My friends and I used to. Back at uni, I mean." Evie smiled at the memories. "There's nothing like dancing on that thing after four Jägerbombs. I can't believe they still make these."

They watched until the end of the song. The lagging dancer sagged at the end, relieved it was over.

"Man," he said to the one who'd passed with a reasonable score. "You owe me big time."

A girl in the crowd next to Evie clapped loudly. "Mark! That was amazing! You were *awesome!*"

The winner, waved happily at her. "Thanks, baby."

Two of the judges whispered intently while the other two scribbled notes. Or what looked like notes; Evie saw one of them pull out a folded piece of newspaper from behind a sheaf of papers and place it on the table in front of her, a half-finished sudoku puzzle prominent on the top. The two whispering judges stopped talking and the one wearing a blazer shrugged as though she couldn't care less.

"Mark," called the other judge, a lean man with a receding hairline. "You're in."

Mark's girlfriend shrieked wildly while Mark victory-punched the air, then high-fived his exhausted friend.

Sudoku Judge sighed and began assembling papers from under the puzzle. The one next to her smirked at something on his phone.

As Mark and his friend left the dance machine, Sarah came up to Evie and Bailey, hands wringing guiltily. "Um, guys, sooo, Tyler is my friend, and he's one of the dancers doing this competition thing, and he was saying that they're short on people and well . . ."

Bailey held up their hand. "Hell no."

Sarah's eyes went big and puppyish. "Please. I said we'd go on the machine *once*, just to draw some people in. I want to help him out, *please?*"

"Your friend is a dancer?" Evie looked around Sarah at the dancers she'd been talking to. They were all gorgeous: a woman with a sweet face talking on the phone, a vest-clad, sparkly guy staring in shocked disbelief at Mark, who approached him with forms in one hand and the other held high, and a grumpy-looking lean black guy next to the sparkly guy. Grumpy caught her staring, and Evie felt something like an electric shock go through her. *Oh. What was* that? He scowled, then turned to his friend.

Hmm. Pleasant. She couldn't imagine Sarah being friends with someone negative, so clearly Tyler had to be the sparkly guy.

"—do you mind?" Sarah asked her.

Evie pulled herself back to reality. "What?"

"Going on the machine with me?"

Evie looked at the dance machine. Dance on that thing with Sarah? Well, if Bailey wasn't willing, it was a no-brainer. "Of course not. I can do those things in my sleep."

"You can, eh? Go easy on me."

Minutes later, when they were standing there eyeing the countdown on the screen, Evie remembered that university was five years ago and that she hadn't danced on one of these since her second year of uni, which really meant six years of not doing this. Also, she'd never done this sober.

Bugger.

New experiences, Evie. Dancing on a machine in front of a crowd of strangers. No sweat.

The beat started, and she focused on the arrows in front of her. A tinny Britney Spears track trilled from the machine, but she barely noticed as she caught the first few arrows without a problem. Step. Step. Too lightly and the machine wouldn't register, too hard and it would slow her down. Stomp, stomp, step.

The song kicked into the bridge, and a flurry of arrows started scrolling. Evie stomped, her arms flying in time to the rhythm while her feet struggled to coordinate with the arrows and the beat. She missed a few and joined back in on an easy step, carelessly swiping at the sweat on her face. Christ, when had this ever been fun?

Oh, right. After four Jägerbombs.

Four frantic minutes later, the song finished and she sighed in relief. Her score ran across the screen, pleasingly high considering she hadn't done this in years. She looked over at Sarah to see her panting and wide-eyed.

"Holy shit-snacks." Sarah pointed at the screen. "Look at that score!"

"Eh, it's all right." Evie became aware of a low roar behind her, and she turned to see a sizeable crowd cheering and clapping. She grinned and bowed, receiving more cheers. She turned to Sarah. "That was fun." Surprisingly, she meant it.

"I need to sit down. I'm too old for this." Sarah hobbled off the machine. "Tyler owes me a drink."

Evie went to join her but found her way blocked by two of the judges, the ones with the receding hairline and the expensive blazer. Blazer looked annoyed while Receding was excited.

"Ma'am," he said, "that was the highest score today."

"Really?" Evie said. If she was the highest score on that machine, they had to be scraping the bottom of the barrel for this . . . What *was* this for again?

She turned to read the signs scattered around the tent, but the judge kept her attention.

"My name is Derek Hastings, and this is Justine Cherry." He held out his hand and Evie shook it, unsure why he was so excited. "We are the directors of QS Dance and Cherry Studios, respectively, and I would just like to congratulate—"

"You on partnering one of my dancers for the competition," Justine butted in, shaking Evie's hand firmly in turn. Very firmly.

"Competition?" Evie struggled to remove her hand from Justine's grip.

"You definitely don't want to embarrass yourself with one of *them*," Justine added, pointing at the nearby dancers.

"Justine, you've allocated your dancers' partners already," Derek hissed at her.

"We'll swap. She's a smart girl." Justine's green eyes flickered to Evie. "You're gay, right?"

"*Excuse me?*" Evie asked coldly.

"Please excuse us a moment, Miss—er," Derek faltered, having not gotten her name. "Er, ma'am." He spun Justine around and leaned in close to her, whispering fiercely.

Oookay. Time to walk away from the strange, rude people. Evie side-stepped around them, only to see the sudoku woman approach her. She held forms in her hands but, unlike Derek and Justine, didn't intrude into Evie's personal space.

"I'm Jean Hastings, assistant director for QS Dance. You're good." She smiled at Evie. "What's your name?"

What in the world was going on? Who *were* these people? "Evie Whitmore."

"Evie, please consider taking part in our competition. Do you have three hours free every day for the next week?"

Evie blinked, then finally turned to look at the signs littered around the stall. *Perform at Pride! Be partnered with a dancer from two of the best dance schools in Toronto! Learn to dance in seven days! LGBTQA2S and allies welcome. Must be comfortable appearing on film.*

Things clicked together.

Oh bollocks.

"I'm very sorry," she started, "I didn't really know about—"

"She'll do it."

Startled, she looked over to see the lean, grumpy dancer at her side. *When did he get there?* He was her height, with dark curly hair and light-brown skin, and he glared at her as though she were some kind of idiot. But he had to be one of the most gorgeous men Evie had ever found abruptly standing next to her—not that she was an expert on the matter.

And like all vaguely good-looking men, he came with entitlement and an apparent inability to mind his own business. Or perhaps he was just as rude as his boss.

Time to end this nonsense.

"*She* can speak for herself," she said, crisply enunciating every syllable.

His eyebrows raised. "Sorry."

That strange feeling shot through her again. She ignored it and turned back to Jean. "I'm terribly sorry, but my friend didn't tell me that this was an actual audition, and I'm afraid I can't—"

"Evazilla, do it!" Sarah joined them, practically flinging herself into their little circle. Next to her, the stocky cameraman aimed a camera at Evie, occasionally panning to something over her shoulder. Evie glanced behind her—the judges were hissing in each other's face. *Hmm. Professional.*

Sarah's voice drew her back to the conversation. "You should totally do this. You're on vacation! You have the time."

Jean and the dancer's faces turned crafty. Evie was going to kill Sarah for revealing that.

"You will be compensated for your time," Jean said.

"No, I won't," Evie told her. "Tourist visa."

"It doesn't have to be monetary." Jean seemed pleased. She nudged the dancer.

"It's a really good opportunity," the dancer said, as though that should be obvious to her. "Please do it."

Evie stared at them all: Jean looked hopeful, Sarah was excited, the cameraman looked bored but gave her a thumbs-up when she caught his eye, and the grumpy dancer waited with his arms crossed. Behind her, the two judges—directors?—still argued.

"Justine, this kind of behaviour is beneath both of us," Derek said.

"I didn't organize this in order to lose," Justine responded coolly.

Christ on a stick. What the hell was wrong with these people?

"Please," the dancer repeated. Meddling and scowl aside, he seemed sincere about her doing it.

Dancing. Her? *Really?* A week of learning something new, then showcasing it at Pride; that would definitely be a challenge. Evie didn't know the first thing about dancing, but all these people seemed to think she could do it. Plus, hadn't Sarah said something about them struggling to find people?

Evie sighed. While it was a pleasant novelty to have a gorgeous guy begging her for something, she couldn't stretch this out any longer.

She turned to Jean. "Three hours a day?"

Jean smiled triumphantly. "Yes. More if your schedules can support it. I'll ensure you're compensated somehow for your time. You will be matched with Tyler, who'll be responsible for your performance and who will perform with you at Pride."

Tyler. Right. Sarah's friend. This would probably be fun with someone like him. Evie had visions of jazz hands and flamboyant spinning. "... Fine."

"Yes!" Sarah crowed, hugging her. The cameraman managed a double thumbs-up while balancing his camera on his shoulder.

Jean thrust the forms and a pen under Evie's nose. "Please fill these in. We require a deposit, to be refunded when you complete the performance next Saturday." She glanced over Evie's shoulder and pulled one form from the bottom of the pile. "I would appreciate it if you signed this one now."

Evie skimmed the form as Sarah bounced next to her. On her other side, she was strangely aware of the dancer staring at her. What was his problem? She raised an eyebrow at him.

He was smirking. "Did Sarah just call you *Evazilla*?"

Jesus Christ. Evie felt herself blush. Wasn't it time for him to disappear? Why did he care anyway?

Sarah's friend hadn't seemed flustered at all until he'd asked her about that name. She'd come off the stupid dance machine with the highest score of the day, bowed to the crowd like a pro, handled Justine and Derek well considering they'd practically ambushed her, and only *now* did she look even a little self-conscious.

She went adorably red, then sputtered, "It's a nickname."

Tyler couldn't help grinning. When he'd spoken to Sarah on the phone, she'd said a British friend from the internet was visiting and that she was a lot of fun. So far, so true. Her accent made her outrage seem that much more furious. It tapped into his inner flirt and made him want to tease her more, which was odd because he hadn't seen his inner flirt since way before breaking up with Lucette.

He tried to damp it down, but, "Oh yeah? What kind of nickname?" came out despite himself.

"One that's none of your business, thanks."

"How mysterious." He grinned. "You're an international woman of mystery."

The look of furious disbelief he got was worth it.

Sarah shook her head. "Ty, stop. Her name is Evie."

Evie did a double take. "*You're* Tyler?"

He waved. "'Sup."

Evie crossed her arms. "You must be joking."

Sarah glanced between them, a big grin on her face.

Maybe this could be going better.

Jean tapped the form. "Evie, focus."

Evie glared at him again, then returned to reading the form. Long seconds later, she signed it. Tyler released a breath he hadn't noticed he was holding. Jean pulled the paper away and left to add it to the forms from the previous people who'd agreed to this joke of a competition. Sarah clapped her hands and bounced around some more. Trust her to be more excited than the people actually taking part.

Behind Tyler, Derek exhaled sharply. "Justine, we've scared away the crowd and it's lunchtime. I'm too hungry to have this conversation with you."

"Then don't."

Tyler watched as Justine dropped a thin hand onto Evie's shoulder and Evie instantly twisted out from under it. She regarded Justine with open disapproval, for which Tyler couldn't help giving her a mental high five. Justine wasn't known for being nice for the sake of it.

"Sorry about that," Justine said breezily. "Where were we?"

"Leaving," Jean said from the judges' table. "She signed with us."

Justine arched an elegantly plucked eyebrow. "Oh? That is . . . unfortunate." Tyler took a step back; she was *pissed*. She fixed Evie with a wide smile, one so forced Tyler thought he could almost see her cheeks straining. "You can still back out of it. My dancers are far more experienced and highly trained than—" her eyes ran over Tyler, unimpressed "—these people. It's not a problem to swap over to my school. We would love to have you." Behind her, Derek ground his teeth audibly.

Evie glanced at Tyler and muttered something that sounded suspiciously like, "Don't tempt me."

Seriously?

"What?" Justine asked.

Evie smiled like a shark finding a school of fish. "I'm most *terribly* sorry, Justine, but the answer is absolutely not. See, I don't mind *these people.*"

Damn. *Damn.* Her tone was so cold it was freezing Justine's face all on its own.

"Though, I *might* be persuaded if you could answer one little question for me," she continued. Sweet though she sounded, her eyes bored into Justine's. "What's my name?"

"Excuse me?" Justine asked, obviously taken aback. "Your name? It's . . ." She fell silent, lips thinning. Behind her, Derek turned red.

Tyler looked between them. Wait, no introductions had happened back there? Ha. Amazing. He'd expect no less from Derek and Justine, given how cutthroat they were being about this. But Evie didn't know them, and she didn't seem willing to play ball.

"Exactly." Evie's smile dropped from her face. "Where I'm from, we appreciate good manners. You're incredibly rude." She glowered at them: him, Katie's camera guy, Derek, and Justine. "In fact, you're all vultures. It's just a bit of dancing. Sarah, we're late for lunch." She marched off, forms crumpled in one hand.

Well. Shit. Tyler crossed his arms, impressed. He wasn't sure he'd ever seen someone tell Justine off before.

Sarah winked at him before following her.

Jean called after them, "Get those forms back to me when you show up for your first session!"

Justine's lips had turned nonexistent. She turned on Derek. "Keep her. I don't need some oversensitive tourist asking me stupid questions." Then she marched off, a perfect example of a pissed-off white lady. Her business partner, Patrick, stood with a sigh, shook Jean's hand, and walked after Justine.

Derek gave one long exhalation and quirked a smile at Tyler, Jean, and the camera guy. "That went great, don't you think? We got good people in the end."

Tyler wanted to scoff. *I mean, yeah, Derek, we did, but the one* I'm *partnered with hates us all.*

The camera guy, whose name was Brock if Tyler remembered correctly, shrugged and walked over to Katie, the film student. She had watched all proceedings from a spot beside the stall, making notes, chewing gum, and generally being as unobtrusive as her mother, Justine, wasn't.

Tyler turned to gaze after Evie. She, Sarah, and Bailey were walking towards the other end of the park. He'd been waiting most of the morning to be assigned a partner to teach, so he was relieved to finally have one, especially someone who seemed promisingly able. But, magnificent as that display of temper was, it was also a little worrying. What if she was a diva? What if she was difficult to teach?

Worse, what if she was another temperamental freak like Lucette?

Speaking of temperamental freaks who also happened to be divas, one of them draped an arm over Tyler's shoulders. "She's a fucking firecracker," Gigi said.

When Evie and Sarah had first stepped up to the machine, Gigi had made joke after joke about their appearance, like he had about nearly every single person who'd auditioned, earning him a smack on the back of his head from Carmen. He'd only stopped when he'd realized Evie was a natural, and switched like lightning to requesting a swap. Apparently Mark the Jock wasn't quite to Gigi's tastes. It would've been funny if Tyler wasn't so used to Gigi being, well . . . Gigi. Tyler had said no at the time, preferring talent over brawn, but after that flash of temper, he was tempted to reconsider it.

"I'll say," he agreed.

"Thighs like Eddie's, did you notice that?" Gigi remarked.

Tyler bit the inside of his mouth. He didn't want to think about her thighs. "I don't care about her thighs. Why do you? She's promising, but she might be trouble. You still want to swap?"

Gigi laughed, then pretended to think about it. "Hmmm, Mark the hetero bro-child with hips, or Lady Chubs-Tottington with a shitty attitude. If I'm going to do this, I'm going to at least enjoy the view. No, not a chance, man. As Shakira says, 'Hips don't lie.'"

"Evie moved a hell of a lot better than Mark did."

"Mark moves fine. He also doesn't shout at people or expect formal introductions. And I like being able to lift the girls I dance with."

For fuck's sake. "Gigi, stop being a misogynistic dick and tell me I haven't made a huge mistake by letting Derek make me a part of this."

Gigi leaned in close, smirking. "She can move, sure. You know who else can move? You. The moment she was saying no, you were there quicker than a toppy daddy at a leather convention. She is so your type, and there is no way I'm stopping you from dancing with her."

Tyler closed his eyes, mortified. That was true. He'd seen Jean's face fall as Evie was clearly refusing, and before he'd known it, he was next to her and begging her to say yes. What the hell had come over him? Sure the auditions were going to close soon, and they'd been having trouble finding three people for the QS dancers, but Tyler wasn't so invested in this that he had actually been desperate. In fact, if he'd had to pull out for lack of a partner, that would have been ideal. So why had the sight of her killing it on the machine given him a sense of hope? What had made him rush to convince her?

Really, it was like he'd been possessed.

Tyler's phone buzzed. He pulled it out to see a text from Sarah: *Join us for lunch?*

Oookay, no. Hadn't he (along with everyone else) made a terrible impression on Evie? Surely the last thing she'd want is to see him again . . . *Hold up, Davis*—they were dancing together now, so they *had* to see each other again. They had to organize the sessions. Tyler wanted to mash the screen at his own stupidity. What was *wrong* with him today? Yeah, he was joining them for lunch.

He responded to Sarah: *Where?*

Her reply came straightaway: *Sushigasm. Opposite the fountain.*

Gigi slapped his shoulder, because obviously he had no boundaries and had read Tyler's screen. "Go make nice, and check she doesn't overeat."

Someone cleared their throat behind them. Tyler and Gigi turned to see Carmen standing there, hand on hip. Behind her stood Mark and his girlfriend. "You guys cuddled enough for today?" she asked archly. "Because I have a class, and I can't babysit these two any longer."

Oh God, that was embarrassing. Carmen had been paired earlier with a thin woman called Claude who sported an amazing undercut and many piercings, and she had been muttering about even leaving before Mark auditioned. And now she looked pissed.

"How long have you been standing there?" Tyler asked. Carmen's eyebrows raised, signalling, *Long enough.*

Mark grinned at Gigi. "Hey, man, you mean that? About my hips?"

His girlfriend nudged him. "Babe, you got *awesome* hips."

"Yeah, you know it," Mark leered.

Gigi's face fell.

Tyler could have gagged. "And on that touching image, I'll leave you to get acquainted." He patted Gigi's shoulder.

He retrieved his bag, said good-bye to Jean and Derek, and jogged through the park to the fountain at the other end. He saw Sarah, Evie, and Bailey going into Sushigasm and hustled after them.

"Four people, please," Sarah was saying to a server as Tyler lumbered through the door. They turned to look at him and Sarah gestured at him. "See, here's our fourth!" He risked a glance at Evie's face, but if she wasn't pleased at him being there, she didn't show it.

The server led the four of them to a table near the window and settled them with menus. Sarah ended up next to Bailey, leaving Tyler to sit beside Evie. She immersed herself in the menu, apparently more interested in the difference between the Sunshine Ramen and the Mountain Ramen than in talking to him. Wait, was this lack of a reaction actually her reaction? That boded well.

"Hey, Tyler," Bailey said.

"How's it going, Bailey?" Tyler asked.

Bay shrugged. "It goes."

"I completely did *not* expect this to happen," Sarah said. "What are the odds? And Evazilla, I'm so mad."

Evie looked up, startled.

"You totally held out on us! You never said you could dance."

"I can't."

"You beasted that machine."

"The dance machine isn't real dancing." Evie's eyes flickered to Tyler. "I only did so well because my uni friends and I didn't have better taste in arcade games."

At least she knew there was a difference between the stupid machine and the real thing. "She's right," Tyler said.

Sarah raised her eyebrows.

"I mean, about the dance machine," he added. "I don't know why they wanted to use that as a way of auditioning people. It doesn't show skill."

"It doesn't?" Sarah looked hurt.

Ah, God. He was on a roll of saying the wrong thing. Was she hurt on Evie's behalf?

He glanced at Evie—who was frowning at the menu. So . . . didn't care? "I mean, it's a physical game," he clarified. "Dancing is more than timing the machine right."

Sarah still seemed upset.

He sighed. "That said, it standardized the audition, a lot of people had fun on it, and we got an *idea* of how people moved."

Sarah pouted. "Jean said she was good."

"Jean's the finance department," Tyler retorted.

"She's married to a dancer. Her opinion has to have some value."

"Have you *met* Derek?"

Evie pointed at the menu. "You know, I think I'll have the teriyaki salmon."

"Same," Bailey said.

Nope, she really didn't care, and Sarah was distracting him. He had to rescue this. He turned in his seat to face Evie—who looked up in surprise—and pointed at her arms. "Your arms were good."

She seemed unconvinced.

"You did these great unconscious movements with them during that song." He demonstrated. "Like, you have rhythm, and you understand the beat. Maybe you think you can't dance, but I can definitely teach you something in a week."

Evie put the menu down. "Your teaching abilities aren't in question here."

Well, that was something. He still got a sense that she thought he was total scum.

More importantly, why did he care so much?

"Good," he said uncertainly. "We, uh, we have to organize the practice sessions. We only have a week."

The server took their drinks orders, and Sarah picked up the menu. "Oh, she's got loads of free time."

"Actually," Evie sounded irritated, "we're going to Niagara Falls on Tuesday. I also have a few meetings scheduled. So while I *am* generally free, I do have things to do."

Right, she was a tourist. That would make things easier for him. She could accommodate his schedule better without the work commitments students usually had. He could keep his classes rolling and keep some of his shifts at the coffee shop. Awesome. One less thing to stress about.

"Okay." Did he sound excited? Maybe he could sound more enthusiastic. "That's cool."

An awkward silence fell on the table. He opened his menu and scanned the lunch options, happy for an excuse not to talk.

"I'm glad it's you doing this," Sarah said abruptly.

"Me?" Tyler asked.

"Yeah. I haven't seen you perform in anything for months. Definitely nothing partnered."

"This wasn't really my choice," he said. "Derek kinda steamrolled me into it."

"Maybe you needed that though."

Drinks arrived, and they ordered food.

Sarah stirred, then sipped her lychee juice through her straw. "We haven't been out in ages. It's so good to see you again."

Tyler shrugged, not wanting to discuss Lucette in front of Evie and Bailey.

"Plus," Sarah grinned, "you'll be an amazing representative at Pride."

Tyler waved dismissively. "I'm a fucking Venn diagram of representation."

"That's exactly my point."

"And mine. Did Derek tell me to do this because I'm talented or because I fit the queer brief?" *Or the ethnic-minority brief.* Tyler was pretty sure Derek was looking out for him, but he couldn't help having doubts about Derek's motivations.

Evie sipped her green tea. "A bit of both, I imagine."

"Exactly," Bailey agreed. "But it doesn't matter. You're awesome."

"Whatever the reason, you're still doing it." Sarah looked ready to hug him, she was so pleased. "I'm super proud of you, and I can't wait to see you and Evazilla storm the stage."

Evazilla. Seriously, what kind of nickname was that?

"So." Evie seemed ready to have a conversation. "How do you know each other?"

"We met at a queer society mixer," Sarah said.

Tyler smiled at the memory. He'd been attending college for dance, she'd been at university for law, and their respective LGBTQ societies had had a joint meet. He'd found her spiking the already-alcoholic punch with cheap rum, and the rest was history.

"You were as crazy then as you are now," he said.

Sarah turned her happiness up to full beam. "Oh yeah. And you were such a Casanova."

Tyler smiled wryly. He'd churned through a lot of curious queer girls, grateful for the attention. It had been fun at the time, but now he had mixed feelings about those memories. He definitely wouldn't be grateful for that kind of attention now.

Their food arrived, and they tucked in. Quietly. When Tyler felt the silence had dragged on too long, he swallowed the sashimi he was chewing and asked, "How did *you* two meet?"

Sarah and Evie glanced at each other and grinned. Tyler didn't like those grins. They seemed to hint at something he maybe didn't want to know.

Sarah began to play with her straw, lifting it in and out of the juice. "We're both on Tumblr."

"And we like a lot of the same stuff." Evie used her chopsticks to load a big mouthful of salmon and rice.

"I followed you because you reblogged so much Eren/Armin slash." Sarah's voice had gone dreamy.

Evie swallowed her food. "And I followed you back because you liked the same yaoi I did. Remember how you found that link to the *Sekaiichi Hatsukoi* OVA the day it was released? And how I went totally apeshit in your messages?"

"Yes! It was so *disappointing.*"

Evie nodded. "Anime creators love teasing fujoshi."

Tyler hadn't understood any of that beyond *Tumblr*. They were net denizens; that much was clear.

Evie must have noticed his confusion. "Basically, we met via social media about three years ago." Her chopsticks somehow scooped a bite-size amount of rice, a feat Tyler had never quite managed to pull off. Dextrous fingers.

"And this is the first time you've met each other in person?" Tyler asked.

"Yup!" As she talked, Evie's expression actually brightened. "It's been so nice to finally meet her. I'd always wanted to come here and see the place where she lived." Evie waved at the view out the window. "She described Toronto so vividly that I recognized places from her descriptions. I've been here for two days, and it's everything I thought it would be and more. Sarah and Bailey have been wonderful hosts."

Really? Maybe some people liked having someone with the energy of fifty million puppies around.

He must have looked unconvinced, because she emphasized the point. "Really wonderful. Sarah is as sweet and cheerful in real life as she is in her emails."

"Oh, Evazilla!" Sarah stood, pattered around the table, and enveloped Evie in a tight hug. "Right back at you, honey! I'm so happy you're here!"

Bailey smiled at the sight of them, and Tyler couldn't help smiling too. Clearly Sarah had yet to show Evie her truly evil side.

"You're over here for sightseeing?" he asked Evie once Sarah had returned to her chair.

"Yes. Also for Pride." Her smile left her face. "I had an opportunity to come here, so I took it."

Sarah waved her hand at Evie. "Forget all that stuff. You're here now. Focus on fun."

"Oh, I am."

Tyler glanced at Bailey, hoping they'd know what *that stuff* meant, but they just shrugged. Tyler dug into his sashimi.

The conversation moved on to afternoon plans, which involved a photography exhibit Evie wanted to see at some gallery on Queen Street and a movie Bailey suggested. Sounded nice to be a tourist. Tyler couldn't remember the last time he'd gone to the movies.

Near one o'clock, Sarah noticed the time, yelled something about being late, and threw down her chopsticks. She dropped money, hugged Tyler, promised to meet Evie for drinks later that evening, then ran out.

The conversation flowed a little more slowly after she'd gone, and Tyler noticed Evie rarely addressed him. Once they paid, left, and were strolling back over the green, he decided it was time to force the issue. His stomach churned at the prospect, but he shoved the feeling down.

"Evie," he began, "when are you free for the first practice?"

She shrugged. "Whenever you're free. I imagine you're far busier than I am."

So British. "You imagine right." He pulled out his phone and checked his schedule. He had blocked off the next afternoon preemptively. "Tomorrow, 2 p.m. until 6 p.m.?"

"That suits me." Out came hers and they exchanged numbers.

So far, so good. They could do this. *He* could do this. "Great. Wear comfy clothes and shoes, and bring water and a snack. And the forms and deposit for Jean."

She nodded distractedly, still doing something with her phone.

"It was nice to meet you, Evie."

She finally looked up at him. Blue eyes—and how was he only noticing those for the first time? What a deep blue. The churning in the pit of his stomach faded, to be replaced by a slow, pleasant heat that radiated out to his fingertips and toes.

Evie gave a small, oddly shy smile, and held out her hand. "I won't say it's been a pleasure meeting you, Tyler, but I look forward to getting to know you better."

Oh hell, she was English all right. She sounded so polite he almost hadn't realized what she'd said. *"I won't say it's been a pleasure."*

Jesus.

Well, in fairness to her, the audition *had* been ridiculous. He'd take *"I look forward to getting to know you better,"* though. Tyler shook her hand, fist-bumped Bailey, and started walking towards the subway.

As he slipped earbuds on, it suddenly sank in that Evie, a tourist from England who was great at eating with chopsticks and making insults sound like a compliment, was actually the best kind of dance partner he could ask for. She didn't live here. She didn't seem to give a shit about being good. She didn't even seem interested in him. She'd learn the dance, make nice for the cameras, wow Sarah and Bailey, then go home, and he'd never have to see her again. All he had to do was get through this one week with her. That was it.

He instantly felt better about the whole thing.

Evie and Bailey met Sarah at a bar near her office in the city centre, a place with exposed brick walls and copper pipes snaking along the ceilings. Bailey left to work in their studio not long after Sarah arrived, leaving Sarah and Evie to stare at the mess of forms for the competition.

"I can't believe some of these." Evie spread them out on the table beside their beers. "Injury waivers, fine, but an allergy form? A questionnaire for the dance school?"

"Just covering their bases, honey," Sarah said.

"And this from Pride." Evie held up the volunteer questionnaire. In addition to the statistics questions asking about her ethnicity, age, sexual orientation, gender, preferred pronouns, etc., they wanted her home address and email, which to her meant one thing: spam. Maybe she could leave that out.

It was still sinking in that she was even doing this.

"It's so *exciting*!" Sarah wiggled in her seat.

Evie wondered if there was anything Sarah *didn't* find exciting about this. "It will be an experience, certainly," she murmured, looking over the temporary member form for QS Dance.

"You're not into it?" Sarah frowned, instantly concerned. "Were those directors really that rude?"

Evie had actually forgotten about them in the wake of exchanging contact details with Tyler. Tyler, who seemed so diffident about this competition. Tyler, with the dark eyes and curly hair and perpetual frown. Tyler, who no doubt thought she was a complete lunatic. There were reasons Evie hadn't shared her Tumblr account with her friends and family, and his reaction was exactly why. *Evazilla*. It had been funny at the time she created the account, and she did maybe sort of slightly like it, but good God, five years hadn't aged it well. She'd never been more mortified.

Plus she'd snapped at him and his boss. Called them all vultures. She'd tried to be funny about it when she said good-bye to him, but as with a lot of things that sounded good in her head, it had come out awful in real life. He'd hesitated to shake her hand. Now she'd have to dance with the guy. What had she been thinking back in that stall?

New experiences, Evie. That's what you were thinking.

Sometimes new experiences were better left new.

"Evie?"

"Sorry? No. No, they weren't *that* rude. If anything, I was just as rude." Evie couldn't remember the last time she'd felt so overwhelmed. That had to be the only reason for her behaviour. Her mother would've had a fit if she'd seen the way Evie had spoken to Justine.

"No, it's just . . . um . . ." She couldn't say Tyler's presence seemed to make her more awkward than she already was, not to someone who knew him so well and who seemed prone to reading into things. "I, uh, I'm not a dancer, Sarah. I jog slowly and do aerobics and lift weights when I remember to. Not dance."

Sarah rolled her eyes. "Listen to you. 'I'm not a dancer. I only do every other form of exercise.' You can handle this."

"I can barely touch my toes."

Sarah took one of Evie's hands in both of hers. Perhaps it was just Sarah, but Evie had a feeling Canadians were a relatively touchy-feely bunch compared to the British.

Sarah's hands were warm and dry, and she gazed steadily at Evie. "Honey. Relax. *Relax.* I kinda think that's the point of this thing. Tyler's a teacher. It's his job to teach you from scratch." She patted Evie's hand. "You're in good hands."

Like she'd said at lunch, that wasn't the point. "I don't think I made the best of impressions."

"Whaaat? No way, you were great! All in everyone's faces and not taking shit and *raaar.*" Sarah made claws. "Very Evazilla."

Evie frowned. "Yeah, but that's not really okay. I was brought up to be decorous and accommodating." It would be helpful to at least not snap at people, especially if they were Tyler and dancing with her for the next week. *Oh dear.* Trust her to start off on the wrong foot.

"Overrated," Sarah declared, sipping her beer. "This is Canada, not England. We're polite, but we're not doormats."

"That's not what I meant—"

"It is, Evie." Sarah turned uncharacteristically serious. "You weren't rude, you just gave their shit back to them. You sassed Justine. You think she liked you before that? She didn't. Her and Derek, and yeah, even Tyler, they didn't give a crap about who you are and that you have manners and are supposed to be—what was it, decorous? You know? You fixed a problem for them, and now they like you fine. What you said doesn't matter. What you *did* does." She smiled. "You're good people, Evazilla, but you can't care about what strangers think about you like that. You can't be perfect to everyone."

Evie opened her mouth to say she didn't care what Justine thought, but stopped when Sarah's point sank in. Hmm. Maybe it wasn't as bad as she thought it was.

"Especially when they crowded you like that," Sarah added. "My God, you should have seen Derek and Justine behind you." She held up her hands and mimed two mouths snapping at each other.

"I did see that. I think everyone saw that."

"And," Sarah's eyes sparkled with glee, "everyone's going to see you dance on stage at Pride."

Evie's stomach plummeted. *Bugger.* She hadn't quite taken in that aspect of it. She picked up the event sheet and skimmed the description. Static stage somewhere on Church Street. *Static.* Not the parade. Thank Christ.

Sarah reached forward and picked up the release form for the documentary. "This documentary should be fun to watch. I hope the crew releases it on YouTube for public viewing."

What?

Sarah pulled out her phone. "I mean, someone's already put a video up, but I think the proper camera will be better quality, eh?"

"There's a *YouTube video*?" Evie hauled Sarah's phone around and watched as Sarah hit Play. Someone's fuzzy mobile camera had caught her dancing around on the machine. It was from behind, so at least her face wasn't visible. She bounced and side-stepped and paused with the music, arms and shoulders swaying, her whole body getting into the swing of it. The title of the video was *Girl kills on the dance machine*, and it had two thousand views.

Oh God. How was this happening?

"I'm seriously rethinking this," she said.

"Why?"

Evie wanted to throw the phone at whoever had filmed her. "You know I'm not out to my family. What if they see this online somehow?"

Sarah frowned. "Honey, you know I don't advocate coming out before you're ready. But maybe you should have considered that before deciding to do something as public as this?"

Fuck. She couldn't win. Evie dropped her face onto the table, past caring. Her phone buzzed in her bag, and she fumbled blindly for it.

"Besides," Sarah continued as Evie turned her face on the table to check the screen, "so what? What happens in Toronto stays in Toronto."

An email from her mum. "You're right," Evie murmured. Looked like Mum had sent a Rowena Whitmore special.

Evelyn, hope you're having a wonderful time in Toronto. Who was it you were staying with again? I hope you've made them a meal to thank them for their hospitality. Richard has received a promotion and we're all so proud. Shep got into the radishes and was very sick, but Dr. Nishan pumped his stomach and he's much better now. What's the latest on the settlement, and have you heard anything about work for the summer? You shouldn't live off savings if you don't have to. In fact, if you have a spare grand or two lying around, you should consider a few ETFs. Your father says they're all the rage in DIY investing these days. Retirement happens to us all! Do let us know when you have a plan in place. Your father says hello by the way. Stay away from poutine, you know how too much grease affects you. All that northern food really hasn't done you any favours, darling. Call us soon.

Good Lord. She thumbed a quick *I hope Shep is all right, hug him for me,* then reread the message. Couldn't she ever stick to one topic? Since Doug—who was her *step*father, thanks, Mum—had received his massive salary increase two years ago, Mum had become insufferable. Investment advice? Really?

"What's up?" Sarah asked.

"My mum is out of touch with reality." Evie turned the screen off. This wasn't unusual. Mum always had been, well, a *handful*. Evelyn was Rowena's middle name, and Rowena loved reminding everyone how Evie was named after her, but "not *too* much after her" because "Evie should be her *own* person." Even after Evie had moved to York, a fair distance from Devon, she still received messages like this regularly. At first, she just thought their relationship was very close. When Evie had been figuring out her sexuality, however, she'd realized that their relationship was less *very close* and more *suffocating*. Truthfully, when U of T had accepted her to the master's program, part of Evie's joy at accepting had come from knowing there would be an ocean *and* a lake between her and her mum.

Not that it appeared to be stopping the emails.

Evie put the phone away. "Do you feel like having poutine tonight?" she asked.

Sarah lit up at the idea. "Fuck. Yes. Let's get as much Canada in you as possible."

As Evie cracked up, she imagined sending exactly that line to her mum. Oh, if Rowena only knew what she was up to.

Tyler opened his bedroom door and walked the three steps to his bed, relishing the sight of it for a few seconds before falling face-first into the comforter. *Oh yeah*. His body sank into the mattress, muscles slowly decompressing like they always did after intense activity.

He lay like that for a while, mind turning over the day. The rest of it had sped by in a blur of classes and shift work, but his thoughts were on a loop of *Class, training, choreography, Evie*.

Over and over again, Evie and her fierce blue eyes and crystal-sharp voice, telling Justine where to go, loudly and proudly and with no hesitation.

He flipped over onto his back and stared at the ceiling.

Evie. He had to choreograph something for her. He'd already blocked a basic routine out, but now that he'd actually met the person he was dancing with, he had to adapt it to her. What he had didn't match the personality he'd seen.

He rolled over to his bedside table where he'd left his choreography notes from the previous evening. He scanned them, noting the words ringed in red at the top of the page: *A dance for the masses*, and the Pride theme, *Fierce*. He smiled. *That* shouldn't be a problem for her. The real challenge was harnessing Evie's natural gifts in moves that looked good, but that a complete beginner could pull off.

Mind ticking over the story of the dance and possible moves, he headed into his combined living room and kitchen. The place was tidy, tiny, and tired, but he loved it. It was the first place he'd rented by himself, and he relished having his own space too much to care about its deficiencies.

He pushed the donated sofa and coffee table to the edges of the room, then started humming the song he'd chosen for the performance and visualizing the opening moves. He blocked them out, adjusted, and quietly felt them out, turning through the room. In his mind, a shadowy partner took form opposite him, reacting to his lead. She spun, met him in a hold, stayed in step and in sync as he tapped out complicated footwork. She floated around him as he stood in pose. He held his part, her part, and their combined steps together in his head, imagining them as though he were an audience member as well as both of the dancers.

Reaching the chorus, he held out his hand and she took it, folding herself into his arms— No. Not like that. That was Lucette. He shook his head and redid the movement. This time the shadow took his hand to throw it away and advance on him, power in her imaginary body.

Definitely not Lucette. He had to remember that.

He matched her step for step. This was a dance of adoration and struggle. He the scorned but tenacious suitor, she the resistant but intrigued lover; it was a classic story that had been told and retold countless times. Just in case the audience didn't get it, it would be set to the fast, furious, and popular "Are You Gonna Be My Girl" by Jet.

The last few bars pounded in his head, and he found himself on his knees watching the shadowy girl stride away from him. She evaporated as she hit the sofa. He sat down hard and reached for his notes, scribbling the moves down while they were fresh in his head.

Oh man. He'd forgotten this. He'd *missed* this. Creating, blocking, twisting the music into his body and releasing it again through muscles. Building the dance, visualizing it, making sure that it fit, that *they* fit. Maybe Derek had been right about needing to partner someone again. He'd forgotten how freeing partnered choreography could be without another person's input.

Without a specific person's input.

Just like that, Lucette was back in his head. He blinked. She perched on the sofa in their old apartment with that perpetual expression of distaste. She lounged in their kitchen, fork in one hand and a bowl of noodles in the other, telling him the choreography for his part wasn't masculine enough. She crushed herself against his chest, crying and telling him she was only trying to help. She danced with him, lovely hard lines in the soft light. She stomped around the apartment in a rage. She looked into his face and said hurtful words about him and his body and the things he lacked as a dancer and as a man, and then she slammed the door on her way out. She flew back in, smiling and begging forgiveness. She lay next to him in bed, dissatisfied and ranting. She danced with him again, lovely and sinuous. Then she resisted his lead. Then she was gone.

His fingers tightened around his pen. Lucette *was* gone. She'd been gone for a year. And what he'd blocked out on paper was good. He knew it was. It wasn't the traditional binary that Lucette had preferred, true, but it was more equal. More give and take. More partnership than lead and follow. More emotion.

Memories of her had no place here.

She was negative and hurtful and she didn't understand you or how to be with you or how to be happy. She's not part of your life anymore.

He closed his eyes. He knew all that, so why did this still hurt? And why did she still intrude like this?

The dance played out in front of him on the sheets of paper. He ran back through it in his head, tweaking his notes anew. When he was happy with what he'd written, he sat back and looked up.

His imaginative shadowy partner stood with attitude, hip out and arms crossed. *Well?* she seemed to be asking.

"I don't know," he said to her, "but I hope the real version of you can carry it off."

She shrugged.

While he was being honest. "I also hope you're nicer to dance with."

She stuck her tongue out at him.

He needed to get a grip. He was talking to his imagination. The clock in his kitchen said it was after 1 a.m. He hadn't eaten. His phone blinked at him from the table, which meant he'd missed a call. Life involved other shit that needed to be dealt with.

"I need to get out more," he said to her. She dissolved.

Typical.

CHAPTER THREE

The dance school was a shortish streetcar ride from the university campus, but Evie had underestimated how long coffee with the course director would take, especially as they'd had to find somewhere that wasn't filled with graduating students. By the time she reached the school, she was out of breath and barely on schedule. Worth the delay, though; Evie was more excited about the course than ever.

But when she reached the front door, she wanted to go back and leave fifteen minutes earlier—Tyler was outside, slouching against the wall and visibly annoyed. The slim redhead and camera guy from the previous day were there too, and they perked up when they saw her.

She stopped in front of Tyler, panting. "Sorry. Had coffee. Ran late."

"It's your time," he said.

If her face hadn't already been hot from running, she'd have flushed. What was this guy's *problem*? He'd seemed mellower during lunch, but now he was back to the bristly obnoxiousness he'd had at the audition.

The redhead stepped forward. "Hi. Evie, right?"

Evie glanced from her to the camera and back again. "Yes?"

"I'm Katie Cherry. This is my cameraman, Brock Stubbs." The camera guy waved. "We're doing the documentary about this dance performance, and we'll be filming part of every session you do."

Cherry? Like Justine from yesterday? Evie took a closer look at her, and, yes, Katie had red hair and thin features similar to Justine's, only softened by youth and a smattering of freckles across her face.

She blew a pink bubble until it popped, then smiled at Evie as she rechewed the gum.

Right. The university project. "Nice to meet you. I think I have a form for you." Evie pulled her backpack off and fished out the release form.

Katie scanned it and nodded, apparently satisfied. "Thanks. Okay, the drill is, ignore the camera. Pretend it's not there. Just be yourself, act natural, do dumb shit, whatever. It's fine, as long as you forget the camera is there."

Evie wasn't convinced. The camera and the cameraman were both a little big to just forget about.

Katie snapped her gum. "I want to interview both of you during breaks or after the session. We won't film the whole thing because we have to get around to the other couples too. When you've finalized your practice schedule, please pass it to me so I can—"

Evie tuned her out when she noticed Tyler looking increasingly pissed off. This wasn't the best of starts. How was she going to learn a dance from him if he was angry?

"—screening in the fall," Katie finished.

Wait, what? Evie returned her attention to her. Katie held out her business card. Bewildered, Evie took it. Embossed writing and a matte finish. Nice.

"All clear?" Katie asked.

"Crystal," Evie said. Damn it. She had no idea what Katie had just told her.

Tyler huffed impatiently. "We done here?"

Katie gestured to the door. "After you."

He pulled away from the wall. "Come on, Evie. There's more admin to get out of the way."

They walked into the dance school. It was in an old industrial building, but the interior was surprisingly warm and bright. The reception area had a welcome desk and chairs, and notice boards studded with staples and the occasional dance poster on the walls. A group of students lounged in one corner, stretching their legs. Three corridors and a staircase led further into the building.

Tyler strode down one corridor, and Evie hustled to keep up. Katie and Brock followed closely.

They stopped outside a door with a plaque reading *Marketing/Finance* and entered to find Jean sitting in front of a computer at a neat desk, complete with empty inbox tray. Evie suspected that Jean was only in the building this Saturday for her and the other contestants. She smiled at the sight of them. "Evie! Tyler! You made it."

Evie dug into her backpack for the remainder of the forms. Her bag gaped, and Godzilla's head emerged. She caught sight of Tyler's bemused expression, and hastily stuffed Godzilla back down. He was only there so she could bring him to the pizza place Sarah wanted to visit that evening. Evie slapped the forms, as well as the refundable deposit, in front of Jean.

"Thank you." Jean smiled before flicking through the mess of papers and sorting them.

All too soon, they were done and shooed out of the office. Outside, they ran into the sparkly dancer, the one Evie had originally thought was Tyler, and Mark from the previous day. Mark chatted happily with Katie while the dancer looked down the corridor, his face red. Brock was also red and staring in the other direction.

"Gigi?" Tyler said.

The dancer turned to them. A grin crept over his face when he saw Evie. "Well, look who it is." He bowed theatrically to her. "Madame High Score, I am Gigi LaMore, née Rosenberg. Welcome to QS Dance, or as we inmates like to call it, hell next to a barre."

"I'm Mark." Mark waved. With his short-cropped hair, basketball shorts, baseball cap, and Nike shirt, he looked the very image of the North American jock stereotype.

She eyed Gigi, unsure what to make of him. He certainly looked the part of a queen, with a leopard-print scarf, diamond earrings, purple hair, and clinging tracksuit bottoms, but there was a defensive curl to his stance and his flamboyance seemed exaggerated. "I'm Evie. Is Gigi your stage name?"

Gigi gasped in faux outrage. "Absolutely not!"

"Yeah, it is," Tyler said drily.

"I like it. How did you come by it?"

Gigi's gaze flickered to Brock before he grabbed her hand and spun her around. "I was a good little girl with a very nice drag mama."

Evie quirked an eyebrow. That seemed like deflection, but before she could ask him his real name, she saw Brock fix Gigi with an intense stare, one that said *I knew it*. She also saw how Gigi avoided looking at the cameraman. Oh. *Oh.* That seemed like a story. She decided she'd leave it for now. "So you *have* seen the film."

Gigi raised an eyebrow. "Film?"

"Evie, we have to go," Tyler said tightly. "We've wasted twenty minutes already."

"I recommend it." Evie pulled her hand out of Gigi's. "You might learn something."

"Oooh, I like her," Gigi said, turning to Tyler. He stopped short, looking Tyler up and down. "Who shoved a stick up *your* ass?"

"Don't give me ideas," Tyler muttered, walking past them.

Katie moved after him, and Evie watched as Gigi very obviously avoided Brock by walking around him and through the finance department door. Mark followed him with all the obliviousness of a puppy. Brock stared at the door, his ears red, then trailed after Tyler. *Interesting.* Evie ran to catch up.

Tyler strode quickly, his entire body stiff. Evie wondered if Gigi and he were friends or enemies. Or . . . oh! Boyfriends? Possibly? Hence that tension with Brock? Tyler didn't strike her as gay, but she didn't exactly have the most developed gaydar in the world.

"Uh, so Gigi seemed . . . nice," she said as they left the corridor.

Tyler gave a sharp laugh. "Don't even try. He's anything but nice."

Not boyfriends, then. "Is he your friend?"

A long-suffering laugh this time. "Unfortunately."

They turned down another corridor. "And he's doing this too?"

"Yes."

"Are you two competitive?"

Tyler snorted. "Do bears crap in the woods?" He seemed less wound up now. "Don't worry about him. He likes to stir things up. Deep down, when it's inconvenient, he's a good guy."

Tyler pushed at a door marked *Practice Room 5*, and Evie walked into a studio space. Mirrors lined two of the walls and a barre ran around the perimeter. Light poured through two windows, and a stereo sat in one corner with mats stacked beside it. She stopped short just inside the door, her nerves clawing up her stomach. Oh good

God, this was real. She was going to dance for the next three and a half hours. Somehow. *Shit.*

Tyler dumped his bag in one corner and pulled out his MP3 player. Katie and Brock walked around the room with the camera, gauging the light. Evie couldn't seem to move. Tyler looked up at her. "You coming, Godzilla?"

She blinked in surprise, then blushed. "You saw him."

"Yeah. I've seen the movies too. You're a fan?" He focused on the MP3 player, picking a tune.

Evie nodded. "Yeah, I liked them."

"I guess that's where Sarah's nickname for you comes from." He seemed very focused on the player.

"It's not, but the name tied in well with my taste in films." She put her backpack down next to his.

"Okay," he said, apparently done with chitchat, "I've choreographed a dance I think you'll be able to do. I'm going to show you both parts, mine and yours, as best I can. Just watch and tell me what you think."

She nodded.

He went to the centre of the room and put his earbuds in. Pressed Play. He stood very still, then burst into dancing.

Evie drew in a small, surprised breath as he danced with an invisible person. The movements, as far as she could tell, were a mix of swing and fluid, interpretive stuff. Fast, controlled, elegant, and smooth, he moved as though what he was doing was easy. The steps were also crazy quick. Her heart sank; no way could she do that intricate footwork *and* keep up with him *and* look good doing it. *Shit, shit, shit.*

When he performed her part, though, her doubts increased. *Her* part was all dominance and ownership of the stage. It sat well on him, but she couldn't pull off that kind of attitude. There was a sexual element too. Of course, she could perform it and have fun with it, but if he expected her to dig deep and expose her supposed inner sex goddess for the stage, she was toast. Her steps were just as quick as his, if slightly less technical. By the time he finished, Evie was wondering if losing the deposit was really such a big deal.

"What do you think?" he asked breathlessly, sweat coating his face and neck.

Evie noticed for the first time that he was wearing a tank that exposed his arms and shoulders, because sweat glittered there too. She'd worn her jogging gear, figuring the running tights, tank top, and sports bra were the most comfortable clothes she usually sweated in. Which meant she'd chosen the right thing. Good. That was a start.

"That was amazing, but I think you better lower your expectations," she said.

His entire frame relaxed. "Not possible," he said.

Ouch. Say what you really think.

"It looks like . . ." She blushed. "Like the guy really wants the girl, but she's making him work for it."

"That's the whole thing in a nutshell."

"What's the music?"

He smiled, a genuine full grin that flashed some teeth and completely changed his face. He looked *friendly*, which honestly threw her a bit.

He beckoned with an earbud. "Come here." She walked to him, put the earbud in, and he pressed Play.

The quick beat and distinctive opening bars lit up her senses. Evie knew this song. She *liked* this song. "Jet? Really?"

He nodded.

"Excellent choice."

"You're going to hate it after this week."

She pulled out the earbud, nervousness building in her stomach. The moves were fast, the music was fast, the footwork was complicated, and she was dancing with a gorgeous guy who seemed unimpressed by her. *Great start, Evie.*

New fucking experiences.

They warmed up, getting Evie's blood pumping and releasing some of the nervous energy building inside of her. Then he showed her the first few moves and had her copy him. When she had them down to his satisfaction, he clapped out the beat and told her to match the movements to it. She messed up instantly.

"It's quick," he said.

"No kidding," she gasped, glaring at him.

He did the moves over again for her. "You've got the stage at the beginning. You have to keep the audience's attention and make use of the stage *and* finish in the right position for me to grab *your* attention." His tone reminded her of primary school teachers telling her she knew how to do her homework, so there wasn't any excuse for not doing it. "You can't take it slow and you can't try to hide."

Good God. Keep the audience's attention? No *hiding*? Since when had she tried to do that? She was in the middle of a bloody studio, there was nothing to hide behind. How was she going to do this? No way could she do this.

Her dubiousness must've shown, because he frowned at her. "Hey, you can do it. You did it at the audition."

"At the audition?"

"Yeah. Attitude. Channel it. Let it lift your body up and out." His posture and body rose and extended as he spread his arms and straightened his back.

Evie copied him. Energy thrilled through her as she spread out into the space. Her body felt taller, her arms longer, her legs poised to . . . to do something, to move or to take flight. She felt centre stage, even though she was near one wall of the room. Exposed, but thrilling.

Ah. Amazing what a simple movement could do.

He nodded, looking pleased. "That's it."

Wait a moment. "This has just been me so far. So this isn't even the part where we dance together?" Evie asked.

"What you just learned was the first nineteen seconds of the song."

She stared at him in shock. "No way. I haven't learned that. I've learned the two-minute-long, take-my-sweet-time version." The reality of what she was trying to do hit her. "Oh God, we only have a *week*."

He shook his head. "Yeah, Godzilla. It's not a walk in the park."

"Bollocks." She gazed at her feet. How the hell was she going to do this?

"We'll get there." He sounded as though he was trying to convince himself rather than her. "Have some water and we'll go over it again."

And they did. Over and over again. Attitude notwithstanding, she felt completely exposed and incompetent. She got every other step wrong, on camera and in front of Tyler. Eventually, the first few steps came together, but her head was starting to get fuzzy with the effort of trying to remember each step in order. An hour later, Evie was too ready to flop down on the ground for a break. She dropped where she stood and spread out on the floor. Immediately, Brock and the camera were in her face. Katie angled a microphone at her mouth.

Evie frowned. "What the—"

"You look tired," Katie said from her right side. "How are you doing?"

Evie gave a weak thumbs-up. "Tired."

"Is this easier or harder than you thought it would be?"

"I didn't think about it at all," Evie admitted. She realized as she said it that no, she hadn't considered this in terms of her holiday plan. She'd just agreed to do it and fit the holiday around the dancing. How . . . utterly unlike her.

Katie nodded and leaned in closer. "You seem to be getting along well with Tyler."

"I *suppose* . . ."

"He's kinda cute, eh?"

Evie lolled her head to her left and looked at him. He was swigging Gatorade and gazing at them, apparently listening to every word. She lolled her head back and shrugged. "He'll do."

She heard rather than saw Tyler choke on the Gatorade. Brock panned the camera up in time to catch Tyler clapping a hand over his mouth to stop it dripping. Evie smiled, and Katie winked at her, red hair flashing in the light.

"So," Katie said, "tell us about yourself. What's your name?"

"Evie Whitmore."

"You're not from Canada, judging by your accent."

Evie would hope so. "No. I'm from England."

Tyler tried to mop up as best he could without snorting more of the Gatorade into his sinuses. Shit. *Shit.* Smooth, Tyler.

This session was going way better than he'd thought it would. Sure, she'd shown up late, but she was listening and taking direction.

She moved conscientiously, which made him suspect she exercized and knew how to listen to her body. A body that had pleasantly surprised him; she was a natural at dancing. Lots of people were, but she was fluid and responsive. Plus, uh, nice to look at. Especially now when her hair had escaped her braid and frizzed around her face. Great legs.

Focus, Ty.

Best of all, she *liked* the choreography. God, that was a weight off his chest.

If she wasn't a tourist, Tyler suspected he'd be in trouble. Liked his moves, dry humour, excellent accent, pretty, could handle Gigi, *and* she could dance. Gigi was right—she was completely his type. But he couldn't afford to think like that.

He pulled out his phone to distract himself and found a text from his sister, Shana: *Bro, will you freaking call me back already? How hard is it to return a call?*

"So what brings you to Toronto?" Katie asked.

"Well, it's a bit of a long story," Evie began.

What the hell is up with Shana? He called her, but got her voice mail instead, and listened to the automated "This person is not able to take your call right now" message with a frown. Okay, so Shana *had* been calling him a lot lately. The message she'd left on his phone the night before had been nervous chatter about random crap in Calgary. That was unusual for her. But until she said what the problem was, Tyler wasn't sure if he should ask.

The beep sounded.

"Shana, call me back when you get a chance," he said, then hung up.

If he was honest, he had other things to think about, like how his next paycheck was a week away, and he was eating beans, rice, and canned vegetables to make his money go further. Oh, and how this stupid competition was throwing Lucette's ghost up into his head.

"Congratulations!" Katie was saying. "We'll definitely be in touch. Now, if you don't mind telling us, are you queer or an ally?"

Tyler turned to watch as Evie replied without hesitation, "Oh, queer."

"Lesbian, or . . . ?"

Evie paused.

Please don't be a lesbian. Wait, what? Where the hell had that come from? He knew multiple lesbians who'd smack him one just for thinking that.

She took a deep breath, then said, "I'm asexual. Well, ace spectrum."

Asexual.

Asexual?

His heart dropped. He missed Katie's next question through a buzz of noise in his head, soon damped down by remembering she was Sarah's friend. *Sarah's.* The person whose first words to him had been, "I'm an aromantic cuddlewhore. What's your poison, honey?" while respiking *punch*, for fuck's sake. And she'd met Evie on Tumblr through "mutual interests." Angsty Japanese media notwithstanding, he could see being asexual as strong common ground on which to base an internet friendship. Especially if you wanted to offer a place to stay while someone came over *for Pride.*

Frankly, it was a surprise he was surprised.

You idiot, Ty. What were you starting to think?

He refused to answer that.

"Not out to family, but I am to certain friends," Evie was saying.

"Is that a problem for you?"

"No." Evie shrugged, still on the floor. "It's never really come up. I've told my family about my boyfriends and some of the girlfriends but—"

"You've dated?" Katie blurted.

Evie arched her eyebrow. "Yes." She leaned towards Katie conspiratorially. "I've even had *sex.*"

Katie went pink and Brock cleared his throat.

Evie made a scissoring motion with her fingers. "Apparently I'm very good with my hands."

Tyler's crotch went heavy, and he sucked in a breath. He'd forgotten how hot hands could be. *God*damn*, girl.*

"*Okay,*" Katie sputtered. "So, your family is okay with apparent bisexuality, but not with asexuality?"

Evie frowned. "They don't really believe in queer people, period. I mean, they know about who I've dated. My dad and my stepdad never talk about it. Mum said once that she went through an experimental phase as well and got through it without any problems, and that I would too." She grimaced. "I decided not to pursue the topic."

Katie smiled grimly. "Sounds rough. This is good for us, though. I don't think there's another ace participating in this. You're a rare bunch."

Evie shrugged. "Not really. One in one hundred. It's the same ratio as redheads in the general population."

Katie's smile froze. Tyler turned away to hide the smirk on his face, and to put his phone away. Much as he enjoyed watching Evie mess with the film crew, the break had to end.

He turned in time to see Evie stand from a perfect squat. Her leg muscles shifted under the material of her jogging pants, and something about her body clicked in his mind. Strong legs. He studied her arms and shoulders. Somewhat bulky, yeah, but it wasn't fat. No, it was *muscle.*

"Is this your first time dancing?" Katie asked her.

"Yeah. Normally I run and lift weights," she said. "But dancing is new—"

"You lift weights?" he asked. If that was true, then that opened up an awesome range of moves for them.

Evie's attention snapped to him. "Yes," she said, tilting her chin as though he were going to argue with her.

Like he would. He was too excited by a new idea. "What weight can you lift?"

She eyed him uncertainly. "Depends on the muscle group."

Katie and Brock retreated, camera rolling.

He glanced down at his body. Since starting T, he'd bulked up, but his basic frame hadn't changed. He was roughly her height and weight. "Could you lift me?"

Whatever she was expecting him to say, it wasn't that. "You?" she echoed in disbelief.

"Yeah."

"Seriously?"

"Yeah."

She eyed him up and down thoughtfully. "Maybe. You're not talking about some fancy over-the-head lift, are you?"

"No. Just pick up and put down." He walked up to her. "Try it."

She looked uncertain. "Are you sure? I'd need to grab you here." She pointed at his abdomen. "You're all muscle, so you're heavier than I am. The lower I go, the easier you'll be to lift."

"That's fine." He held his arms out loosely. "Go for it."

She hesitated.

He beckoned. "Come on, Evie. Keep your back straight. Do it slowly, and don't hurt yourself." *Or me.*

She stepped in closer, and he caught the smell of her: herbal shampoo, cottony deodorant, and a base note of spicy sweat. Nice.

Tyler. For real. Freaking focus already.

He tensed his core as she crouched down, wrapped her arms around his hips, and straightened with her legs. Just like that, he was up and supported. He looked down at her. She was staring into his shirt with immense concentration. She held him securely for a beat, then gently put him back down. *Easy. Awesome.*

"Perfect," he said, patting her shoulder.

She smiled. "I've never had a guy say that to me after I picked him up."

"You pick up guys often?" fell out of his mouth before he could stop it. *Oh dear God, Tyler. What are you doing?*

Her eyes glittered at the innuendo. "Nope. My style of picking people up isn't to everyone's tastes."

Ha. "I like it. I like it so much, I'm going to work it into the dance."

Her face fell. "*What?*"

"It'll be great." His mind was running through her part of the dance and reworking a quick part that involved them battling each other for attention and space on the stage. He stepped away and went through the moves, seeing how they fit together with the beat. Evie watched him patiently, her arms crossed. When he was happy, he retrieved his notes from his bag and quickly scribbled the basic lift in there. This was going to be fun.

"Okay." He rose and returned to her. "Do it again, but instead of putting me straight down, move me to your right side."

He directed her through the lift, making sure she knew what she was doing. Every time her arms closed around him, he felt tingly, aware of her strength and care. It had been a long time since someone had lifted him, and he'd forgotten how great it felt.

When they were done, she stood red-faced and sweaty before him. She'd done so well, it was only fair to return the favour.

"I also pick *you* up in this routine, if you want to practise that too," he said.

There was an awkward pause.

"Uh, just while we're doing lifts anyway," he added. *Stay cool Tyler, it's just a lift.* "You know. Keep the right mindset going." Or something.

She slowly nodded, eyeing his arms. "Do you lift me in the same way?"

"Almost. What you did is a basic lift. This is a straight lift. I'm going to hold your waist, just under your rib cage, and lift you right up in front of me." He demonstrated how far up. "You're going to help me by jumping into the lift and keeping your core stiff. Really tense it. Also put your arms on my shoulders so you have a platform to support yourself on."

She bit her lip, that look of concentration back. "Okay."

He moved closer. "Ready?"

She nodded.

He put his hands on her waist, and she lightly touched his shoulders. Small shocks skittered up and down his arms. He swallowed, then croaked, "Jump."

She did, and he lifted her. Her arms straightened on either side of his head, weight bearing down on him, her core tense, her legs straight. A natural. Those core muscles were strong and tight under his hands and *wow* he shouldn't be this interested in those—

"You guys look great!" Katie called.

He'd forgotten she and Brock were still there.

"You okay?" Evie asked uncertainly, looking down at him. Her fingers curled, bunching the material of the tank on his shoulders. Yeah, he was okay. He was *good*. He could gaze at those eyes all day.

"Yep," he said.

"I'm not too heavy?"

"Nope. Just heavy."

She cracked a smile, and Tyler started easing her down slowly, unable to look away from her face. She gazed at him, and just like that they were anchored into each other by sight as well as by muscles and hands. His breath caught somewhere deep in his chest. Thoughts scattered, throwing up similar images of her flushed and lowering to him, not to touch the ground but to kiss him. He shook his head to clear it. Her weight dug into his shoulders until her feet met the floor. They paused for a moment, looking at each other, then both of them let go.

"That was awkward." Evie looked away, face pink. "All of this feels really awkward."

"There's a trick that helps with that." His voice had gone rough.

"Oh?"

"Yeah. Keep doing it." She snorted, and he backed away. Enough lifts now. They had to move on with the routine, otherwise he'd never teach her anything. "Which means we're going to go over from the beginning again."

She groaned.

He grinned.

This was officially fun. Partnering with Evie was *fun*. He couldn't remember the last partner who'd made him snort his Gatorade or who'd given him snark while also truly trying to work with him (mostly because she would have been way before Lucette). That Evie was strong and gorgeous and made him remember what his libido felt like was a bonus. This was excellent.

It can still go wrong, that negative part of his head chimed in.

Partnering was, by its very nature, intimate. A good bond had to be built between partners in order for the dance to work. Sometimes when the routine told a romantic story, people were too drawn into that bond, too liable to think the acted chemistry and physical closeness indicated deeper feelings. It had happened with Lucette. And here he was now, already wonderfully aware of Evie's physicality.

Luce had always hated him dancing with other women.

Man, Luce is not here.

He took a deep breath. *Chill, Ty.* If things got weird, he knew better now. He could spot the warning signs. And Evie was a tourist; she would leave.

But there wouldn't be any problems. Evie was no Lucette. Evie was lots of things, but she didn't seem poised to misread the physical acting component of the routine as something more. Hell, her being asexual might even mitigate some of the physical stuff. She probably wouldn't even notice it, let alone read too much into it.

Relief bloomed, and he truly relaxed for the first time since the session started.

By the time Evie collapsed next to her bag at 6 p.m., her legs and arms were shaking. Katie and Brock had long since disappeared to film Gigi's session, meaning Tyler was the only one to hear her moan like a cow in distress. It didn't matter how much she jogged at home, it was nothing compared to dancing for three and a half hours. *Nothing.*

As she blindly dug in her bag for a cereal bar, she caught Tyler smirking at her. She held up one finger. "No. Don't look so smug, Mr. I-do-this-for-a-living. I'm dying."

"Me? *Smug?*"

"You. Smug. Right now." She bit into the bar and chewed. Never had anything tasted so good. "Oh God, I won't be able to move tomorrow."

"You'll have to," he said.

"Don't remind me." She crunched away as he pulled a towel out of his bag. *Hmm. Must remember that.* She'd sweated like a pig in the Sahara today. Attractive.

Not that she cared about being attractive.

Not that Tyler appeared to care either.

"This was good." He sat next to her, towelling off.

Yeah, right. She raised an eyebrow at him. "Don't. I'm a complete beginner. I know I'm not good."

"I said *this* was good. I'm a teacher. I work with beginners all the time." He pointed his towel at her. "You follow directions, you try things, and you're picking it up. So yeah, this was good." He paused. "If it makes you feel better, you're a good beginner."

That made her chuckle. "You're very kind."

He looked away. "I'm really not." His phone buzzed, and he checked it. Whatever it was made his face cloud over, and he turned the screen off with a short, angry motion.

An awkward silence filled the space between them. Evie dug through her bag and pulled out her diary and pen. "Let's arrange the sessions for the next week."

Tyler nodded and tapped his phone awake. He quietly read out the gaps in his schedule each day for the next week, and Evie wrote them into her diary.

She'd turned to the week after the performance when he said, "I'm guessing that's when you leave?" She'd written in big letters *FLIGHT HOME*, and the flight details on the Tuesday following the performance.

"Yes."

"You're not here for long."

"No." She winked at him. "Put up with my terrible footwork for a week, then you'll never have to see it again." She flicked the pages back to the current week and crossed out the session they'd just had.

He pressed closer against her. "Oh hey, cool."

What was *with* him? She looked up at him to tell him off for reading over her shoulder, but he was gazing with open admiration at her diary. Every week was a two-page spread, with spaces for each day of the week. Doodles ran throughout this week, odd things she'd seen and wanted to draw: sushi, the CN Tower, two figures on a dance machine, a mess that was supposed to be poutine, chibi versions of Bailey and Sarah, a maple leaf, and a miniature Godzilla.

"You draw?"

She wouldn't quite call it that. "I doodle."

"They're cute." He tapped Godzilla. "Especially this."

She blushed. "Godzilla's easy to draw." Which was true.

"I couldn't draw like that."

"Look." She angled the diary so he could watch her. She slowly redrew the little Godzilla. "See—an oblong, two little eyes, more oblongs for the body and legs, some triangles for the claws and scales and teeth, and you're done."

Tyler huffed in amusement. "Sure, whatever." He pointed at Sarah and Bailey. "I recognize these two."

Drawing chibi versions of them was as easy as doing Godzilla, but the reactions had been hilarious. In fact . . . Evie eyed him over, taking in his distinctive features—the curly hair, defined jaw, angular face—and grinned.

He quirked an eyebrow in confusion. "What?"

"Stay still."

She picked up her pen and quickly sketched out him as a chibi figure. Big eyes, big curly hair, big head, with a toddler body wearing dance clothes.

He laughed, short and delighted. "You make it look easy."

"You make dancing look easy." She gestured at herself. "I know I'm going to be in pain tomorrow, and you've barely broken a sweat."

"I might not be in pain, but—" he fingered his tank "—I'm kinda gross right now."

"Me too." Hers was stuck to her, and she peeled it away from her body. Jeez. When she looked back up, she found herself gazing into dark, appreciative eyes.

"I wouldn't say that," he said.

Oh *wow*. That was completely unexpected. *Those eyes.* A lump rose into her throat, and she couldn't find anything to say.

He blinked, then his mouth twisted bitterly and he moved back. "Uh—"

Something thudded in the corridor outside. Uncertain if she was upset or grateful for the interruption, Evie stood on wobbly legs and opened the door.

Gigi stood a few doors down, chest heaving. Brock was against the wall, staring at Gigi in shock. Bags lay around their feet. To her surprise, Gigi was visibly upset: all wide eyes and defensive stance.

"Gigi," she called before she could think about it.

Their faces snapped towards her. Brock straightened. She grasped for something to say. "We're done here," she managed. "So if you're waiting for Tyler, he's free."

Gigi nodded jerkily, picked up his bag, and almost ran towards her. At the door, he paused and whispered, "Thanks."

Evie watched as Brock lurched away from the wall. He ignored her as he picked up his bag and left. Whatever had happened, the aftermath left her feeling a little uncertain and off.

Gigi didn't seem affected. Once in the room, his entire demeanour changed. He tossed his bag aside, did the straightening, uplifted posture Tyler had shown Evie earlier, and strode across the room as though he owned it.

"Ty," he announced, "you will not believe how much crap the hetero is giving me. I need at least four cosmos to get over this afternoon. *At least.*"

Tyler snorted as he stood up. "Your game plan is to drink your way through this competition?"

She walked to her bag as Gigi imitated an inept Mark. "'Bro, I'm, like, bugging. Dude, I've, like, never danced with a dude before.' I swear to God, if he calls me 'bro' one more time, I'm going to *grand jete* his nuts into Lake Ontario."

"He's trying to be nice," Tyler said. "That's how straight guys act when they want to be friends."

"How the fuck would *you* know?"

Tyler exhaled sharply. "Jesus, Gigi. Who the hell tied your panties in a knot?" Tension filled the room as the two men stared each other down.

Bloody hell.

Evie took that as her cue to leave. She quietly picked up her things just as Gigi made a strangled, frustrated noise. He burst out with, "I'm sorry!" and started tromping around the studio, arms swinging.

Yup, time for her to leave. "Tyler, I'll see you tomorrow."

He nodded and waved wearily. "See you, Evie."

She pulled her backpack on and left the room, aiming for where she thought the reception was. Brock was nowhere to be seen, thankfully. She wondered what had happened between him and Gigi. Then she thought about Tyler's eyes and that bitter expression, and wondered what was going on with *him*. She didn't think that bitterness had been aimed at her, but it had been weird.

Especially since today had been so fun. Tyler wasn't as grumpy as he'd first appeared. Turned out he was actually patient and funny and maybe even a little sweet. Evie had to admit, she'd had a crazy moment where she thought he'd freak out when she had revealed her orientation in her interview. Crazy, because if he was friends with Sarah, he should be fine with asexuality; and crazy because of course he *was* fine. Had barely blinked.

She enjoyed the dancing too. It felt good to move her body in new ways, to express something through her physicality. And the lift! He'd lifted her effortlessly, which was a first for her. She'd loved that. Really loved it. Finally those moments in dance movies where the guy held the girl up actually made sense to her. She couldn't quite put her finger on it, but it was something about feeling supported yet uplifted. Like she could do anything. And in the movies there was probably some sexual stuff implied in the movement, but she didn't need that to feel good about the lifts. Given that Tyler had to have lifted lots of women when dancing, she doubted he found it sexual either.

She also liked the power she'd felt lifting him. That was sort of uplifting too. She liked that he trusted her to handle him that way. No guy had ever asked her to lift him except as a dare. Tyler had been excited about it; he'd lit up as soon as he knew she was strong.

It had been quite a while since she'd spent time in another person's space like that. It was strange, but good, to dance with someone, to *properly* dance, not just bounce along in a club. Not that it was anything special for him. She knew that. But there couldn't be anything wrong with enjoying another person like this, not when it was so—

"EVIE!"

She stopped short and looked around her to see Bailey and Sarah running up to her. In her reverie, she'd walked straight past them where they stood outside the school.

"Girl, you were on another planet!" Sarah threw an arm around her shoulders. "How was it?"

"Fun?" Bailey asked.

"Yes!" Evie described the session and demonstrated a few moves as they walked to the streetcar stop. Once on the streetcar, she collapsed into a chair, legs alarmingly wobbly. "I'm good for nothing except a shower and that pizza you promised."

Sarah and Bailey smiled.

"For sure. That's no problem," Sarah said.

"You totally smell," Bailey added with a grin.

Evie good-naturedly flipped them the middle finger.

"How was Tyler?" Sarah asked.

Bailey shot her a look, and it was one Evie had often seen in couples and friends who really understood each other. The kind of look where they talked to each other without using words. What was that about? Why were they worried about Tyler?

"He was fine," Evie said slowly. "Very patient. Should he not have been?"

Sarah bit her lip. "It's just that . . ."

Bailey nudged her. "Sarah."

"I *know*, Bay. Evie, it's just some history with his last dance partner." Sarah shrugged. "It's not my story to tell, and it's definitely not your problem to worry about. If he wasn't freaking out, then that's good enough for me. It's kind of awesome, actually."

That was . . . interesting. Tyler might've been grumpy, but he didn't seem the type to freak out about anything. Evie hadn't noticed anything strange, and she said as much. "I'm not exactly a permanent dance partner," she added. "I'm around for a week. Three days after the performance, I'm gone for a few months. I doubt he's that invested in this, you know?"

"You're right," Sarah said. "I'm sure he's not."

Evie's phone buzzed. She picked it up and saw a WhatsApp message from Tyler: *Gigi is flipping his shit on me. Did you see anything in the hall?*

She frowned and tapped out her answer: *Not much. I think he and Brock had a tussle and dropped a few things. Brock looked like he was shoved into a wall. Maybe an argument? Idk.*

"Who is it?" Sarah asked.

"Tyler."

"Tyler? He texted you?"

Evie looked up to see Sarah and Bailey doing it again, the wordless communication thing. A little odd, considering how chatty Sarah normally was, and how many people were talking around them on the streetcar. A small moment of silent communication in the middle of human noise. Her phone buzzed in her hand.

Tyler: *Thanks. That clears something up. Good thing you opened the door when you did.*

Evie: *Why? Would something bad have happened?*

Tyler: *Not necessarily, but it's better nothing happened. Gtg, G has disappeared somewhere.*

Oh dear.

"Evazilla," Sarah said a little too innocently. "What are you smiling about?"

"Nothing," Evie said.

"Nothing, eh?"

Time to turn the tables. "You sounded *so Canadian* right then! 'Nothing, *eh*.'" She made sure to beam with delight.

Bailey chuckled, and Sarah laughed and leaned against Bailey. They swayed with the movement of the streetcar. "Maybe we can watch you practise sometime."

Evie shook her head. "No. *No.* I'm terrible and you'll be bored stiff."

"Oh, I don't know about that." Sarah grinned.

"And what is that supposed to mean?" Evie demanded.

Sarah said nothing, merely did the look thing again with Bailey.

Evie put her phone away, baffled. Normally Sarah would and did spill out whatever was in her head. Whatever she was keeping back about this dancing and Tyler stuff had to be serious . . . right? Considering this was Sarah, Evie didn't know what to think.

Honestly, it was just dancing.

Tyler blinked and tried to focus, but the colours were starting to ripple together. Two doors to choose from: noxious pink for the girls, neon blue for the boys. He looked around for a single or disabled washroom, but there wasn't one in sight. The best option not available, he'd have to go for the next best. The crowd in this bar was mostly young and hipster, so he doubted he'd get any crap. He *hoped* he wouldn't. He sighed, focused on the blue, and strode in there. Straight past other guys, into a stall, lock. Do his business, flush, wash his hands without looking at anyone, out.

Gigi was right where he'd left him: draped over the table with a glass of water, using ten empty shot glasses as a pillow. *Ten. Jesus.*

Tyler knew better than this; however, Gigi on a bender was nigh unstoppable. At least Gigi had drunk most of them.

"Still awake?" Tyler asked, poking Gigi's face.

"U'for—unfort— Yeah." Gigi moaned into the table. "Fuck men. Aaallll assholes."

"Yes, yes, I know."

God, this took him back. Who knew gay men and straight women talked about similar things when wasted? He took it as a reminder that men had a habit of screwing things up. It was a point of principle to not be a screw-shit-up man now that he'd transitioned.

But Gigi's mention of guys seemed promisingly close to the nub of Gigi's meltdown. Maybe they could finally talk this shit out and go home and *sleep*.

After Evie left, Gigi had apologized again for the straight men remark—and Tyler had only forgiven him because he knew how thoughtless Gigi could be when upset—then had resumed bitching about Mark and his sin of being heterosexual. Reading between the lines of his complaints, it sounded like Mark was actually doing well with Gigi's routine. So clearly something else had riled him up. Really riled him up. Enough to drag Tyler out for happy hour at a bar close to the dance school, with a promise of paying for Tyler's drinks and having two, max.

Of course, he'd hit the rum and Cokes so hard he'd been slurring within an hour. Tyler had managed to make out something about a guy and the name Brock, but nothing more than that before Gigi had gone to the washroom for the longest time and come back with shots.

Since then, Gigi had crumpled onto the table and moaned about life being awful. Evie's response to Tyler's message had confirmed a growing hunch: Brock and Gigi had had words and now Gigi was freaking out. Tyler made him sip the water while trying to gauge the total alcohol units they'd both consumed and whether that was okay for his testosterone levels. So far his head was telling him *lots* and *probably not*. Right now it wasn't the biggest of deals.

"You." Gigi glared, pointing a finger in his face. "Yooouuu're damn han'some, you know tha'?"

Well, no, but it was always good to hear. Tyler smirked. "Course I am."

"Beh you never ha' any issues in high school."

The fuck? "Hey. Hey. I *transitioned* at the end of high school. I thought I was a messed-up dyke for a long time. *Plus*," he gestured to his skin, "you know, black?"

Gigi waved dismissively. "I was fat."

Oh *hey*. Hey now. Not like it was a competition or anything, but he was pretty sure racism and gender dysphoria at least equalled obesity in terms of fucking your life over. Tyler wasn't in any condition or mood to argue with a wasted Gigi about it, though. Especially not if the memory of said high school obesity was fuelling this rage drinking. *Goddamn it, Gi.*

"You complain you're fat now," Tyler pointed out.

"Yeah, buh I was ac'shly fat back then. Chubby little gay who was into theatre arts and dancin', that was me. A teenage *cliché*." Gigi flicked a shot glass across the table. "High school fuckin' sucked, man, and *not* in the good way."

"It sucked for everybody."

"Yurr not *lis'nin'*." Gigi sat up, gulped some of the water, and began gesturing wildly. "So. There I was, okay, the chubbiest little queen-in-waiting you ever *seen*. G'ttin' beat up, locker graffiti, insults, allovit. An' there was this . . ." he screwed up his face ". . . guy. Yanno? A *guy*."

Tyler did not, in fact, know, having always been into girls, but he knew exactly what that tone meant. This wasn't just anyone. This was *someone*.

"Crush?"

Gigi closed his eyes in consternation. "Huge. Massive. Fuckin' head over fuckin' heels. Course *I* didn't say anythin' 'cause I liked having all my teeth in my head, yanno?"

"Who was he?" Tyler thought he probably already knew.

"Brock."

Yup.

Gigi sighed dramatically, slumping across the table. "He was *gorjush*." He frowned. "Well, gorjush to *teen* me. If I saw sixteen-year-old him *now* I'd be all like, 'Back in the playpen, child.' Yechhh. Anyway. He did, like, technical shit for the school plays or whatever. Lights'n sound'n stuff. Trust him to show up now with a fucking *camera*."

Yeah. What a total douche-canoe. "Word."

They stared morosely at the pile of empty, sticky shot glasses.

Tyler poked Gigi's forehead. "So what happened?"

Gigi frowned at him. "Huh?"

"High school. Brock."

Gigi covered his face, almost knocking over the water. Tyler rescued it and took a gulp for good measure.

"He kissed me."

Tyler choked and sprayed the water out.

Gigi didn't seem to notice, because he continued despondently. "It was after rehearsal this one time. Erryone was packin' up an' I was g'ttin' my crap from where I stashed it an' he totally ambushed me. Heh, *bushed*. Sayin' stuff like, 'You were good tonight,' an' bein' all friendly an' shit. An' I was all like 'Oh em *gee*, I'm gonna die from happiness' 'cause he was *talkin'* to me. Jus' talkin'. Then he kissed me. And I was all like—" Gigi swept his arm around grandly "—whhaaat the fuuuck? Ya*nno*?"

Tyler protected the water. Gi had totally lost all, like, spatial awareness and stuff. And Ty needed water because water was like life. Second only to Gatorade.

Gigi sighed. "We made out an' gave each other handjobs for like three weeks, then his frien's saw us, an' tha' was the end."

Tyler winced. That couldn't have been good. "Aw, Gigi, I'm sorry."

Gigi reared back up. "*Yurr* sorry? *I'm* sorry! I was so fuckin' happy he liked me, I didn't fuckin' *think*." He rapped his own forehead, then winced. "Ow. So his frien's catch him kissin' the chubster queer, right, an' he was gone. Vroom! Said it was *my* fault. Said I came on to *him*. Closeted prick." Gigi's face fell. "Never spoke to me again. Bullied worse." The expression on his face made Tyler want to hug teenage Gigi. "Stayed that way till I graduated an' got the *fuck* out of Dodge."

Well, Jesus. That sounded awful. Why were people so crap in high school? This was kind of reminding Tyler of Sarah's stories about *her* town. She'd never come out there, but being... Well, she hadn't known she was asexual back then, but she'd totally not sexed people at all, and apparently that had sent rumours flying around, which meant she had been bullied for being a lesbian *and* for being a prude. Somehow. He wondered what Evie had had to deal with. Man, it would suck if Evie had had to deal with that too.

Though, now that he was thinking about it, *his* school had been relatively okay with LGBTQ people. There had definitely been bad times for him too, not least heightened by the fact that he couldn't seem to do the girl thing in any way. Hindsight explained all, but at the time he'd felt like someone had given him a stick shift to drive and he only had the instruction manual for an automatic. He could still sort of drive it, but he knew he wasn't doing it right and it felt wrong and made everything just that much harder.

God. People sucked. Life sucked. Why did it all suck so much? Suddenly he felt so unbearably sad for him, and Gigi, and Sarah, and everyone else who'd had to take crap from people just for being themselves. Ordering another round of drinks looked downright necessary.

Huh, maybe the alcohol was getting to him more than he'd realized. Melancholy didn't usually set in this quickly.

"That's really shit." Tyler patted Gigi's shoulder heavily. "Like, total fucking remove-someone's-nutsack-and-shit-on-it shit."

"I know, right?" Gigi sat up straight. "So. I graduate. I get to Toronno. I drop eighty pounss. I enrol in dance school. I go out. I fuck whoever the fuck I wan'. I have boyfrien'ss. *Ssss*. Like, plural. Life is fuckin' sweet." His hands exploded out from the table. "Then Closeted Assface shows up with his fuckin' *camera* an' tells me he's *sorry*."

"That ass— Wait, wha'?" Tyler wasn't sure he'd heard right. "He apologized?"

Gigi scoffed. "Yeah. Says he's sorry an' I'm gorjush an' can he make it up to me. Canyu b'lieve him?" Gigi's face darkened. "Make it *up* to me? He broke my chubby little gay heart. He does *not* get t'make that up to me now that I'm sexy. Thass *not* how it works."

Tyler nodded. "Totally." He paused. "But he apologized?"

Gigi snapped his fingers. "Tyler! Honey! I'm *sayin'* that he can't jus' waltz in here, say he likes me, and expect me to be *okay* with it."

"Nah, nah, it doesn't sound like that. He said he wants to make it up to you. That's a better thing." Apologies were good things. They were awesome things. He'd know.

Gigi peered at him suspiciously. "Whose side're you on?"

"Yours. Duh. Always. But, Gi, if you really didn't care, you'd've walked away or fucked it out." Tyler thought about it. "Definitely fucked it out."

Gigi grinned. "And then sashayed away. Like a boss. Like a *queen.*"

Tyler stacked two shot glasses, thanking the breakup gods that he hadn't done this with Gigi when he'd broken up with Lucette. Like he needed more vague memories of feeling anxious and exposed in public; starting to transition had been bad enough. "But, Gi, like, my point is that you only drink shots when you're upset."

"So?"

"So, he got to you. You still like him."

Gigi blinked at him, then moaned and face-planted onto the table. "Nooo, Ty. Fuck. Fuck. 'M a fuckin' mess. Stop showin' me the mess I am. An' I don't like him. I hate him. Him an' his stupid face an' 'mazin' shoulders. Why does he have such a great body? How is *that* fair? Why?"

Tyler knocked on the back of Gigi's head. "Hey. Hey. You're, like, proving my point. He's your first love. Let him make it up to you."

Gigi raised his head to glare at Tyler. "*How* is *he* my first love? My first love should've been grand! Poetic! Passionate! His closeted ass tossed me to the fuckin' *wolves.* Wolves, Ty!"

Tyler knew from experience that first love could be all those things and still end in heartbreak. Or wolves. "But he apologized."

Gigi did seem to be thinking about it. "Revenge sex is too good for 'im."

"Did I say go easy on him?"

Gigi peeled himself off the table and picked up the water glass. "I guess I could *consider* indulging him." He was still wasted, but seemed much calmer now. He fixed his gaze on Tyler with surprising focus as he swallowed a gulp of water. "Sooo what's *your* mess? Who keeps texting you?" His eyes narrowed. "It's not the Überbitch is it?"

Heh. Überbitch. Oh hey, he probably shouldn't find that funny. "If you mean Luce, no." Tyler balanced a third shot glass on top of his stack. "Shana's the one hassling me right now. I have no idea what's up with her and—"

His phone buzzed and he checked it. Evie again: *Shots are always the answer. Is he okay?* Aw, she was asking! That was sweet.

"You know, Evie saw you and Brock in the hall." He tapped out a positive response. "What happened there?"

Gigi waved his hand dismissively. "Assface came on too strong an' I told him to back off is wha' happened." He leaned forward and rested his chin in his hand. His elbow slipped on the table, and he almost ended up face-first in his water glass. "Sooo," he said, recovering. "You're messaging *Evie*."

"She *is* my dance partner for the next week." Tyler's voice came out a little sharper than he'd expected. He fidgeted with a nearby shot glass, feeling uncomfortable now.

"Baby Marky Poo an' I are partners, buh you don' see us textin' each other our boy problems." Gigi's eyes gleamed. "She an' her magnificent thighs live up to tha' high score?"

Tyler rolled his eyes. Gigi was definitely back to his usual levels of drag wit. "You have to stop it with the weight cracks. It's not funny. She, like, asked after you. Such a waste."

"Tell her 'm fabulous an' you totally look like someone slipped you E."

Tyler dropped the shot glass. "What the hell?"

Gigi pointed a finger at him. "You look *happy*."

"Well *excuse me* for getting along with her."

"Her thighs mus' be *amazin'*."

"I don't wanna think about her thighs."

Gigi grinned wickedly. "Yeeeaaah you do."

Tyler scowled. Maybe he did and maybe he kind of already had, but where was the need to point it out? "Why don't you drink your fucking water and think of revenge stuff for Brock to do for you?"

Gigi lifted his glass to Tyler. "Jus' sayin' she's, like, sexy-nice. Tha'sss all." His face darkened. "Better'n Bitchface. Oooh, girl, nah. An' waaay better than Marky Mark the het'ro puppy. Did I telyu that his girlfrien' texted him like *seven times*? At practice? An' that he ac'shlly texted back?"

Only about fifty gazillion times. "You did."

Evie hadn't responded—which, okay, that was okay, she probably had other things to do than watch this soap opera from afar—so Tyler put his phone away. Gigi seemed to have talked himself out of his funk. Suh-weet. Tyler could tell this would be a night where Gigi stayed over. The edges of the world seemed a little less blurry now, and he figured with more water, he might just avoid a hangover.

CHAPTER FOUR

Evie walked into the school on time the next morning, ready to dance once more. Tyler hadn't messaged her again since yesterday, so she wasn't sure where to go. Were they using the same practice room? She had no idea.

Katie and Brock were in the reception area, heads together over a laptop. When they saw her, Brock went red and Katie stood quickly and waved. Evie joined them, noticing that Brock avoided her eye—embarrassed? Unsure? Who knew. Katie seemed cheerful though, with a cup of coffee in hand and gum going voraciously. Quite how those two flavours meshed was beyond Evie.

"Check out the interview we did with Mark yesterday." Katie swivelled the laptop around.

Mark's wide grin filled the screen. Katie pushed Enter and his face started moving. "I'm on?" He looked beyond the screen. "Like, now?"

"Yes," Katie could be heard saying.

"Wow, awesome!" He waved at the camera. "Yo, Mom!"

"Please ignore the camera. Could you tell us your name and what you do?"

"My name's Mark Castle, and I'm studying economics at Ryerson."

"Why are you doing this dance competition, Mark?"

He looked excited. "I'm doing this because dancing is *boss*. And my little bro is gay too, so it's like personal for me and stuff. And my girlfriend said I should totally do this."

"You're straight?"

"Oh yeah!"

"You don't mind dancing with a guy? Your girlfriend doesn't mind?"

Mark waved dismissively. "No way! We're solid, Frannie and me. Totally solid. She's super excited about it. Like I think she's more excited about it than I am, and I'm *really* excited about it. I've never danced with a guy before. It's way different than dancing with a girl."

"Who's leading?"

"I am," Gigi called from offscreen.

"Yeah, you are, bro!" Mark raised his hand. "High-five me, man!"

Gigi gave him the most lacklustre high five Evie had ever seen. God, watching these two interact was hilarious. She had high hopes for their dance at the competition.

Katie paused the video, the corners of her mouth twitching.

"He's certainly . . . enthusiastic," Evie said. That was the nice way of saying *ridiculous*, right?

"He's adorable." Katie's smile broke through. "Clueless, but adorable." She winked at Evie. "Brock hates him. He glowered at him the entire time we filmed that."

"I did not," Brock muttered.

"You totally did. You did it again this morning."

Brock went even more red and turned away to do something with the camera.

Katie shook her head and focused on Evie. "Which room are you in today?"

"I don't know. Isn't Tyler here already?"

Katie shrugged. "I assume so."

One of the reception staff called over to them and directed them to a nearby practice room. The three of them walked together, Brock still very intent on the camera. Tyler stood outside the room talking to Gigi and the third QS dancer in the competition, the one with the sweet face.

Gigi noticed them first. "Evie's here with her entourage. I'm out. Don't forget, Ty: go see Jean." He clapped Tyler's shoulder as he walked past, nudging Evie when he reached her. "Give him hell, girl."

Evie grinned. Someone seemed back to normal today.

Tyler met her eyes, face weary and body slouched. He'd pulled his hair back, which looked good. Better than the rest of him did; Tyler was very obviously hungover.

"How does Gigi look so fresh and you don't?" she asked.

"Because he sold his soul to Satan." His voice was gravelly.

"It's because he's younger than you. Hi," the dancer next to him said, smiling at Evie. There was a soft Spanish lilt in her voice. "I'm Carmen."

"Evie." They shook hands.

"Carmen's scoping out the competition," Tyler said.

Carmen gasped. "I am not!" She shoved him and turned back to Evie. "I just wanted to say hello and good luck."

Even if she was their competitor, Evie was inclined to like her. Carmen oozed warmth and empathy, and combined with everyone's friendliness, Evie could feel herself melting a little. How was everyone so nice here? "You too," she said.

"I'm going to set up," Tyler muttered, stepping into the practice room.

Carmen rolled her eyes. "He's just grumpy because Gigi kept him up until 3 a.m. He'll be better once he's danced a bit." Evie noticed Brock scowling, possibly at Carmen's choice of words. She decided she definitely liked Carmen. Especially when the dancer leaned in and murmured, "Take a tip from me? He might be leading, but you're in charge." She winked. "Good luck, sweetie."

Carmen swished past, her feet barely making a noise.

Evie entered the room and put her stuff down. Tyler was stretching in the middle of the room, facing away from her and glaring at the mirror. Behind her, Katie and Brock settled into place. Evie shed her jumper and joined him in his stretches. "Fun night?" she asked.

He scowled. "Don't ask."

"Wow, that good?" She didn't really expect an answer.

He huffed.

Evie had been where he was; she'd gone to university in London, after all. She left him to stretch by himself.

As she had expected, she'd woken up in pain. Her muscles were decidedly not happy at being used like this. So she'd stretched before breakfast and went through the moves she could remember under Bailey's watchful eye; now she felt almost all right again.

Certainly more all right than Tyler, judging by his expression.

Ten minutes later, he crouched next to her as she stretched her legs.

"Sorry," he said tersely. "I'm not a morning person."

"It's 11:30 a.m."

"I woke up an hour ago."

Be nice, Evie. "I'm not a morning person either. I get it. You sure you want to do this now?"

"No time later. You done stretching?"

She nodded.

He stood and held out a hand. "Let's go over what we did yesterday."

Evie let him pull her to her feet.

Out into the centre of the room she swayed, reliving that expansive, stage-owning pose, then forgetting the next step. With his help, she managed to fumble through her part of the opening routine a few times until they thought she had it.

But when he joined her, it was disastrous. She did the opening bars, bumping into him when she turned, misjudging where he'd be. They corrected, then he took her hand for their first moves together and promptly stepped on her feet.

"Sorry," he muttered.

"I thought *I'd* be the one stepping on *your* feet," she joked.

"I have your moves in my head as well as mine. They're all mixing." He dropped her hand, shook himself out, then took her in hold again. "Slowly."

They bumped their way through the routine, miscounting, stepping on each other, mixing up turn directions. Elbows jabbed, knees knocked, and more toes were squashed. Her feet started hurting, and every time she bumped into him, it was slightly painful because he was a solid mass of muscle. Evie's heart sank lower and lower the more they messed up. The final straw was when Tyler accidentally kicked her leg. Pain exploded across her shin and Evie hopped back, cursing in surprise.

Tyler looked aghast. "Oh God." He extended his hands to her. "I'm sorry. Fuck. I'm really sorry."

"It's fine!" She put her leg down. It would bruise, but it wasn't bad. "I'm not hurt."

Tyler sank onto his heels. "The fuck is wrong with me today?"

Evie glanced at the clock on the wall. 12:30 p.m. He was hungover. Awake for just a few hours. Grumpy. Stressed. She guessed he'd had to rush here. Had he eaten? An idea came to her, and she went to her bag. She returned with a cereal bar.

"Here," she said. "It's not a proper meal, but it's food."

He glanced up at her, then took the bar and ate it. She crouched next to him.

"I'm really sorry." He crumpled the wrapper in his hand. "I don't normally hurt my dance partners until at least the third session. Promise."

Humour was always a good sign. "It's fine. Honestly. I can barely feel it now."

He didn't look like he believed her. He looked almost wary, actually, crouched like that, eyes jumping between her face and the floor. Was this just the hangover talking? Evie wasn't sure anymore.

"Tyler," she said uncertainly, "I was more surprised than hurt, you know? Not a big deal. We're cool."

"Thanks, but that's not what I'm here to do."

Oh. He was meant to be the professional dancer. Was that it? "You know, I missed the part of the form that said we had to get this perfect straightaway."

His expression lightened, and his mouth quirked in a small smile. Evie smiled back. What was going through his head? She wasn't sure until those dark eyes flickered to Katie and Brock and he whispered, "I wish they would go."

Evie had forgotten all about them. *Ah.* "Give them some good material, and they will," she whispered back.

"Like what?"

"It's not *so* bad," she said loudly. "At least we haven't fallen yet." Then she reached out and pushed his shoulder. He sprawled on the floor, the look on his face so comical Evie couldn't help laughing.

"Look at that." She batted her eyes at him. "My leg feels so much better."

An evil grin wormed itself across Tyler's face. "Oh, you're in trouble, Godzilla." He swept one leg under her, sending her to the floor too.

She rolled back up into a crouch. "Have to try harder than that, Ronaldo."

He gathered himself and lunged as she skittered back. She stood, jumping away from him, ready for when he surged to his feet, so she could dart around him with a burst of laughter. He chased her around the studio, finally cornering her in a hold, and knocking her feet out from under her. She found herself literally hanging in his arms and grabbed his shoulders instinctively. His scent unfurled around her as he lowered her in a dip: masculine, musky, slightly sweet, and possibly tinged with last night's tequila. He dipped her back, lower and lower, an evil glint in his eye.

Evie might have misjudged this.

"*Who* hasn't fallen yet?" he asked as he dropped her. She gasped as she fell all of one inch onto the floor, then started laughing again when she realized what he'd done. He sat next to her, grinning.

"Arse," she managed once she'd calmed down.

"I try."

She smirked. "You smell like tequila."

He sniffed his armpit. "Yeah. That's not from last night or anything. That's how I smell permanently."

"Must be difficult staying sober with all those fumes. No wonder you were all over the place just now."

"Hey. Hey." He poked her leg. "Who's the professional here?"

"I don't know. All I see is some hungover—"

"Ahem."

They looked up to see Katie with the microphone.

"I hate to interrupt"—she raised her eyebrows—"but as you're not rehearsing, I thought I'd get Tyler's interview down."

Tyler stood.

Evie pushed herself up and walked with him over to the bags, a little disappointed and confused at her disappointment.

Katie positioned him facing the light, and Brock trained the camera on him.

"Please tell us who you are and what you do," she said.

"I'm Tyler Davis, and I'm a professional dancer."

"What's your background in dancing?"

He shifted his weight. "I did ballet when I was a kid all the way to high school. I started experimenting with more contemporary dance styles, including swing and interpretive, when I was in my late teens. I decided I wanted to try going professional and did a dance performance course at college, with a side certification in dance education. I met Derek through the course and joined QS Dance when he set the company up. Now I teach and perform."

"What sorts of things do you perform in?"

He shrugged. "Music videos, live performances, research presentations . . . whatever I can get."

"Why did you decide to do this competition?"

Evie could tell he wanted to say, *Because my boss told me to.*

Instead he recited, "I'm queer and I think it would be inspirational for other queer people of colour to see someone like me excelling at dancing professionally."

Well, that was also true and important.

"If you don't mind telling us, what's your orientation?"

He ran a hand over his neck. His eyes flickered to Evie, then back to Katie. "My queerness doesn't come from my orientation. I'm a straight trans man."

Tyler was transgender? Evie hadn't expected that. *And why not, Evelyn Whitmore? Stop assuming people are cisgender, especially in a place like a queer dance school.* Of course, knowing that people came in a variety of genders and that sometimes people had to make physical changes to transition to their true gender was one thing; remembering it and applying it when looking at people—interrupting the socialized, automatic need to identify everyone's presented gender—was another.

At least she'd read him correctly as male, especially after being lifted with those powerful arms of his yesterday. Imagine all the training behind that strength. Imagine training as a female-bodied dancer, then learning moves for male roles with a transitioning body. Imagine going professional, despite all the odds. Imagine still being open about that kind of identity in front of a dance company and friends and an audience and a camera.

Wow.

"You're into girls?" Brock blurted.

Tyler crossed his arms and grinned. "Yeah."

Relief lit up Brock's face, making Evie smile. *Ha. Interesting.*

Katie glared at Brock, then turned back to Tyler. "And how are practices going from your point of view?"

"As you can tell"—Tyler swept his hands wide—"awesome."

Evie chuckled as she stuffed her spare cereal bar into her mouth and checked her phone. Another email from her mother had come in while she'd been practising.

Hello darling. Doug's asking after you and wondering if you need a place to stay in London when you come back from Toronto. He has a third flat near King's Cross. Let me know. I saw your pictures of poutine on Facebook, and I have to say that I hope you're eating proper meals as well as junk. Do remember what I told you about holiday eating. Shep was sick again, from damaged dog food I think. Was sick all over the hydrangeas. I took him to Dr. Nishan and he ran a few tests. Will get results back in a few days. Rich sends his love. By the way, he told me to watch a YouTube video of someone who looks very much like you. I'll send the link to you later, the resemblance is uncanny. When are you visiting Niagara Falls?

She plunked the phone back into her bag with mixed feelings. Good thing that fucking YouTube video was blurry.

"Cool," Katie was saying. "I hope you don't mind me asking, but did transitioning change anything about dancing for you?"

Tyler shifted his weight. Again, he looked at Evie. Maybe he was nervous talking about this in front of her? She smiled at him and saw his shoulders relax.

He cleared his throat. "A few things. Some of it was simple, like learning how to lead or building up my upper-body strength. Other aspects of it are less simple to deal with."

"Is there transphobia in the dance industry?"

"There's transphobia everywhere," he said, "but we're not unheard of as dancers. I don't shout about it, as I think my dance skills speak for themselves, but I have had the occasional job purely because of my trans status." He shrugged. "That's life."

"Why dance?"

He straightened and smiled. Not the polite one he'd flashed during the interview, but the one that transformed his face. "I love dancing the way I love breathing. I've never been able to see myself doing anything else."

Katie smiled at him. "Gigi said the same thing."

"He would. We're definitely not doing it for the money."

What passion. When was the last time she'd felt that strongly about anything? Drawing, maybe. Only she'd never taken her drawing as seriously as Tyler took dancing.

"I think we've got what we need for today," Katie said.

Tyler twisted away instantly. "Great."

Katie and Brock gathered their things and left, Brock in particular avoiding eye contact as he shut the door.

Evie stood and held up her hand. "Teamwork."

Tyler high-fived her. "Damn right."

"So about Brock and Gigi . . ."

Tyler groaned and dragged his hand through his hair. "Oh God. Gigi and his fucking meltdowns. Don't get me started."

Meltdowns? "Was it serious?"

He gave her a *really?* look. "No. They were in high school together. They have history. It's not great history, but I think Brock wants to make up for that." He smirked. "He wants to, and Gigi will make it very difficult for him."

What a relief. "When I saw them yesterday, I thought there might be something really bad going on."

Tyler shook his head. "Nope. Just teenage drama returned in adult form."

Evie nodded. "Good." She held up her arms in what she hoped was perfect frame. "Shall we?"

The rest of the session was way better than the start of it. That granola bar she'd given him was the only thing he'd eaten so far today, and he'd needed it. Needed it and the horsing around and the subsequent removal of the camera crew. It was somehow much easier to swing her around and guide her without people watching them. Way easier to iron out fumbles without having them captured on camera too.

By the end of the session, they could manage about half the routine without major mishaps. Evie was having difficulty with a few of the partnered sections, especially where she had to be aggressive and dance a frenzy around him.

When she found things hard, deep lines formed between her brows, and she occasionally bit the inside of her lip. Not that he'd noticed that *particularly* or anything; he just liked her focus. He liked that she was trying, really trying.

Also she hadn't treated him any differently after finding out he was transgender. He hadn't thought she would, but he'd misjudged people before (and nope, not going to remember just how badly). So far, she seemed all right with it.

And with him kicking her. It had been a while since he'd done something like that, and okay, injuries were par for the course in dance, but he never felt good accidentally hurting someone else. But she'd been chill about it. More chill than he'd been.

While crouching on the floor after that frankly stupid-crazy series of mistakes, Tyler had heard Lucette's voice in his head telling him that if he had to fuck up, could he please do it away from an audience and not embarrass himself and her. He'd been trying to talk himself out of it, desperately aware of the camera and of Evie, when she'd shoved him. It was like a spell had been broken, and he could ease back into the zone of teaching. Maybe eating had helped too, but Jesus, the girl could give him shit whenever she wanted to if it made him feel instantly better like that.

They were cooling down in the Jet-free quiet, Evie sitting up for static leg stretches instead of slumped on the floor like she'd done during their breaks yesterday. She rose out of the stretch and dug in her bag. "Today was good, wasn't it?"

"Yeah," he said.

"I mean, I felt like I was getting it."

He nodded. "You are."

She took a long drink from her water bottle. He watched her throat move as she swallowed, then tore his eyes away, feeling... Ugh.

This was the point where people made conversation, which seemed impossible to do if they didn't have a step or move to talk about. His fingers played along the lid of his Gatorade as the silence rang loudly in his ears.

Ask her something, Ty.

He grasped for something to say. Anything. *Anything!* "So . . . what have you been doing in Toronto?"

She shrugged. "We've done a lot of the touristy things. Bailey and Sarah are busy this afternoon, so I thought I'd go down to the island and walk around. We're meeting for dinner at seven with some of the Toronto aces from Tumblr."

"Sounds fun."

She smiled. "It should be. The last meet I went to was in London, for Pride last year. It was fun, but not quite the same as having dinner and sitting around chatting." She stretched out her legs, and he noticed their nice shape, how her calves tapered into her ankles. Just noticed it, the way he noticed that her water bottle had left her lips all moist.

Jesus.

He resolutely ignored her thighs. "So, you don't hang out with many, um, ace people at home?"

"Not really." She leaned over, touching her toes.

What the— Tyler looked down at his Gatorade, needing to . . . what? He saw women stretching around him all the time. But Gatorade deserved focus and attention. *Riiight.*

"I have plenty of friends, queer and otherwise," she was saying. "But a local asexual group in *York*? No, it's not really a thing."

"That kinda sucks." He had the transgender artists group and enjoyed the meets he could make. He couldn't imagine not having them there; it was such a great feeling to be around people who were like you and just *got it.*

She shrugged. "It's not the end of the world." She glanced over at him. "What about you? What does the rest of your day look like?"

He grimaced and set the bottle down. "Work, mostly. Jean wants me to look over a few things for Pride, and I have an interpretive class, then a shift."

"Shift?"

He nodded, easing his arms into a triceps stretch. "I work part-time at a café to cover my bases."

"Ah. I did that during uni." She immediately looked guilty. "That is, I did that to contribute something towards my student loans while I was still studying. I was lucky I found other work right after graduating."

That was the dream. Now that she'd mentioned it though, he had no idea what she did for a living. "What is your work? I never asked."

She shot him a puzzled look. "I work in engineering. I told Katie about it yesterday."

Engineering? She was an *engineer*? "I guess I didn't catch that part of the interview." Whoops. Shit.

"I do electrical engineering. Stuff with computer and network design." She shifted her weight, suddenly awkward. "It's interesting and pays the bills."

"I can imagine." He couldn't imagine it at all. Sitting in an office all day, staring at screens and data, dealing with photocopiers and colleagues . . . Nightmare. The money was probably amazing though.

Amazing enough to buy a two-week trip across the Atlantic.

Maybe he should rethink the nightmare aspect of it.

They gathered their things and left as the next class piled in. In the hall, Evie hesitated. "I was wondering if there are showers here?"

"Down the hall." He pointed. "You got everything you need?"

"Yes." Her face lit up in a smile. "Today was really fun. Thank you."

What was she thanking *him* for? He had a sudden urge to shuffle his feet in embarrassment, but forced himself to look her in the face instead. "I had fun too. Enjoy the island."

"Will do. See you tomorrow." She turned and walked down the hall.

Tyler moved away in the other direction, his feet suddenly heavy. He wished his schedule wasn't full. He couldn't remember the last time he'd been on the island. It was a glorious day, perfect for exploring. She was going to walk around by herself, and he honestly would kind of like to walk with her, and he literally couldn't afford to think like that because he needed the money that teaching this next class would give him.

He sighed and kept going. At the Marketing/Finance sign, he knocked and waited for the requisite "Come in" before entering.

Jean smiled at him. "Tyler! Take a seat, please." She gestured at the chair in front of her desk.

He sat. "What's up?"

She fished an envelope from a drawer. "Pride sent this for you."

"What is it?"

She shrugged. "Dunno. Also, here." She pushed a few Post-its towards him. "People called us looking for you."

"Huh? Why?"

"Pride released details of the competition on their website, and it seems there's quite a few people interested in speaking to you."

Tyler picked up the Post-its. *Nikki Johnson, the TDOT Blog. Chell Houseman, the Dance Ontario Association. Jules Mitchell, the Globe and Mail.* "About what, exactly?"

Jean shrugged. "I'm your employer, not your agent."

Oh God. Jean or Derek representing him to outside parties. They were good people, but she was definitely more suited to the numbers side of things. "I'm always grateful for that."

Jean leaned back in her chair, crossing her arms and fixing him with her usual insightful frown. "How are things going?"

Was she talking about the competition or generally? He hedged his bets. "Good."

"Evie doing all right?"

"Yeah. She's picking the routine up okay." He thought back to the way she twisted and moved fluidly. How she responded to him, how she anticipated his own movements, how she concentrated. "She really is a natural."

Jean nodded. "Katie showed me her interview. Evie's full of surprises, isn't she?"

Surprises? Oh right, her asexuality. "You mean her orientation?"

"That too. She's an interesting person. I was thinking of offering her a year's free membership here as compensation for doing this competition. You know, so she could do classes and things. What do you think?"

Huh? *Membership?* Why the hell would she want that when she was leaving in ten days' time? "I don't know, Jean." He smirked. "Maybe she'd prefer a key ring."

Jean laughed. "Good one." She pulled a notepad filled with crossed-out scrawl towards her and wrote something down. "I'll ask her."

"Was that it?"

"Just one more thing." She sat up. "I know Derek pushed you into this, but I hope it opens up more opportunities for you. I think you've had a rough year, and I'd like to see more good things happening for you."

He could tell she meant well, and he appreciated the sentiment, but given how competitive the dance world was, he could hear an unspoken criticism of him not taking opportunities when he should've. Maybe that was Luce's voice in his head, but he still straightened in his seat. "Jean, if I haven't been doing my job—"

She frowned. "No, that's not what I mean. Your work is fine. You were one of the first dancers we scouted for this company, and I hope you consider Derek and me friends as well as bosses." She pierced him with a serious yet caring look that reminded him of his mother. "I noticed you tucked yourself away after breaking up with Lucette. I think you're out of it now, and it's good to see. Keep it up. Okay?"

He nodded, throat thick.

She waved him out. "Get going. Thanks, Tyler."

"Bye, Jean."

He closed the office door behind him and glanced at the Post-its in his hand. Tyler had been dancing at gigs and performances and live events for a few years now, and none of it had generated interest like this. Typical: do all the artistic and boundary-breaking stuff for years and get nowhere, but the moment he was in a shticky dance-off between QS and Cherry Studios as very obvious rainbow representation, everyone was all over him. He wanted to scrunch up the papers in his hands and throw them in the trash. Sure, he was trans and black, but he was also a dancer, for fuck's sake.

But everyone had their spiel. If working in the creative industries had taught him anything, it was that you had to exploit who and what you were if you wanted to get ahead.

People had looked at him all his life and seen his skin first. Derek and Jean, much as they said they hired him for his dancing, knew that they needed people of colour if they wanted QS Dance to be the diverse place they'd dreamed of. Not that he begrudged them that. People like them were part of the solution. But this is what life was like: being good just wasn't enough; he had to be better than the cis white competition. And if he wanted to be known, he'd have to work as many angles as he could.

It still felt like selling out.

He stuffed the Post-its into his pocket for later. He'd *consider* contacting these people over lunch.

As he headed to the canteen, another thing Jean had said returned to him, and he pulled out his phone to message Evie: *Jean wants to see you whenever you're free.*

That done, he went over to the canteen's microwave to heat up his homemade rice and peas with a side of veggie frittata. *Food of the health-conscious dancing gods*, he mused sardonically as he waited in line for the microwave.

Someone cleared their throat behind him, and he glanced over his shoulder.

Brock stood there, looking pained and awkward. "Uh. Hey."

Oh *hell* no. Tyler held up his hand. "Nope. I do *not* want to be involved."

"Please, Tyler, just a few minutes."

The girl ahead of him took her food from the microwave, and he shoved his in. Punched in three minutes, Brock hovering at his elbow like an anxious puppy.

"I mean it, man." Tyler glowered at Brock. "Get lost." If he was still there three minutes later . . .

Brock didn't seem to get the message, because he straightened his shoulders and stood his ground. "I'm serious about him."

"Tell *him* that, because I don't care."

"You know him best."

"I really *don't care.*"

"And I'm desperate."

"Talk to Gigi, because I. Don't. Care."

Brock blanched. "Why? Isn't he your friend?"

"Yeah. But his relationships aren't my problem until he gets hurt." Tyler glared at him. "Actually, you already hurt him. Years ago. You're the real reason for my fucking hangover today. Get the hell out of my face. And talk to *him*." When Brock opened his mouth, Tyler leaned in. "Not. Today."

Brock shut his mouth, nodded, and walked away.

Tyler rubbed the bridge of his nose. After way too many shots of tequila, he was done with Gigi's love problems. For fuck's sake, he'd just gotten over his own. That was it: he was done with *everyone's* love problems, period. The microwave beeped food readiness, and he pulled his Tupperware out.

Settling at a chair, he drizzled hot sauce—which he kept in his bag for precisely this purpose—over it and dug in.

Of course his phone rang. He checked it to see it was Shana, sighed at the timing, then answered.

"And where the hell have you been?" she demanded.

"Hey, sis." He continued forking food into his mouth.

"I have been calling you *all day*."

"I was asleep, then I had rehearsal. Cut me some fucking slack, seriously."

"Jesus. Would it kill you to call me more?"

"Would it kill you to not call me so much?"

She sighed straight into the receiver, and he jerked the phone from his ear.

"Look, Ty, it's just that it's hard up here, you know? Darrell has his shitty friends and life on the other side of Calgary, and Mom's busy with all her clubs and things. Sometimes I feel like you're the only one who gives a shit about what's going on with *me*. And Mom misses you. We all miss you. Why aren't you here?"

"Shana, what do you want me to say?" Ugh, that probably wasn't what she needed to hear. He should kick himself after saying that. "Look, you know I miss you too. And Dar." He really did miss his siblings, but there wasn't much of a dance scene in Calgary. There was barely one in Toronto . . . Wait, that niggly feeling in his gut was back. "What is going on with you?"

The silence at the end of the phone said it all.

"Shana Davis, you're never like this and you've been calling me for days. Talk."

"I'm pregnant."

His fork fell into his food as his entire body went numb. His jaw dropped open like a goddamned cartoon. "Oh *wow*."

"I'm pregnant, but Ray doesn't want it."

He exhaled sharply and leaned back in his chair. Big freaking surprise there. He'd only met the guy twice, and twice was enough. Shana had been with Ray for just under a year, and while they'd hit it off at first, Ray had turned out to be a nonstarter and Shana had been complaining about him a lot lately. He and Darrell had been waiting for one of them to kick the other to the curb. Had thought it was only a matter of time, actually.

Guess again.

"Screw Ray," he said. "What do *you* want?"

Shana hesitated. "I want it. I definitely want it. I want to keep it and raise it and be a mom." She paused and Tyler waited for the *but*. "The thing is, I want it to have a dad. And Ray doesn't want to be that dad."

Tyler closed his eyes, hating what he had to say next. "Seems pretty cut-and-dry, Shana."

"I know." She exhaled, a low, sad sound. "I've been trying to decide what to do, and I can't make my mind up. I have a good job and savings, but I don't know what the maternity leave is like, and Mom *is* here, but you know how her health is, and what if I can't provide for it, and Dar is being a dick about it all, and I just really want you to be here but you're not, so . . ." She broke off. "I went to the clinic and had it checked out. I'm six weeks. *Six weeks.*"

Six weeks seemed like forever. No wonder she'd been anxious on the phone. Tyler pushed his food around with his fork. "Sounds like you need to do more thinking. You gotta decide, Shana. But whatever you decide, I'll help you out. Even if I'm not in Calgary, you know I have your back."

She sighed. "Thanks, bro. I knew you'd get it."

"For the record, there's no wrong decision, all right?"

"I know. Thanks. I love you." She sounded better.

"Love you too." He mashed his fork into his frittata, which was going cold. The clock on the wall told him he had ten minutes before class. "I have to go, okay? Call me if anything comes up with Ray."

"Okay."

She hung up, and Tyler shovelled the food in.

He paused.

He might become an *uncle*.

And what was he doing? Who was he and where was he going? Tyler was twenty-five and maybe about to become an uncle, and all he had to show for it was a ruined relationship, a bunch of batshit friends, and a stalled dance career.

At least he could work on one of those things. Out came the Post-its and his cell. Several calls later, he had a few interviews scheduled. Once that was done, he imagined life with a miniature Davis in the family—maybe with Shana's big dark eyes and Ray's jaw—put his face down on the table, and groaned.

"Chill out, man." Eddie patted his shoulder as she passed by. "It's only a competition."

Once her business with Jean was done, Evie headed to the waterfront and took the ferry to Centre Island. It was a pleasant Sunday, so the crowds were out in force. She walked through the amusement park and took pictures of the antique rides. She petted the animals in the farm. She even considered paying for tickets to go on the rides, but decided against it because they would have been more fun with other people.

Finally, she found herself on the pier on the other side of the island, facing out onto Lake Ontario, which extended to the far horizon. From here, it was like being on an island in the ocean rather than a lake. Lake Ontario was so huge it probably qualified as a sea.

The peace of the landscape jarred with the chaos inside her. Her head chattered at her in circular threads of dance moves, job settlements, a new city, moving in sync with a boy, Canadian friendliness, food, her friends, the ace Tumblrites, Tyler's smile. Tyler's patience. Tyler's humour. His laugh. The cues she thought were maybe there, but maybe weren't. The way his face had clouded after that messy start. The way he'd grinned when she'd sent him to the floor.

She meandered down the pier onto Manitou Beach—or Centre Island Beach, the signs weren't consistent—took off her shoes, and revelled in the sand under her feet and the fresh breeze off the lake. She walked and walked, letting her thoughts drain from her head and the aches fade from her body. The quiet and relative solitude eased her while the unfamiliar scenery distracted her. When the weather turned, clouds curling towards the city with dark purpose, she made her way back to the ferry terminal. By the time she reached it, rain had begun spitting, and when she was back in the city centre, the weather had completed a total one-eighty into a storm.

As she had an hour to kill before meeting Sarah and Bailey for dinner with the aces, she found a nearby café with wi-fi and settled in with a cup of tea. She answered Mum's message with a simple, *Hope Shep's okay. Holiday is going great. Love to you all*, then scrolled Facebook. The cream of her friends' lives spilled across her screen: parties and babies and exotic locations and new jobs. She'd never noticed before, but it was the same stuff, just from different people, over and over again.

She lifted her head to survey the café interior. People dressed in suits hunched over laptops. A couple snuggled each other on a sofa. It could have been York, but for the little differences that made the scene foreign: the dollar signs, the local wording in the ads for soup and breakfast foods, the accents in the conversational buzz. The people and experiences foremost in her mind.

For the first time in far too long, Evie felt something close to content. Like this direction, new and intriguing, was a good one.

She turned off her phone, opened her diary to the back pages— the notes section that no one ever used—and started drawing.

CHAPTER FIVE

Tyler woke up refreshed. He rose and stretched, feeling out the kinks in his body. Checking the weather outside brought a smile to his face: the sky was a washed-out blue, promising a beautiful day after the previous evening's rain. Glorious. He went through his morning routine with a sense of cheerful purpose, smiling at himself in the mirror as he lathered for a shave. He was so full of energy, he almost bounced on his way to meet Gigi for coffee near QS Dance.

Gigi, on the other hand, showed up with bags under his eyes and wearing black and grey. Only rainbow earrings brightened his outfit, which was worrying.

"Morning!" Tyler greeted him as they joined the queue.

"Good morning, sunshine." Gigi yawned.

"You look like you slept . . . well."

"Who says I didn't?" Gigi stared longingly at the pastries on display.

He was in a pastry mood. Underslept. Tetchy. Tyler put two and two together. "Something happened with Brock."

Gigi closed his eyes. "I got dinner and the best fucking blowjob of my life."

"Next," the barista called. Tyler stepped forward and ordered his usual black filter. Gigi requested a large syrup-laden frothy monstrosity, and Tyler wondered (as always) how he handled training with that amount of milk sloshing in him.

At the hand-off point, Gigi slumped against the wall, a dreamy expression on his face. "Seriously, he's good."

Oh, ew. "I don't care."

"You should, because *fuck* I needed it."

"I really don't want to know." There was one thing he *did* want to know. "How did dinner happen in the first place? I thought you were gunning for revenge."

The dreaminess dropped from Gigi's face. "He apologized. He *begged* for forgiveness. He actually got on his knees in the fucking street and begged. Fantasy brought to life." He didn't sound happy about it, though. Tyler thought Gigi was trying to be gleeful, but he couldn't carry it off. It took Tyler a while to decipher the expression on Gigi's face because he'd never seen it there before, but once he figured it out, he knew what the problem was.

Gigi felt guilty.

"You let him buy you food, blow you, and then you ran out," Tyler realized.

"Yeah."

"You're a dick."

"Yeah."

"You're a chickenshit dick."

"Yeah."

"Black filter, up!"

Tyler retrieved his coffee. When he came back, Gigi seemed to be fluctuating between desperate justification and misery.

"Look, it's the least he fucking deserves after what he did. I don't feel guilty about running off." Gigi scowled. "Don't look at me like that. I don't, okay? At least," he relented, "not much."

Tyler rolled his eyes and sipped his coffee.

"It's just . . . He was in the street." Gigi wrung his hands. "He said he was still crazy about me. That he was totally gay and out of the closet now and was never going back into it. Everyone was looking at him, and he didn't care."

That had to be nice. Tyler couldn't exactly relate. "Good for him."

"Then dinner was fun, like actually *fun*, and he just looked so delicious . . ." Gigi gave him the wide-eyed puppy treatment. "What do I *do*?"

Oh good God. Tyler was ready to smash Brock's and Gigi's heads together. "Talk to him," he said drily.

"I can't do that!"

"Vanilla almond extra-dry latte, up!" The barista eyed Gigi as he came up to collect it. "You should definitely talk to him."

Gigi retrieved his coffee, blushing madly, and they left the café. As they walked to QS, Gigi wailing the entire way, Tyler couldn't help looking forward to lunchtime practice with Evie. She would be relatively soothing after this soap opera of a coffee run.

Training went perfectly, no doubt because he'd actually slept well for once, and he emerged from it feeling amazing. Gigi was ambushed by an enthusiastic Mark straight afterwards, and Tyler avoided them as he made his way to their practice room. He'd booked the same one, so he wasn't surprised to find Evie there already, sitting on the floor listening to music.

She looked sad.

As soon as she saw him, though, she smiled and pulled out her earbuds. "Good morning."

She *seemed* okay now. "Hey."

She put away her MP3 player. "Where's the film crew?"

"Hopefully watching Mark torture Gigi," he said.

She smirked. "Better him than us."

"You wouldn't believe the drama this morning," he said.

She shook out her legs and started warming up. "Drama? Do tell."

He filled her in on the coffee run as they stretched, making her laugh.

"Brock has his work cut out for him." She rose gracefully to her feet.

Oh, those legs. He coughed. "Technically, Brock is reaping what he sowed."

She smiled at that.

Oh, that smile. *Jeez, Ty, head together, please.* Tyler set his player into the studio stereo, fiddling with it longer than strictly necessary so he could get his shit together enough to remember the routine. He turned around to see her going through the steps, so he stayed where he was to see how she did. She knew the routine up to the first chorus, then she fumbled, struggling with the move order. Those lines appeared on her brow, which meant it was time for him to do his teacher thing.

"Lindy, kick, lindy, then spin, then kick," he instructed, performing the steps for her.

She nodded and repeated the moves, her whole body slow and heavy. None of her usual verve was there today.

He frowned. That was worrying. There was definitely something bugging her.

They walked through the routine, then took it from the top, almost getting it right the whole way through. The trick with the routine was to do it right *and* quickly. He'd hoped they'd have the routine down by this third session so they could focus on speed and precision for the rest of the week.

Stop stressing, Ty. There's still four sessions to go.

Four.

Yeah, that's plenty; it's fine, it'll be fine.

An hour and a half into the session, Evie was doing all the moves in order and with only basic prompts from him. She did the final march away from him and spun to face him at the end. Still lacking energy, but she was trying.

"It's getting better," she said, slightly out of breath. She said it like he'd say the weather was okay outside. Total lack of enthusiasm.

He reached for something to say that would break her mood, something to lighten her and really make her move. Something that would help her the way she'd helped him yesterday. Only, he'd been in this situation before, with a girl who'd never liked any of the things he tried to say in consolation. None of his words had been enough, and they'd soon dried up. But for Evie, he wanted to dig them out again.

"Yeah," was all that came out.

Nice one, Tyler. Smooth.

She shook out her shoulders. "Could we take a break?"

He nodded.

She turned away from him and dug into her bag. He craned to get a glimpse of her face in the mirror and, yep, she wasn't the lively person he'd been dancing with the last two days. Had it really only been two days?

Some words finally came to him.

"How was the island?" he asked.

"Lovely. Just what I needed." Her voice was warm. That was good, right? "I walked along the beach and watched the rain come in off the lake. Stunning."

"You were out in the rain?"

"I managed to avoid the worst of it." She checked her phone, actually glowered at it, and tossed it back into her backpack. Something about her bag was off too, now that he'd noticed it. Something was missing.

"Sounds nice," he said.

"It was." She saw him looking at her in the mirror and smiled reflexively.

Ah, he got it: Godzilla wasn't in the bag.

Something definitely wasn't right if that dumb toy wasn't kicking around. "You okay, Evie?"

Her smile turned flat, then left her face completely. "I'm fine. Just tired." She stood up. "I'll be back in a sec." She left the studio.

Nice job, Ty. Super well done. Tyler paced around anxiously, then did what always helped to release energy, and turned his MP3 player on so he could freestyle to his own music. He dusted off a few rusty contemporary and street dance moves to loosen out his legs from the routine, to help shake his frustration at himself and his inability to say the right thing. When he next looked at the door, Evie was leaning against it watching him, a soft smile on her face.

"You're incredible," she said.

Warmth pooled in his stomach. "I'm just messing around."

"Your messing around is incredible."

She sounded like she meant it, and she looked at him as though he was the best dancer she'd ever seen. Her hair was all wispy around her face, and the way she leaned stuck one hip out, creating a rounded, elegant series of curves from shoulder to thigh. *Gorgeous.* A lump rose in his throat, and heat churned in his belly.

Without any conscious decision on Tyler's part, he extended his hand and went over to her. She took his hand and allowed herself to be led into the middle of the room. His MP3 player thumped out Lauryn Hill, and he repeated a few of the easier contemporary moves, making Evie copy him. She let herself be swung and pulled around, the most relaxed she'd been all session.

"You know, you're a natural at this," he said.

She blushed. "Shut up."

Fuck, that was cute.

"Seriously. If you'd started when you were little, you could have gone professional."

"You really think so?"

"Yeah." He spun her around. "You got moves, girl."

"I'll settle for not being completely rubbish on nights out." She paused. "I got your message and saw Jean before coming to practice. She said nice things too. Gave me a key ring. You're all so friendly here."

Hmm. "Not all of us." He could think of a few times when people hadn't been that friendly to him.

Her expression shuttered. "You're right. Not all of you."

Ah. "Who's giving you shit, Evie?"

"No one." She scowled. "At least, no one you know. Seriously, it's my problem. Don't worry."

"Yeah, but your head's there and not here. It's affecting your dancing." She looked surprised, and he spun her around again. "See? You're slow. Sluggish."

She frowned, her gaze inward. "You know, I hadn't even noticed that? You're right."

"Spill it, Godzilla. Sharing is caring."

She sighed. "It's nothing. Well, not *nothing*, but . . ."

"Evie."

She slowed down, her face going distant. "You know I met a few aces from Tumblr last night for dinner? It was going well until the topic of coming out came up between me and this one girl." Evie stopped moving. "I told her I wasn't out to my family, and she took it so personally. As in, in-my-face-telling-me-I'm-doing-the-wrong-thing personally."

Ugh. Judgmental people. "You said in the interview your family wouldn't get it." He remembered *that* part of it.

"They wouldn't. Being straightforwardly gay would be easier for them, but because I've dated men *and* women, they think I'm still figuring it out. I've tried to explain it, but they don't get it. And the nuance of not needing sex in the relationship would be beyond them." She crossed her arms. "We don't talk about things. We just say what's happening and people accept it or not. My brother Richard was bullied at school, and my mother told him to fight back, and that was it, problem solved, never brought up again. It didn't stop, but he couldn't complain about it anymore because the solution had already been given to him."

"So your family sucks at communication." That sounded rough. Sure, his family sometimes felt like they were suffocating him with all their chatter, but he'd rather have that than not. "You tried to come out, but it's not exactly sticking. That's different from pretending you're completely straight. Is that what this girl thought you were doing?"

She shrugged. "I guess so, but I didn't get a chance to explain it like that." She scowled. "She went on and on about how it's so much worse the longer you wait and I'm lying to them by omission and I owe it to myself and to them blah blah bloody blah. Unbelievable," she said, fury making her whole body lift and sending her arms gesturing.

Tyler couldn't help appreciating how those movements made her breasts lift and emphasized the curve of her waist.

"She just wouldn't let it drop! I mean, for fuck's sake, she just met me! She doesn't know me. What the hell gave her the right to lecture me on my choices?"

"You tell *her* that?"

Evie actually growled. "I tried, but she was too busy giving me some sob story about her cousin's bad coming out." She flung her arms up in the air. "Like, I get it, you know? It's sad. But I've heard that story before. We all have. What the hell does her cousin and her family have to do with me and mine? You know? I ended up moving seats just to get away from her. Do you realize how that was for me? It's like the British equivalent of a slap in the face."

For real? He snorted. "Hey. She was out of line. You're right—it's your choice. If you think it's better you don't tell your family, then it probably is."

"Right? Thank you!"

"So why the anger?"

Evie seemed to deflate. "I just . . . I don't know. I guess I didn't expect that kind of judgment from another queer person. Or perhaps it was more the outrage that she showed. She was so *angry.*"

Evie's fingers went to her hair and worried at a loose lock. Tyler's fingers itched to reach over and tuck it back for her.

"It was like she implied I was letting the side down. What 'side,' I don't know, because I didn't join anything. I just turned out to be what I am. I'm not just asexual or biromantic; those are aspects of me.

It's private. It's important, because I had to do the oh-so-minor thing of taking apart and rebuilding my *entire outlook* on relationships and sex, but at the same time, that doesn't mean I'm duty-bound to be a freaking activist."

He nodded. "I get it." Oh, did he ever get it. He'd processed similar thoughts when he realized he liked girls and that he definitely was a guy. Coming out as a man had been absolutely necessary for him, but before and during transition, the visibility of gender had sometimes been so difficult to handle. His relationship to his own gender was something so private that it had seemed crazy unfair it also had this public aspect to it. There were days when he'd wished he could just not be seen, to not be so visible and always have to explain himself. In his experience, there was one consistent thing about being queer, no matter what shape it took: sometimes just existing was exhausting.

"Like, I know that having the choice to be open or not is a luxurious viewpoint to have," she added. "Now is a good time to be out. There's never been a better time. I saw *Milk* like everyone else." She paced. "I guess I was just . . . startled. Because, despite her baggage and rudeness, she had a point. I spent last night and this morning thinking about how my personal story fits into the wider political one, and what I owe my family. What I owe myself. If I owe anyone anything at all."

"Jeez, Godzilla. You think a lot. It's chill to take a backseat sometimes, you know?"

She stared at him, then laughed. She looked so relieved, that Tyler reached out for her. He couldn't help it. His hands settled at her waist like they were meant to be there, and by some miracle, the words were there too, because this was easy to talk about.

"If you want my opinion," he said, moving her into an easy sway—and Jesus it was magical the way she just followed him like that—"it doesn't matter about the bigger issues. It sounds like your family isn't exactly helping you out much. When I transitioned, it wasn't fun or easy, but it was made way better because my family was totally on board. Like, my mom read up about it and joined a bunch of forums and groups for parents of trans teens." He smiled at the memory. Those groups were mostly excuses for his mom to go out these days. "My family, we're in each other's business all the time. Like, *all* the time. I tell them everything that's going on. But with you, and tell me if I'm wrong, it sounds like your family isn't like that. Yeah, they won't kick you out, but they're not exactly going to join AVEN and play happy rainbow families with you."

She drifted in sync with him, eyes on his. "You're not wrong."

"Then no, you don't *owe* them this. Not when they're not on board for the smaller stuff, like who you love and who your friends are and how to deal with childhood bullies."

He spun her around slowly and *there* it was—she moved way better. Lighter. She returned to his hold and, to his surprise, initiated a reciprocal spin. Ah, she was definitely back if she was taking the damn lead from him.

"See how easy you move now?" he pointed out.

She turned to face him, blushing but smiling. "Yes, I got it. Thank you for letting me vent. You're good to talk to."

Pride filled his chest. "Girl, I had so much therapy when I was younger, I should be charging you for this. Dr. Davis's patented dance therapy."

She stroked her chin thoughtfully. "I see, I see. I'm indeed grateful, Dr. Davis. Is this first consultation free?"

Ha. "Hey now, nothing's free in this world."

"Then how should I pay you, Dr. Davis?"

"For starters, you can stop stealing the lead."

She dipped him. "Never."

Tyler blinked up at her grinning face. Fucking hell. He hadn't been dipped in *years*. Where had she learned *that*? "Buy me lunch," slipped out of his mouth. *Buy me lunch and tease me.*

Surprise flitted over her features. Surprise and something that looked like hope. "All right." She brought him back to standing. "Lunch it is." Her gaze flickered to something over his shoulder. "Oh. Don't look now, but we have an audience."

Evie hadn't noticed Katie and Brock come in. How long had they been there, filming them? Oh God, how much of the last half hour was on camera? And Tyler's cheeks darkened when he saw them—was that a blush? *Cute.*

After a long moment, Evie and Tyler separated.

"Hey guys." He waved.

Katie leaned against the wall with her arms crossed and eyebrows high, chewing thoughtfully. "Oh don't mind us. Please, continue whatever you were doing."

Tyler cleared his throat and looked at Evie. "Uh, back to it?"

She nodded.

Talking to Tyler had been brilliant. Somehow, he'd lightened the massive load that had weighed on her chest since yesterday. Sarah had fussed over her all evening after the disagreement, but honestly hadn't helped much. Really, all she'd wanted was some quiet to process her thoughts, *then* to talk them out. So Evie had gone to bed grumpy and woken up all tangled inside, unable to let it go. It was good to have someone help her tease out her feelings instead of just agreeing that yes she was angry and yes that anger was valid.

The difference it made physically was astounding. She'd found the first part of the session okay, but not that fun. No energy, no real connection to the moves, her body just going through the motions. Now though? Tyler was right. Everything in her felt physically lighter and dancing seemed easy. How had she never noticed that before? He had to be some kind of genius.

And they were going to have lunch together. That was . . . also good.

Tyler's finger prodded her forehead. "Hey, Godzilla, focus."

She batted away his hand. "Yes, yes, sensei, got it."

Amazingly, she was starting to get the steps down. Not perfectly or quickly, but she could do the entire routine from start to finish without forgetting a step. It was an odd sensation for her, a mix of conscious preparation and association. Each step needed the one before it; if she started in the middle of the routine, she would be lost. Sometimes her body moved before her mind did, and she wasn't used to that at *all*. If she thought too much about it, the balance fell apart completely.

Also new was the sense that she was telling a story. Her character was interested, yes, but resistant to Tyler's character's attentions. Every move she made not only had to be technically correct, it had to be full of personality and attitude in order to convey her character's emotions. And that wasn't something she'd ever done before. She'd never had to think about how her hips tipped and what that did to her pose, or how to angle her shoulders and arms in order to convey an idea. Doing it, feeling out the limits of her physicality and self-awareness like this, was exciting. She felt like she'd discovered another part of herself.

Definitely a great new experience.

When they paused for another break, Katie swept up to them, Brock keeping them both in frame as he approached with the camera.

"So," Katie asked. "How's practice going?"

"Better." Tyler glanced at Evie, annoyed. Hmm. Seemed like he was as done with them as she was. "How's the documentary coming?"

"Good. We're getting loads of material." Katie leaned forward. "Evie, what's Tyler like to dance with?"

Evie made sure to school her expression. "Awful. He's a control freak. I can't do anything right."

Tyler's jaw dropped, and he huffed in disbelief.

"Really," Evie continued, "I'm having second thoughts. We keep being distracted, he's such a klutz, I'm not sure we're well matched—"

Tyler muttered something and scooped her up over his shoulder. Abruptly, she was upside down, facing his butt and legs. *What? How?* "Hey!"

"Excuse me, I need a word with my dance partner," he said to the camera.

"Put me down!" He'd swung her up like she was a doll. Absolutely no fear. *Bloody hell.* As he walked away from them, Evie looked up into the camera and mouthed, *Control freak.*

He patted her leg. "Behave, Godzilla."

"I *am* behaving."

He stopped still. "You're a visitor to my city, but I have a reputation to maintain."

"*Your* city? Excuse you, you're not the only—"

"Get back here," Katie called, "we're not done!"

"As long as Evie doesn't get to speak." Tyler swung around to face the documentary makers. "Much more," he added.

For fuck's sake. Evie slapped his back. "Put me down already."

"Hey, I have a new idea," he said. "Why don't I just do the whole routine with you on my shoulder like this?"

"Why don't I just knee you in the face and we can spend the next two days in hospital?" Evie wriggled them threateningly.

He scoffed but grabbed her knees tightly. "That's nothing. It's not a dance rehearsal if you don't spend time in the ER."

Evie laughed despite herself. "Come on, I can't feel my legs anymore."

"Okay, here's how this is playing out." He turned around so she could look up and face the camera. "I'll let you down after you say something for me. Repeat after me: I, Evie Whitmore."

Evie rolled her eyes. He let her slide farther over his shoulder and she shrieked, grabbing his shirt. "If I go down, Davis, I'm taking your shirt with me." God, this felt too close for comfort.

"I, Evie," he insisted.

"I, Evie," she intoned.

"Do solemnly swear."

"Do solemnly under great duress swear."

He jiggled her legs. "That my partner, Tyler Davis."

"That my partner, Tyler Davis."

"Is without doubt the most talented, insightful, understanding, and handsome—"

"Oh, *really* now—"

"—dancer and teacher I've ever had the privilege of working with."

Evie sighed and faced the camera. "He's great."

She felt Tyler chuckle under her and her legs were pulled forward. She clenched her core instinctively and rose up so she looked down at him from what was now an impromptu lift. Her abdomen and hips were held tightly against his chest. A nameless emotion rolled through her when she realized that he *had* her. And he was enjoying it.

"You swine," she choked, clutching his shoulders.

"You're still buying me lunch, right?" His gorgeous brown eyes laughed up at her.

"Jesus, you two, get a room," Katie groaned.

Oh. Really? Evie felt a blush creep over her face. She seemed to be doing that a lot lately.

Tyler set her down quickly. "We tried," he said, deadpan, "but these people with cameras keep interrupting us."

Katie rolled her eyes. "Have you seen the other couples' routines?"

"No," they said in unison.

Tyler made a face. "Carmen's really good, so I have no idea what to expect from her. I think I'd end up intimidated."

Brock and Katie shared a knowing look.

Aha. Evie would bet money Tyler's instincts were right. She crossed her arms. "I don't suppose you two want to share what you've filmed?"

"No," Katie said. "Contractual obligation." Evie snorted. A likely story. They wanted primed but real drama to capture on the actual day.

After a few more questions the camera crew left, thankfully leaving them alone again.

Tyler caught her eye and grinned, prompting butterflies in her stomach.

Alas, they had to get back to business. This time, she *really* noticed a difference. Messing around had lightened the atmosphere, and now they kept interrupting each other with sly pokes and rude hand gestures. Her body twisted and turned, Tyler keeping pace easily, because somehow they were more in sync than before. The feel of his hands in hers was second nature, and she could sense where he was by some strange association between the routine and her body. She kept catching his eyes on her, focused and lively.

Evie definitely wasn't used to being physically in tune with someone like this.

Even better, *Tyler* seemed to be legitimately enjoying the session. Even though she was a beginner, had brought her worries with her, and he'd had to listen to her vent, he still liked dancing with her.

The thought did more funny things to her stomach. Oh Lord, this really was a thing, wasn't it? Beyond nerves and dancing, beyond making a new friend, and finding unknown parts of herself, this was . . . This was special.

Despite all the warm fuzzy feelings, come the end of their session, she was ready to crawl back to bed. Instead she collapsed where she stood, body shaky and stomach empty. Tyler stood over her, stretching his hamstrings in a way that made his legs look slightly disjointed.

"I can't move," she said.

"I noticed."

"I thought I'd get used to the exercise."

"You are. Your body's just complaining about it."

"Uggghhh."

"Eat something. You'll feel better. Oh look, it's lunchtime."

She narrowed her eyes at him. "I see your cunning plan, sir, and I disapprove."

He crouched next to her. "Do I have to carry you out of here?"

"No." Christ. No one had any business being as strong as he was. She flopped over onto her front. "I'm moving." She crawled to her bag. "See?"

Tyler scoffed and stood. "People are waiting."

Evie wanted a chair. A motorized scooter thing. Yes, that would be good. Something that would transport her with minimal effort on her part. She pulled herself up to standing and picked up her backpack with a grimace. "Lead on, sensei."

"What do you want for lunch?"

"Whatever's closest," she replied grimly.

Ten minutes later, they were settled in an Italian sandwich place and Evie had an iced tea in front of her. She gulped it down and closed her eyes during the ensuing sugar rush. "Oh God, that's good."

"Sugar makes everything better," Tyler remarked.

So true. Evie let the rush subside, then opened her eyes. "Katie looked ready to kill us."

"If she hasn't cracked by the end of the week, she'll be a documentary director for real."

"Have you seen Mark's interview?"

Tyler's eyebrows rose. "No."

"It's a thing of beauty. Oblivious hetero man beauty."

He snorted. "I can imagine."

Evie sipped thoughtfully. "We should get Brock to show us footage. Bribe him with drunk Gigi stories."

Tyler groaned and covered his face. "*No.* I don't want anything to do with their drama."

She leaned forward and peeled a finger off his face. "Gigi's your friend. His drama is your drama."

"And don't I know it. It's ridiculous." He peeked at her with his mouth half turned up in a smirk though.

"*You're* ridiculous—"

Evie's phone buzzed. So did Tyler's.

She glanced at him, then they both pulled their phones out. Evie saw a message from Sarah that simply said: *LOOK OUT THE WINDOW.* Evie looked up at Tyler, whose eyes were wide. They turned together to the window.

Sarah and Gigi waved at them excitedly from the street. Gigi laughed and Sarah rushed to the door. Evie couldn't help feeling a little disappointed. She turned to Tyler and— Was it her imagination or did he look disappointed too? "How did they find us?"

"I don't know." He seemed tense.

"Hey, guys!" Sarah trilled, sliding next to Evie.

"Isn't this *cozy*." Gigi grinned, nudging Tyler meaningfully as he sat next to him in the booth. Evie was amused to see how unimpressed Tyler was.

"I was going to surprise you for lunch," Sarah said to Evie. "I bumped into Gigi, who said he saw you two walking out of the studio together. We followed you and you had no idea!" She picked up the lunch menu and started scanning it. "This place looks great. Ooh, salt beef."

"Shouldn't you be somewhere apologizing to someone?" Tyler said pointedly to Gigi.

Gigi gazed at him with wide, innocent eyes. "Why would I do that?"

Tyler's smile could have cured *and* salted beef. "It's so great you joined us. You should have the chicken."

"Oh, I already ate," Gigi said.

Evie couldn't help wondering what on earth Sarah and Gigi were so happy about.

The waitress approached with Tyler's and Evie's orders. She blinked at the newcomers, then took their orders and bustled away. Evie picked up her pulled pork slider and took a bite. Heaven couldn't taste any better than pulled pork at that moment. Her eyes might have rolled back in her head. When she returned to reality, she saw Tyler grinning at her.

"How was practice today?" Sarah asked.

"Great," Tyler said. "Evie's doing well, and we're on track for Saturday." He turned to Gigi. "How's Mark?"

Gigi threw his hands up. "He asked if his girlfriend could watch us practise."

"So?"

"*So,* no! The last thing I need is them slobbering over each other while I'm trying to teach him open fucking hold . . ."

As Gigi settled into his rant, Sarah leaned against Evie. "That sounds really positive, especially for Ty. Things must be going *super* well, eh?"

What the . . . No, Sarah. Just no. "I owed him lunch."

Gigi leaned over the table and grinned like a shark scenting blood. "That's not what Brock said."

Evie could play this game too. "How *is* Brock? Have you apologized yet?"

Gigi gasped. He whacked Tyler's arm, forcing him to put down his sandwich. "You told her? How could you tell her about last night? What the fuck, man?"

Results. Evie smiled. "He didn't tell me anything, but you did. Just now. Last night, huh?"

Gigi gaped at her, then narrowed his eyes. "You play dirty, Whitmore."

She sipped her iced tea.

"Who's Brock?" Sarah asked.

Tyler picked up his sandwich again. "No one."

"The camera guy," Evie said.

"A mistake." Gigi sat back and crossed his arms.

The waitress set down drinks and Sarah's sandwich, distracting them. Evie met Tyler's eyes over the table as he chewed, looking thoroughly amused. He closed his hands around his sandwich as though holding a long, thick object, and she tried not to choke on her food with laughter. Sarah's delighted expression instantly put her on full alert, and she swallowed her food. "So, Sarah, you wanted to surprise me?" she said.

"Yeah! I have news. Do you remember Vaughn from last night?"

Evie had a vague image of a mop of dark hair and expensive clothes and art talk. "I think so."

"He's the art gallery curator. You talked to him about Postimpressionism and colour theory. Or something. He wants to come with us to Niagara Falls tomorrow!" Sarah beamed. "It'll be four of us now."

Tyler coughed and gulped some water, Gigi patting his back in concern. Once Tyler could speak, he asked, "You're going to Niagara Falls tomorrow?"

"Yes. That's why we scheduled the practice in the evening," Evie said. "I thought I told you?"

He nodded. "Yeah, yeah, just forgot it's *tomorrow*."

Time was passing so quickly. Evie frowned at her slider. Tomorrow was the fourth session, which meant they were halfway through this competition. She was leaving a week tomorrow. She looked up at Tyler. He set his sandwich down and gazed back at her with an expression she couldn't begin to figure out.

"Omigod, that means you're going back to England in one week's time!" Sarah gasped. She put her arm around Evie and hugged her tight. "I'm going to miss you!"

Evie laughed and hugged her back. "Come on, Sarah, I'll be back before you know it."

Tyler shoved at Gigi. "Excuse me." Gigi let him out, and Tyler walked to the washroom.

Gigi eyed them. "The Falls, eh? I love Niagara Falls. They have an IHOP there."

Sarah blinked. "IHOP? You like the Falls because of *IHOP*? Are you serious?"

Evie tuned out their bickering. Her slider no longer looked appetizing. This lunch, so bright and promising, had fallen dim around her. She felt . . . upset. Why? It couldn't be the idea of going, which was ridiculous because she was *coming back*.

Perhaps, she realized, surveying the restaurant and catching Tyler's eye as he stepped out of the washroom, it wasn't the act of leaving, but what she would be leaving behind.

"Evie!"

She turned. "Yes?"

Sarah scoffed at her. "Weren't you listening? We have *got* to take you to brunch."

"Okay?"

"Believe me, you Brits don't know proper brunch," Gigi said.

"How would you know?" Tyler had reached the table now. "You've never been out of Ontario."

"We'll figure it out." Sarah turned to Evie. "Now, tomorrow, we'll pick Vaughn up on our way out of town. And maybe some cake. Ace field trip to the Falls!"

Evie's head whirled. Brunch, Niagara Falls, this strange funk she was suddenly in—it was a little much, and she couldn't feel excited about Vaughn joining them. From memory, he was really opinionated. Not as bad as the girl who'd decided her opinion trumped Evie's life choices, but still, not someone she could see enlivening the trip.

Evie noticed that Tyler barely spoke during the rest of the meal. Granted, Sarah and Gigi could cover everyone's conversation themselves, but something about Tyler's silence bothered her. She focused on it so much she missed Gigi asking her a question.

"That sounds great!" Sarah exclaimed.

"Sorry, what?" Evie asked.

"Drinks on Thursday," he said. "Friday I'm in class, and we should be resting for the performance anyway. So, Thursday, cocktails with me on Church Street." Gigi waggled his eyebrows at her.

Evie had to laugh. "Yes. Absolutely."

"What about you?" Gigi asked Tyler.

He was focused on what was left of his sandwich, apparently uninterested in their plans. "Can't. Working."

"What, at the café? They can spare you."

"No. It's a dance gig." Tyler shifted in his seat. "It pays really well. Sorry."

Gigi eyed him suspiciously. "You're off the hook this time."

Tyler eyed him back. "You still owe me for Saturday."

Gigi sighed dramatically but didn't argue.

Sarah checked the time and flew into a panic. She hugged Evie good-bye and put down money for her food.

Gigi stood to go as well. "I have a class, so I'll walk you to the TTC, Sarah."

She nodded and they left.

Evie and Tyler were left in a dizzying vaccuum of quiet. Tyler opened his mouth, and Evie held up her hand. "No," she whispered. "Let's just enjoy the peace."

He snickered and leaned forward. "What the hell was that?"

Evie shook her head. "I don't know. If it was just Gigi, I'd expect an ambush, but Sarah too . . ."

Tyler's eyes glinted. "Oh, it was definitely an ambush."

"But why?"

An uncomfortable silence fell as Evie realized that neither of them wanted to answer that. Friends just being friends? Or friends being nosy? She looked out the window at the passing traffic and marvelled again at how *different* everything was.

Tyler set aside his empty plate with Sarah's. "I noticed you didn't have Godzilla today."

He did? She'd left the toy behind because of the course department visit she was making later. She didn't want to risk the course director seeing her lugging some toy around—there had been a few close calls the last time she'd visited. "He was tired after all the walking yesterday," she said.

Tyler smiled. "You go far?"

"All along Manitou Beach. It's gorgeous out there." She pulled out her diary and opened it to her notes pages to show him her doodles. He made the right appreciative noises, and she found herself staring at him.

Evie ducked her head as she blushed. What was *with* her? She seemed to spend half her time with him blushing. He was her dance partner. Nothing more. Even if he was cute and sweet and patient and funny and— Oh. *Oh Evie. You know better than this.*

Time to get a grip. She was impressed by the guy's focus and talent, that was all. That and the way he moved with her, the way his face lit up and his hands waved when he was inspired, the way he touched her like she had substance and presence and— *Stop it.*

The routine. It had to be the routine. All that intensity and pretend passion and physical closeness. It was messing with her perceptions of his behaviour. None of this was romantic. Even if it felt textbook romantic, it wasn't.

But maybe this is platonic and I've made a new friend.

She glanced at him. He was still looking at her silly drawings, really admiring them. Guys like him, who were surrounded by dancers, a group of people universally beautiful and more disciplined and interesting than her, couldn't be into someone like her, not when they had so many better options. No way was he even on the same level as her. Nope, it seemed fairly straightforward.

Who are you kidding, Whitmore?

"You know," he said, "I read a bunch of web comics, and I really think this is on the same level." He pushed the diary back towards her.

Evie forgot the drawings. "Web comics? You do? Which ones?"

Tyler laughed and started listing them.

She took another bite of her slider.

The next hour sped by in a whirl of iced tea and conversation. Comics and the internet, the games they liked to play when they had spare time, TV shows and movies and hobbies. Their tastes overlapped a lot, which meant Evie could have talked with him for hours. But he had class, and she had to continue feeling out her new territory. Alas, responsibilities.

She paid for lunch and they left, moving stiffly. Tyler stretched outside, grimacing. "I shouldn't have sat around for so long." He caught her eye and winked. "Not that it wasn't worth it."

She smiled. She couldn't seem to stop smiling. "I'd like to do this again."

"What, buy me lunch?"

"Rant at you and then buy you lunch, yes."

He grinned. "That sounds good to me. Thanks for today." He checked his phone. "I have to run. Have a good time at the Falls, and I'll see you tomorrow."

"See you."

He hovered uncertainly, then waved at her and jogged away.

Evie sighed, watching him go. Her stomach flipped over and chills raised goose bumps along her skin. Her mouth went dry, despite all the tea. The world seemed to shift and reassert itself into a brighter, more beautiful place. She felt so powerful and uncertain she couldn't speak.

Shit.

Shit. Shit. Shit.

Evie.

This *wasn't in the plan.*

Tyler spent the next class trying to sort out the mess of emotions in his head. Somewhere between being pissed off that their lunch had been interrupted, and being shaken by Sarah's announcement of what seemed like a double date, this weird feeling of possessiveness had curled into his chest. He didn't like that. Not when nothing had happened to warrant it, nothing except the small thing of Evie being fucking adorable and clueless about Sarah's scheming.

Because what else could that double date be? He couldn't imagine anyone called Vaughn the Art Curator willingly driving two hours to the Falls and clicking photos with the other tourists just because it was a fun thing to do. Even if the guy was asexual (*like Evie*) and into art (*also like Evie*) that didn't necessarily mean—

And where is that thought going? Quit it, Davis. She lives on the other side of the goddamn Atlantic. Back to reality, dude.

There was still a pang in his chest at the idea of Evie seeing the Falls with someone else like that. Someone who was more like her than he could ever be, in ways that mattered.

His musing was interrupted by a text from Gigi in the middle of his class: *Vaughn's not even in the picture. Don't worry about tomorrow. I got your back.*

Oh God. This he did not need. What the hell did *that* mean? Gigi being up to something was the last freaking thing he wanted.

Tyler: *I don't know what you're talking about. Whatever you're planning, don't do it.*

Gigi: *:)*

After class, he went to the reception area and waited for the writer from the Dance Association. This was the first of the interviews he'd scheduled, and this half hour was all he had free today. The fact that he'd just spent a whole hour on lunch with Evie wasn't lost on him, but he was electing to ignore that.

Lucette would have been appalled. She'd always hated how he prioritized things.

Whatever. It was *his* career. And wasn't it telling that he didn't need her around at all in order to do this? *Hell yeah.*

The idea kept him smiling through introductions. Apparently that was a good thing, as the interview went more smoothly than he'd expected. The Dance Association writer mostly wanted to know about his dance background, but she asked a few questions about being transgender in the dance industry and whether he felt transitioning had affected his prospects as a dancer. He answered as honestly as he could.

The best part of it was posing for pictures. He stood in the centre of the practice room, lit by small, powerful lights, and let himself go. He stretched and leaped and dipped and flexed, those good feelings from lunch and professional attention filling him up and bursting through his muscles. He even pulled out a few breakdance moves, making the photographer laugh.

When he was catching his breath after a deep straddle, the interviewer threw a question he wasn't expecting: "Weren't you Lucette Poignier's dance partner?"

He choked on a breath and coughed. Oops. He bent over and took a deep breath. Rubbed at his thighs to hide his expression. "Ah. Yeah," he managed, straightening. "For a while."

"I think I remember you and her performing at the dance festival last year. She defected to Vancouver, which I thought was a shame for Toronto's scene. Are you still in touch?"

"No. We fell out for, uh, artistic reasons." If you could interpret Lucette being a volatile head case as *artistic*. And people remembered them? Still?

"That's a shame. You two danced well together." She smiled. "Dancing with a complete beginner must present a whole other challenge."

He couldn't even begin to compare Evie and Lucette in terms of dance ability. They were worlds apart. That wasn't a bad thing though. He moved on the spot, trying to tease out his thoughts while keeping his focus on the photographer.

"It does," he said eventually. "But Evie's been fun to teach. In a way, it's ideal that she's not a professional. She doesn't take things so seriously. This competition isn't about who's the best, so I don't find this a challenge. I find it's closer to what I love about dance."

"Oh?"

He scrabbled for the right words. "I . . . love dance. You know? It's how I express myself best. It doesn't matter if I can do a perfect high arabesque or just the merengue, it's all the same to me. It's been fun working with Evie because she's like that too—she doesn't care about technique, she's just enjoying it. Yeah she'll never be a professional, but it's not about that for her. It's about learning to express herself in a different way. For me, teaching her is getting back to basics and remembering why I do this."

Jeez, that was cheesy. He felt his face heat up.

The reporter had a soft smile on her face. "That's a wonderful answer. Thank you."

And just like that, they moved on. More importantly, Tyler felt okay. Six months ago, discussing Lucette like that would have left a bad taste in his mouth and a shaky feeling in his stomach. Having the competition and Evie to talk about helped immensely. Mentally rewinding the interview as he sunk into the warrior pose, he could honestly say the entire interview had been pretty great. *Hell yeah, I can totally do this.*

Course it helped that there weren't any more bombshell questions.

True to form, Derek stuck his head around the door at the end of the interview. "Am I interrupting anything?" he asked, raising his eyebrows and smiling knowingly.

"No, we're done," Tyler said, managing to resist an eye roll. Trust the owner to try to worm in on his action. He introduced Derek to the Dance Association people and together they walked them to the front door.

Derek shook hands with the writer. "It's been great meeting you," he said. "Thank you for coming here."

"Thank *you* for letting us do this in your studio," she said.

"If there's anything I can do to help you with your piece, just let me know." He handed her his business card and a key ring. "We're very supportive of our dancers, and I'm thrilled you're interested in Tyler. He's one of our best. Oh, and here, let me get the door for you."

Oh, real subtle, Derek.

Tyler waited until they were gone before glaring at Derek. For someone who hadn't lifted a finger to help organize the interview (apart from say yes to using QS space, but Tyler refused to acknowledge that), Derek looked very satisfied.

"I think I made a good impression," he said.

"Mine was better. Keener."

Derek nudged him good-naturedly, and they turned back into the school. Derek cleared his throat. "Hey. I saw your and Evie's interviews."

Tyler sighed. Of course he had. "And?"

"I made a good choice, didn't I? Evie is perfect for you."

Intelligent, funny, works hard, hot . . . Derek, you have no fucking idea. Also, you didn't choose, she did. "I thought the dance machine thing was dumb, but she's actually good at this."

Derek nodded enthusiastically. "Yeah, yeah, exactly. You know, it's probably not great if I admit this, but I was really surprised when she said she was an engineer. She doesn't look the type, you know? Don't normally get engineers here as students."

"The *engineer* thing threw you?"

Derek screwed up his face. "Well, yeah. That's mathematical smarts, right? Normally mathematical people go for music as their creative outlet. It's like a proven thing."

He didn't have time for this. "Whatever. I have a class to get to."

"You and she are cute together too," Derek said as Tyler walked away.

"That's irrelevant, Derek," he tossed over his shoulder.

An engineer and a dancer. *Cute.* Tyler wondered what adjective would describe an engineer and an art curator.

CHAPTER SIX

Evie stared at the Falls in complete awe. Thousands of tonnes of blue-green water poured over sharp cliffs into a frothing pit, mist glittered in the sunlight, and she could see the sun glint off camera lenses on the American side of the Falls. The sky was summery blue and yawned above her, emphasizing just how *big* this part of the world was. She and Vaughn drank in the sight, relishing the relative quiet left behind by Sarah and Bailey ducking away to buy drinks. Sarah had kept the conversation up effortlessly the entire drive to the Falls—apparently very glad to have more time off work—and to Evie's relief, Vaughn had been more friendly than opinionated.

"This is stunning," she said.

"Isn't it?" Vaughn agreed. He rested his elbows on the guardrail and smiled at the sight of the Falls. "I've been here more times than I care to admit, and I've always been blown away."

As it turned out, Vaughn was fairly well versed in Ontario's landmarks. Evie mostly remembered his art knowledge from the meet-up, but he was something of a traveler in his own country. On the car ride down to Niagara, he'd talked about the visits he'd made around the province, including the vineyards near Niagara, Lake Superior, Hudson Bay in the north, Ottawa, and Algonquin Provincial Park. She'd decided her impression of him from the meal had to have been coloured by the coming out altercation; he was actually quite fun.

He also cleaned up better than she remembered: that mop of dark hair was combed back today, and he wore a linen blazer, crisp white shirt, maroon jeans with the cuffs turned up, and deck shoes. Evie was fairly sure his sunglasses cost more than her master's tuition. Vaughn wasn't the kind of person she'd expect at a meet-up for aces from Tumblr—he screamed gay rather than asexual or net denizen—but that was the beauty of the intersection between the internet and real life. It meant she could meet a man who would fit in nicely in the posh areas of London or York but who also enjoyed video games and discussing the intricacies of queer theory.

He was also an instant fan of Godzilla. He insisted on taking multiple photos with the toy, then holding him as they strolled along the viewing rail.

"There's probably more pictures of the damn monster than of me," Evie muttered, looking over the pictures on her camera.

"I think it's novel," he said. "I'd never consider taking a mascot on my trips." Vaughn stared at Godzilla for a moment. "I have to say, I'm very glad I decided to tag along. I don't normally go to meet-ups, but the other night's was fun. Today isn't how I'd usually spend my time at Niagara." He glanced at Evie. "It's been such a pleasure to visit somewhere I love with other asexual people."

She was touched. "Thanks, Vaughn. It's been lovely meeting you."

"When are you going back to England?"

"Next week, but I'm back in the autumn to study. We should meet up."

Vaughn bounced Godzilla in glee. "Absolutely. We can drink free sparkling wine and pretend to be snobs at art exhibitions."

"Only pretend?"

"Ha! Art snobbery is always pretence."

"As long as there's wine involved, I'm there."

He cast her an approving glance. "I think this is the start of a beautiful friendship, Evie."

They'd strolled past Second Cup now and turned to go back. Sarah and Bailey were taking forever.

"Sarah mentioned you're doing a dance competition while you're here?" Vaughn said.

Evie nodded. "It's something I accidentally joined."

His eyebrows raised. "How do you accidentally join a dance competition?"

She described the audition, how Sarah knew Tyler, and the practice sessions they'd been having.

Vaughn nodded throughout. "Sounds brutal. Three or four hours a day? Your legs must be pure muscle."

They *were* more solid, but hardly pure muscle. Mostly just sore. Evie looked down at them. A deep bruise stood out on one shin—the souvenir from Tyler's hungover mishap. "They're getting there. Honestly, they've never looked this good."

"What's the routine like? Is it difficult?"

"Yes. It's complicated but fun." She snapped yet another picture of the Falls. "I mean, it is for me. For Tyler it's probably fairly tame."

"Tyler is the gentleman teaching you the routine?"

"Yes." And damn her, she blushed *again*. "It's, uh, it's just a stunt that's happening for Pride, but it's been awesome. Meeting new people. New experiences. All that stuff."

"Eminently admirable. New experiences keep life worth living." He smiled slyly at her. "Sooo, what's this *Tyler* like—"

"Hey!" Sarah called from behind them. They turned and were handed iced coffees. "Sorry," Sarah said, "there was a massive line."

"Huge," Bailey emphasized, spreading their hands wide.

It hadn't seemed that big to Evie when they'd walked past the coffee shop. Given how Sarah was looking at her and Vaughn, she decided not to argue about it.

They took more photos, then lined up for the boat tour. When she stood on the deck and approached the Falls, Evie closed her eyes and felt the cool mist sprinkle on her face. It seeped slowly into her skin and hair, soaking her with gentle brushes, and when she opened her eyes, she found herself surrounded by fog. The noise of the Falls drowned out the boat's motor and the chatter of her friends.

Peering into the mist, Evie wondered what a certain dancer would have to say about the natural beauty of his country, and she wished he was there with them. If he could see this mist, the raw power of the water, she thought he might be awed into silence the way she was. Unlike Sarah and Bailey, resolutely chatting despite the noise of the falls, Tyler would probably just lean and watch with her. No words necessary.

A realization that she was being watched startled her out of her reverie, and she looked over to see Vaughn holding her camera.

She smiled at him, saw his finger press down again, then she turned back to the mist and the Falls and tried to imprint the experience in her memory.

After the tour, they had lunch and discussed plans for the evening. Vaughn was going to a slam poetry session, Sarah was climbing with friends at an indoor wall, and Bailey was working on an arts project with their company. While Vaughn and Bailey discussed the logistics of dinner, Sarah leaned towards Evie.

"I can*not* believe he's ace," she said, her voice low.

"Sarah, he's literally opposite us."

"He's nice, eh?" Sarah beamed.

Evie blinked, then frowned. That phrase usually only meant one thing. "Gaybeard, is this a setup?"

"No!" Sarah said quickly. "I invited loads of people from last night. Honest. Vaughn was the only one to take me up on it. And you two seemed to hit it off, so I thought why not? You're having fun, right?"

Why not indeed. The thing was, it now *felt* like a setup to Evie. At least they weren't straight, otherwise this would supposedly be a done deal if all those rom-coms were to be believed. "Of course. This place is amazing. I *suppose* we've 'hit it off.' Vaughn is lovely. But . . ." She glanced at Vaughn. "I feel this is a friends thing."

Sarah seemed to struggle not to smile at this. "Really?"

Evie eyed her suspiciously. If Sarah had really been setting them up, why was she so pleased now? "Yes," Evie said slowly.

Sarah stirred her drink. "Is there anyone else you wish was here instead?"

Evie blushed despite herself. "No," she lied. "This is fab."

Sarah's grin threatened to split her face as she took Evie's hand. "You don't say, Evazilla."

After lunch, they strolled back along the viewing platform and through Niagara to their car. Evie found herself next to Vaughn while Sarah pointed something out to Bailey ahead of them. He asked her when the dance performance was.

"Saturday. It's taking place on a stage somewhere on Church Street." She side-eyed him. "I'm not telling you when. It won't be anything special."

"Perhaps, but perhaps not. But it *will* be fun. Plus you're representing us." He pulled out his phone and tapped at it. "Ah. The performances start at 2 p.m. Consider me already there."

Saturday was four days away. Four days didn't seem like enough. She wondered if Tyler was really as confident as he'd seemed the other day. She wondered how Gigi and Mark were getting on. Hopefully Mark was struggling too. At least he didn't have to deal with unexpected feelings as well as lack of experience. How the hell *she* was ever going to do this, now that her thoughts were filled with Tyler, was kind of beyond her.

She was abruptly hit by a small wave of homesickness. Just enough to make her miss the familiarity and routine of her life back home. Something about the heat of this place, the unfamiliar wide-open landscape, the different accents and people, and the worry of a public performance, all combined to briefly be overwhelming. She took a deep breath, letting it pass.

"You're miles away, Evie. You okay?"

She snapped back to the present. "Yes? Yes. Sorry. What were you saying?"

"That I'm sure you'll do wonderfully." Vaughn leaned in. "Also, I think you're lovely too."

Oh no. Oh Lord, how mortifying. "You heard us?"

"Sarah isn't as quiet as she thinks she is," he said. "And I have the impression that she's been watching you closely. Not sure why, considering you seem very much smitten with someone else. Just so we're completely clear, I'm already totally and very happily taken. Even if I weren't, when I have the bad luck to fall for someone, they tend to be male."

Evie was never going to live this down. "I really, *really* didn't—"

"But I can always use more friends." He winked. "Especially ones who would be willing to revisit the Falls with me and my boyfriend this winter."

Evie smiled, relief trickling through her. "I would love to."

Tyler had barely had time to think. Since opening at the café, his schedule had been packed, so of course when he finally reached the only break he had before the Pride practice, Shana called. He decided to step outside to talk to her, as it was paradoxically more private than indoors; particularly when Gigi was hanging around with an expression that said, *I have feelings and I need to share.*

She didn't even bother with preliminaries. "Ty, I've made a decision. I'm keeping it."

Ooh. Okay. Deep breath. He looked up into the cloudless blue sky, wide and clear and full of sunlight. It somehow seemed appropriate for news like this. "That's a big step, sis."

"It is. I don't care. I know I can do this."

"What about Ray?"

"He's gone." She *tsk*ed. "I told him I was keeping it, and he told me we were over. Threw a fucking tantrum and walked out. I think he's blocked my number. Asshole."

"Wow, Shana. *Wow.* You okay?"

"Yeah, I'm good. Honestly, I'm great."

"Is he hanging around? Looking to cause problems?"

"Please. Boy's too chicken to do shit to me." She sounded more like their mom as her anger revved up, her voice taking on more of a Jamaican lilt. "I told him I'm not chasing him. I'm not taking anything from him. So if he wants to disappear, he can do it and be done with us." She sighed. "I don't think he left town or anything, but I doubt I'll see him again."

"I hope not." Tyler couldn't quite believe *this* was how Ray was being kicked out of their lives. "So, I'm going to be an uncle, huh?"

Her voice turned low and happy. "Yeah, bro. You're Uncle Tyler now."

"I'm not old enough to be an uncle. What the fuck." He was struck by a horrific realization. "Shana. You're going to be a *mom.*"

She made a noise of pure delight, and he grinned.

A car stopped down the street from the school. He watched as a guy in a blazer and deck shoes got out, then held the door open for Evie. He almost dropped the phone. She looked gorgeous. Loose top, skirt, sandals, sunglasses, and her hair down, her skin slightly sunburnt, and a smile on her face as she waved into the car and shut the door. Just *gorgeous.*

Oooh, hell, he was in trouble.

"Ty, you there?"

Oh right, the phone. His sister. "Yeah, still here."

"Mom's feeling a lot better, and I know you're busy and all, but try to get to us sometime this summer."

"I'll try."

"You better. I'll keep you posted about the baby. Miss you, lil bro."

"Miss you too. Thanks for telling me, Shana."

Now Evie was hugging Deck Shoes Guy. Wait. Was he *Vaughn?* He looked like a Vaughn. Tyler had never met a Vaughn, but he was pretty sure they all liked pairing deck shoes with blazers on hot June day trips to Niagara Falls.

"Call me soon," Shana said.

"Will do. Love you, Shana."

"Love you too."

He put the phone down and watched Evie wave good-bye to Vaughn. The car drove away with a honk as Vaughn walked towards the nearest subway station and Evie turned towards the school. Towards him. She saw him, and her face split into a wide smile. Suddenly he couldn't remember what he'd been doing or why he was standing outside.

Oh yeah. He was in *big* trouble.

He waved as she approached him.

"Hi, Tyler." Her accent made his name clear and sweet.

"Hey." He still had a grin on his face. He probably looked like an idiot. It was just Evie, after all.

Yeah, right. She could never be *just* Evie.

"You look happy," she said.

"I do?"

"Yes."

It's because of you. You and this gorgeous day and . . . "My sister just told me I'm going to be an uncle."

She went all soft around the edges. "That's brilliant news!" She hugged him. He caught the scents of sunscreen and now-familiar herbal shampoo. A warm ache bloomed between his legs, and he resisted the urge to turn his face into her hair.

"Congratulations, Uncle Tyler." She stood back and looked him up and down. "You definitely look like an Uncle Tyler."

He scoffed. He was wearing two-day-old dance gear and his hair was pulled back in a man bun. Never was a man more the picture of responsibility. "My sister just found out. I'm still taking it in."

"I'm really happy for you." She looked like she meant it. Oh God. He couldn't tell her the full story of his sister's baby daddy running for the hills and spoil it.

"How were the Falls?" he asked instead.

She lit up. "Wonderful. They're *spectacular*." She dug into her backpack and drew out her camera. "We took photos." Then she was right up against him so he could see as she clicked through the photos of the day. And yeah, the Falls had been spectacular. But the photos of her and Vaughn goofing off with Godzilla sent a barb through him, which he instantly pushed down, then forgot about when she clicked onto one of her on the deck of the tour boat. He touched the camera with one hand to stop her from moving on. The picture was surprisingly well composed—there wasn't anyone else in it, just her and the rail. Mist deepened behind her and droplets shone in her hair as she stared off into the distance with a wistful smile.

"You look stunning there," he said honestly.

She made disbelieving noises. "Vaughn took that of me. I was thinking of . . . of, um, how incredible being under the falls was."

Goddamn *Vaughn*.

Their eyes met, and he realized just how physically close they were. Her face was inches from his. He didn't move, however, and neither did she. She looked back down and kept clicking through the photos. Tyler barely took them in; this close, all his senses were attuned to her. Her smell, her hair, her skin, her fingers, her mouth . . . *Focus, Ty.* He was still half holding the camera, and her fingers brushed against his, causing his breath to catch as the motion sent electricity through him. Evie turned her face to his—

"*There* you two are!"

They jumped apart, then turned towards the doorway. Katie stood there, coffee cup in hand and gum in mouth. She grinned at them. "Ready to start?"

"Y-yeah." Evie turned the camera off. "I need to get changed, so I'll meet you all in there." She walked into the school, past Katie, who fixed Tyler with a knowing look.

"You two look like you're getting kinda close," she remarked.

He wanted to shove her and Brock and the camera and the entire stupid documentary back into 2008 where documentaries like this belonged. "Yeah, friends do that. Let's go." He brushed past her, then past a dour Brock in the reception, and stomped into the practice room.

Once there, he started warming up. Evie soon entered wearing her usual gear, her hair tied up and skin still warm and glowing from a day in the sun.

He pulled his gaze away before it turned into an actual stare, and put on some warm-up music. "I thought we'd try syncing the moves to the music today."

She made a face. "I can't promise anything except that I'll try."

"'Do, or do not. There is no try.'"

She rolled her eyes. "Yeah, yeah, Your Jedi-ness."

He turned and bounced in place to the music while she warmed up. What was this song? Florence + the Machine? Yeah, good to dance to. Tension thrummed in his veins, and he pulled a few ballet stretches to work out some of the nervous energy. Christ, where was it all coming from?

"Tyler?"

Uh-huh, that would be where.

He turned around. She faced him, ready. "Can we run through it a few times first?"

He swallowed. "Yeah. Totally."

She danced away, and he turned off the music, then moved into position, into character, ready to play suitor. As part of him settled down and focused on the routine, another part became more and more keyed up. Evie was full of sinuous energy, whirling around in her set up to the routine. She came face-to-face with him, her entire body alight, and he took her in hold. One beat, and then they were moving together.

It was electric. He almost felt sparks as he led her through the first part. Her character resisted and took the lead, and energy coursed through him as he kept up with her. They managed the quick footwork section, messily, and separated for the slow stare down during the second drawled chorus of the song, and then, *bam*, together again for the instrumental.

Before he knew it, he was on his knees and she was sauntering away. The end of the dance. His breath left him in a rush. There had been lots of fumbles, but that was definitely the best run-through yet.

Evie turned around and beamed at him. "Tyler!" She ran up to him, hands out to help him stand. Blue eyes shone at him in delight. He paused a moment to take in her joy, then gripped her hands and stood slowly, his head still spinning. This was beyond words, how good this felt. How in tune they were. He'd never wanted to kiss someone so much in his life.

"Once more?"

"Hell yeah," he managed.

While they had the steps down now, doing them in time to the music proved more of a challenge. They were both soaked with sweat by the time Tyler called a break. Evie was visibly slower now, and she slumped to the floor dramatically.

"This music is horrible," she said to the ceiling.

Told you so. Instead of saying that, he chuckled, dug into his bag for an energy bar, and tossed it to her. She caught it with one hand and wolfed it where she lay as he sat down next to her. Katie joined them, Brock and the camera at her side.

"The routine's coming together," Katie said. "That looked really good." She blew a gum bubble.

Tyler couldn't speak for Evie, but when he said, "Yeah, we're getting it," she sat up and nodded. Katie smiled and the bubble popped.

"How do you do it?" Brock asked.

Tyler glanced at Evie for guidance, because he sure as shit didn't know what Brock was talking about. She shrugged. Okay. No help there. He turned warily back to Brock. "Practise for three days?"

"No, dude, this!" Brock exclaimed, waving a hand between the two of them. "This connection you have. You two *get* each other. What the hell?"

Oh *fuck*. Evie went bright red. Tyler couldn't bring himself to look her way again. "Uh," he said, "I don't think we're ... That is, we're not actually—"

"Brock," Katie warned.

"Seriously," Brock continued. "Can't you give me some advice? Gigi is driving me insane. *I'm* driving me insane." He set the camera down and sat in front of Tyler. "I'm begging you, man." Desperation was written all over his features.

Why did this keep coming back to him? He wasn't Gigi's only friend, just his best one. Didn't Brock have someone better to talk to? Hadn't he heard of the internet for relationship advice? Given Tyler's record with relationships, Reddit was legit the better option.

"Brock, this is so unprofessional, I can't even deal right now," Katie ground out.

Brock glanced at her. "I'm not a professional, and I'm out of options." Brown eyes back on Tyler's. "I can't pin the guy down. I asked him if we could talk, and he said we could, but now he's not answering my calls or texts. He gives me these *looks* during rehearsals, you know? But then he avoids me afterwards. Today he used *Mark* as an excuse to get out of practice without talking to me. He hates Mark. Jesus, I love the guy, but it can't go on like this."

This wasn't going to go away, was it? "Dude, I . . ." He sighed. "I don't know what to tell you. This is Gigi we're talking about."

"You're in love with him?" Evie asked softly. Tyler risked a peek at her, but she was completely focused on Brock. She slid closer to them so she could lay a hand on Brock's arm.

Katie picked up the camera. "This is totally going in my write-up and in the final cut if it has to, Brock, so don't blame me if you don't get full credit for this." She pointed it at them.

"We can make it a blooper."

"For a *documentary*?"

"And yeah, Evie." Brock's face softened. "He knows that. I don't get why he's running away."

"He's scared," Evie said immediately.

"I know *that* much. But I'm not going to hurt him again."

"Does *he* know that though?" Tyler asked.

Brock slumped. "I hope so," he mumbled. "I don't know."

Evie patted his arm. "I think this might be a case where you have to wait it out. Don't go anywhere, but don't push him. Trust is a difficult thing to build."

Brock appeared the image of misery. "I get that. But how can I build it if he won't let me? This assignment finishes on Saturday. I don't want to do the stalker thing and hang around outside the school waiting for him to talk to me. And I know he wants to talk, he just . . . doesn't know how."

Tyler nodded. That was Gigi all right. "I agree. I'm all for being patient, Evie, but I think this requires a shove in the right direction." He glanced at her. She seemed puzzled for a second, then must've figured out what he meant, because her expression turned cunning.

"Brock," she said, "are you free Thursday night?"

He blinked at her. "I could be."

"Gigi is taking me and my friend Sarah out around Church Street on Thursday night."

Brock perked up like a wilted plant in a bucket of water. "Ah."

"I cannot fucking believe this," Katie muttered, focusing through the viewfinder.

Tyler had to agree with her for once. What the hell was with this week? Why did life do this? Nothing happened to him for months, then *everything* landed on his lap in four days.

And thanks to Brock, he could barely look at the best thing about this week.

Brock pulled out his phone. "What's your WhatsApp name?" Evie retrieved her phone and they traded details. The guy was so pathetically grateful that Tyler almost wanted to pat his arm too. Almost.

"Thanks, guys," Brock said. "Seriously, thank you. If I can't make this up to him, I don't know what I'll do." He closed his eyes. "I just want to make him happy."

Tyler just about felt sorry for him. Jeez. "Yeah, buddy, we know."

"I want what you two have, you know? That talking-without-words thing." He waved vaguely in the air between Tyler and Evie. Tyler could feel himself blushing, and he knew without checking that Evie had gone red as well.

Brock continued, oblivious. "We had it once. I think we could still have it. Oh man, I can't sleep because all I do is think about him, you know? Not in a gross way or anything," he added hastily.

"Just . . . I know Gigi feels something too, but he won't sit still long enough to tell me what."

"You'll get there," Evie said. "You will. Be patient."

"Are we done with the soap now?" Katie snapped. "Because I have a documentary to film."

Brock nodded, suddenly all business. "Yeah. We're cool."

No, they weren't. Tyler couldn't remember the last time he'd felt this embarrassed. This was worse than when he'd finally seen what Lucette had been doing to him and for how long. This was worse than when he was six and Shana had made him laugh during his birthday party and he'd ended up farting super loud in front of his family and friends and made everyone laugh, on camera. Hell, this was worse than that one time he'd tripped while dancing for a music video and knocked over half the set.

"Tyler."

He looked over into serious blue eyes. Evie swallowed, openly nervous, took his hand, and pulled him away from the camera to the other side of the room.

"I have to ask you something," she said, her voice low. "And I hope you'll be honest with me." Her eyes flickered to Brock and Katie, who were watching and trying to listen in. "We're dancing well together, right?"

"Yeah."

"I think we have a good connection." Her voice was becoming shakier with each word. His heart leaped hearing that. "Like, really good. The—the best. The thing is, I don't . . ." She dropped his hand to wring hers together. "I'm not good at judging situations like this. Doing this has made me so aware of myself and, at the same time, so aware of *you*. Is this normal for dancing partners? Or is this something . . . more?"

His mouth went dry. She was gazing at him, waiting for him to speak. Katie and Brock couldn't lean closer without actually moving. Suddenly he was facing a timid and shy Lucette, gazing at him through her lashes as she said, *"You like me, right?"* His throat closed up. Was that happening again? *Don't freak out, don't freak out.*

She went red and glanced away. "I mean, if it isn't, I want to make it clear. Be on the same page, so to speak. I just don't want to make you uncomfortable, or be uncomfortable myself, and assume this is more than it is, because this is wonderful as is, and I don't want to change that or be awkward and, oh God, I'm rambling." She stopped. "Um. Yeah. Shit. Bollocks. I'm stopping now." She crossed her arms.

Snap out of it and fucking speak, Tyler. "No," he choked out.

Her eyes flew back to his, wide. "No?" she echoed.

"No, we're . . ." He eyed the camera. Still being filmed. Still on show. *I'm still not . . .* His gaze flickered back to her. Beautiful, even in the middle of almost confessing—what? That she felt something for him? Something more? Which, okay, he felt that too. He totally did.

But could he rely on that sense of *more* from a basis of four days of dancing? He wanted to. But he also didn't want to, because four days was nothing.

Shit, she was starting to look upset. He needed to say something. But what? Damn it, he was so bad at this. What if he said the wrong thing and she flipped out? Or did what Luce used to do and sulk or, even worse, yell at him?

Think, Tyler. It was kind of a basic question, right? But why was she even asking it? How could she be invested in whatever was happening between them? She was going back over the Atlantic in exactly one week.

Wait, so, even if she did freak out, she'd be gone after a week. He could handle a week of freak out. Or of awkward. But he didn't want either of those things. He wanted the energy they'd just had, so he had to say the right thing to make sure there wasn't awkwardness. As in, like, nothing that would lead her on or make her upset. He could do that.

She glanced at the camera. "You know," she murmured, frowning, "we can talk about this later, because this is less than ideal—"

"No, it's fine," he said, words finally rushing to his aid. "I mean . . . These are, um, unusual circumstances, right, and we do . . . We're dancing super well together." He took her hand. "I think we're good friends. I think that's what's coming across." Something in him slowly curled up and cried as he said that. His throat tightened, and he gripped her hand harder.

She looked down at their hands, then up at him. Her expression made him freeze; she was disappointed, but also skeptical. She knew he wasn't telling the whole truth. The same connection that made him feel like the world sparked into life when they touched pretty much guaranteed she saw straight through what he was saying—and it hurt her.

"All right," she said, sounding anything but. "That's . . . good to know."

Out of all the reactions he'd expected, this was the one that surprised him the most—which didn't really make sense. Because of course she wouldn't fly off the handle. Most people wouldn't. Why had he assumed she would?

Fuck. His head was a goddamn mess.

He couldn't seem to let her hand go. Suddenly, he flat-out didn't want to. "I know Brock said some, um, some stuff there, but, uh . . ."

"He misunderstood," she said firmly. "Yes. I know." She forced a smile, and Tyler wanted to take those words back. He wanted to take the whole conversation back and pull her out into the corridor for some fucking privacy and show her exactly what he *did* feel.

"We're fine as we are," he said desperately. "We're perfect, just as we are." *You're perfect, and I don't want you to go.* The words refused to leave his mouth.

She smiled a little more genuinely. "I agree with that." She swung his hand. "We should get back to work."

"Yeah."

She let his hand go and walked back towards Katie and Brock, who quickly turned away as if they hadn't been trying to film and eavesdrop on the conversation. Brock looked particularly guilty. As far as Tyler was concerned, the two of them couldn't leave soon enough.

Tyler couldn't feel his body. He moved after her on autopilot and took his starting position.

Two agonizing hours later, Evie waved good-bye and walked out the door. Tyler wanted to collapse to the floor in disappointment. That energy had still been there, Evie had been her usual joking self, and they'd managed to get the first minute or so of the routine up to speed; it had outwardly been a good practice session.

He felt like crying. The latter half of the session had been nothing like the first half. The first half had been fireworks and magic; the second half had been harsh reality covered by reassuring smiles and old jokes. Tyler knelt and dug for his phone. It was ten o'clock, but he didn't care; he called Shana.

"Hey, Ty!" She sounded pleasantly surprised. "What's up, bro?"

"Shana, I messed up."

"What happened?" There she went again, sounding like Mom.

"You know that performance I was telling you about? The Pride one?"

"Yeah."

"And the girl I'm dancing with?"

A smile came into Shana's voice. "Oh yeah. I saw that video you sent me. Girl did good."

"It's her. She happened."

"What'd you do? You drop her?"

He leaned against the mirrored wall. "Not literally. We've got this amazing connection, and she asked me about it, and I choked."

"Baby, how long have you known this girl?"

Including the audition? "Five days."

"And are these feelings amazing because of the dancing thing? Because that was part of the problem with Lucette."

"I know. And no, it's not. It's amazing because she's amazing." He closed his eyes and sighed. "She's funny and smart and gorgeous and sweet and . . . I don't know, Shana. I want to pick her up and keep her with me all the time so I can just be with her."

"She feel the same way?"

His throat closed up again. "Yeah," he rasped. "Maybe. I think so."

"So what's the problem? Ask her out."

"She's from England, remember? She's here for another week and then she's gone. Like, what's the point? Plus, I keep choking." He forced the words out. "I keep being reminded of shit Luce would say and do, and it's getting in the way."

"Oh, bro." Shana's voice turned sympathetic. "That sucks. For real, that sucks. But it doesn't mean you can't ask her out."

His eyes flew open. He hadn't expected that. "Huh?"

"Don't 'huh' me. Ask the girl out."

"Shan, I'm struggling with psychological turmoil."

"What's a date going to hurt? Call it practice, if you want. But for feelings. Or something. Just have some fun times with her now, get an international friend for keeps afterwards—it'll all be cool. And good for you."

He pulled his jacket out of his bag and shrugged into it. "I like her, Shana. I really like her."

". . . Oh, *Ty*."

"But I told her this is just friendship."

"She fall for that?"

"No."

"You're an idiot."

"I told you I messed up!" He stood and pulled his bag over his shoulder. "How do I fix this?"

"Tell her you're sorry and ask her out."

He left the practice room and found himself face-to-face with Brock. "I can't do that," he said into the phone, staring at the guy. He hadn't noticed it before, but Gigi was right: Brock really did have great shoulders.

"If you can't, then you deserve the nothing you're going to get."

"Shana!"

Brock retreated a bit but waited for him.

"Sort it out, bro." Her voice softened. "I know it's been a rough year for you, but this girl sounds like a good thing. You have never ever called me up at 10 o'clock because of a girl before."

"Oh."

"Yeah, *oh*. Ask her out. That's my advice."

"Thanks." He thought.

He said his good-byes and hung up. Right. *Right*. He could do that. Ask Evie out. But first, he had someone else to deal with.

Brock straightened as Tyler faced him. "I came back because I wanted to say sorry."

Tyler was suddenly very, very tired. So. Much. *Drama*. "Sure, dude."

"No, I mean it. What happened back there? Because I thought you two had totally gotten together, you know? When I saw you talking like that, I realized you hadn't and I felt like a total asshole."

He looked terrible. Tyler had a sudden urge to laugh at the guy. He was completely inept at this stuff, wasn't he?

"Don't worry about it, man." He realized he meant it. "It's my problem. Hers and mine."

They started walking to the school's reception area.

Brock smiled shyly. "I apologized to Evie too, when she left just now. She was really cool. I kinda thought she might be all British, you know, all pretending it didn't happen, but I guess that's just a stereotype, because she's never been like that during all this dance stuff." He seemed to notice he was babbling, and took a deep breath. "So, uh, I was wondering if I could make it up to you. By helping. I mean, she's helping me with Gigi. I could help you with her."

Tyler shook his head. "Thanks, Brock, but no offence? I think I'm good. I know what the problem is."

"What is it?"

"It's complicated."

Brock nodded, clearly expecting to hear all the damn dirt.

Tyler sighed. Why did people keep doing this? "Look, I got issues. I can deal, but they're there."

Brock stopped short and gave him a hard look. "It's not because of the asexuality thing, is it? Because that would be *low*, man. Like, okay, I don't get it, but if I had that kind of connection with someone who was— Like if *Gigi* was asexual, I'd fucking *make* it work."

Tyler shook his head. He hadn't considered that aspect of it— truthfully, had genuinely forgotten all about it. Somehow it didn't seem to matter. Sex wasn't what drove this thing between them. "It's not her orientation."

"Good. Because you two had the eye thing going on."

"The eye thing?"

Brock nodded seriously. They were in the reception area now. He attempted to demonstrate to Tyler by fluttering his eyelashes in what Tyler guessed was meant to be a seductive, intense gaze.

"*That* eye thing," Brock said. "You know, where you look at each other all the time and you don't look at anyone else like that."

Tyler snorted. "My eyes don't flutter. And neither do hers."

"You know what I mean."

"I really don't."

"Dude, give me a break," Brock grumbled.

Tyler smiled, because it turned out teasing him was fun. They emerged into the Toronto night, neon signs lining the street and streetlights keeping back the dark. The air tasted like tap water and the promise of sleep. He glanced at Brock. "TTC?"

"Yeah, man." They headed towards it.

Despite the weight of the day's events, Tyler did feel better. Perhaps Brock and Shana were right. Perhaps he could trust in this thing between them enough to at least try it.

At a minimum, he owed Evie lunch after today.

CHAPTER SEVEN

Evie woke up and immediately wanted to bury her head under the pillow, never to emerge from Sarah and Bailey's sofa bed again.

What she did was get up.

She went from their living room into the kitchen and made herself a cup of tea. It was still early and the sun inched over the horizon. The view from the kitchen window looked out over their scrap of a garden and the scrap of garden belonging to the house behind them, where dew sparkled on the grass and flowers. The sky promised another hot, beautiful day.

The world was still effervescent. She thought it might have dimmed after his . . . not rejection, necessarily, but certainly denial. Tyler had avoided eye contact until she'd pointedly stared at him, and even then he'd said each word as though they were being physically pushed through his mouth. *"I think we're good friends."* Said like he couldn't believe he was saying it. The strength of his grip on her hand had increased and increased until she'd let it go. Given the way he looked at her and the ease they'd previously had, Evie was less than convinced he really felt that way.

But something had made him say it. Uncertainty? Fear?

Or he meant exactly what he said, and Evie was just trying to see something where there was nothing.

Of course, she'd treat this as friendship now, even if she wasn't wholly convinced it was. After Brock's disastrous assumptions, she'd tried her best, but their dynamic hadn't been the same. The latter half of the session had been awkward and tense, so the routine had been a welcome distraction from her own disappointment.

Brock had been sweet the previous evening. He'd waited for her in the reception, looking so miserable she couldn't help taking pity and listening to what he'd had to say. If he was desperate when he'd crashed their practice session, he'd been more than contrite when he apologized for making things awkward. She'd forgiven him on the spot. And it really wasn't his fault anyway; the fault was hers for asking and Tyler's for *not* asking and theirs for ignoring it until someone else mentioned it.

She closed her eyes. The first half of the session had been . . . wow. Just *wow*. They had known the moves and anticipated each other, and they'd fit together like clockwork. It had been straightforward and simple and mesmerising. She'd been so aware of him, drawn like a magnet over and over to him and his dark eyes and graceful body.

That sounds almost sexual. But it wasn't about sex, not really. It was about being in the same room as him, that strange irresistible, magnetic draw to another person who just *clicked*. She'd felt glimmers of this with other people, had felt it in her previous relationships, but with Tyler it was all-consuming. That was rare, which made her disappointment that much more bitter.

She leaned her forehead against the window. Why was this so complicated?

Motion stirred behind her, and she turned to see a sleepy Bailey step into the kitchen. "Hey," Bailey said.

"Morning."

"You okay?" Bailey asked.

Evie nodded. "You?"

"I'm awake and will soon have coffee. That's always good."

Evie turned back to the window with a small smile and sipped her tea as Bailey made coffee. "Bay," she said carefully, "do you know Tyler well?"

"Sorta, but not as well as Sarah does." Bailey joined her by the window, coffee cup in hand. Their hair was flattened on one side from sleeping, and their pj's had skulls dotted across them. They'd promised Evie a set for when she came back to Toronto.

Evie mentally sifted the words she needed. "Would you say he's a private person?"

"Oh yeah, definitely."

Perhaps the whole problem had been asking him in front of that damn camera. But then, what did *"We're perfect, just as we are"* mean? Because "as they were" had been the burgeoning emotional wonder that prompted her to ask him what was going on in the first place.

"Evie?" Bailey asked.

Evie recounted the previous evening to them. "So that's what happened, and I'm still trying to figure it out. I mean, he *is* sending mixed signals, isn't he? I got that right?"

"I think so."

"But he probably has reasons for sending mixed signals."

Bailey nodded, brown eyes serious for once. "Yeah."

"There's not a lot I can do about it, then." Evie regarded the garden again. "Ugh. I wish I could let it go. Be cool."

"But?"

"I've liked lots of people," she said, "but not quite like this. This is more."

"How so?"

Evie bit the inside of her lip. "Everything looks different. You know? The world seems clearer and brighter. Everything feels better and sweeter. And it's just because he exists and I know him and he likes me." She gestured to the window. "It's going to sound so cheesy, but that view out there? It's beautiful. It's the most beautiful thing in the world, because he's alive and out there somewhere."

Bailey scoffed. "Gross."

"I know. I *know*." She gestured uselessly. "I disgust myself. What's happening to me, Bay?" What was it about this trip? She felt all twisted and exposed and real. The view, the smells of the morning, the taste of tea on her tongue. Her thoughts coalesced, shiny and bright.

"I think this place is good for me," she said slowly. "All the noise and the new people and the course . . . Coming here was the right decision. Being here later will also be right. So even though he's being weird, and I don't understand why, it doesn't matter. I can't be unhappy about any of this. Whatever happens with him," she grinned at Bailey, "I will be here in the autumn, and it will be so great I won't understand why I didn't come here sooner. I can't wait."

Bailey smiled at her. "That's a good attitude to have."

"Can't wait for what?" Sarah came into the kitchen and threw a sleepy arm around Bailey.

"Life," Evie said.

"Always." Sarah nuzzled Bailey. Evie felt like a third wheel for a moment, a slightly envious third wheel, but forced herself to let the feeling go. Their affection for each other sometimes blurred the lines between platonic and romantic, but they were definitely platonic. Evie wasn't a third wheel—she was a friend. She sipped her tea, happy to be there with them in their home for a moment like this.

Bolstered by her morning epiphany, Evie left the house ready for anything. She would get through today's session and tomorrow's and the rest of the week. Awkward or not, she'd be able to handle Tyler. Things would work out the way they should.

And people thought Brits exaggerated the benefits of a decent cup of tea.

Sarah and Bailey were both working, so Evie shopped for souvenirs by herself before the dance session. She scouted the tourist shops near the school, picking up multipack maple syrup bottles and maple leaf cookies and a *Canada, eh?* T-shirt in one store before checking her phone for the latest from the British day. Two messages waited for her: an email from Mum and a WhatsApp from Tyler.

Tyler.

She quickly tapped open the message: *If you're free, do you want to meet for lunch before practice?*

She checked the time. Two hours before the session was due to start. Heart beating like crazy, she thumbed out, *Yes. Meet in an hour's time?* and sent it.

Then she checked her mother's email.

Darling, I hope you're still having a lovely time. I saw your Niagara pictures, and I have to say there was a VERY nice-looking young man in them. I hope you have something you want to tell me. I'm not sure I understand the toy, but otherwise the pictures are stunning and you look beautiful. Particularly that one on the boat in the mist—very atmospheric. It's all grey and gloom over here; the full British summer is in session! Your father says that the latest rage in London are sandwich trucks. Do they have those over in Toronto? Shep lay down in the garden yesterday afternoon as I was doing my weeding and wouldn't move for anything for hours. Poor doggy, he's getting old. I won this week's WI baking competition with my kumquat and orange tart. I'll send you a picture in a sec. Everyone said it was absolutely delicious, but I'll have to take their word for it as I don't eat sweet things anymore. Richard hasn't called since Sunday, and I'm quite annoyed. Tell him to call me, would you? I'm your mother, it's not too much to expect a call every now and then, is it? Can't wait to see you home again dear. Only a week to go!

[tart.jpg]

Blimey. The Women's Institute and rain. Evie was definitely missing out. Honestly, couldn't this stuff keep until she was home?

Her phone buzzed, and she changed back to the Tyler thread.

Tyler: *Cool. Same place as last time?*

Evie: *Sure. See you there.*

Evie put her phone away and kept shopping. Her mind stuttered over that lunch invite as she browsed. *Don't think too much about it. Just roll with it. Friends, Evie. Friends* only.

She found herself with armfuls of things like Nanaimo bar mixes and ice wine–flavoured tea, and swiftly put most of it back. *Focus.* She wanted maple syrup and cookies and a shirt and maybe some moose-related magnets and postcards and ridiculously flavoured tea. That's what she wanted. Yet for some reason she was standing in front of a row of shot glasses shaped like boobs with hockey sticks between them. *The fuck? Focus!*

The hour couldn't go quickly enough. She made her way to the café half an hour early, purchases in an embarrassingly touristy plastic bag, and to her surprise, found Tyler waiting for her outside. He looked tired, as though he hadn't slept much. When he noticed her, a small smile wormed its way out.

"Hey," he said.

"Hi."

Silence widened the foot between them. Evie gripped the handle of the plastic bag a little more tightly. She was British. She was used to handling awkwardness by brushing over it. But this was Canada, not home, and as it turned out, she liked this *new experiences* credo she'd been following here.

Plus, no matter what happened here today, she would be okay with it.

"Food?" he asked.

"Yes. In a minute." She took a deep breath. "I'm sorry about yesterday."

He looked away immediately, his face blushing darkly. "You don't have anything to be sorry about."

"I feel I do. I put you on the spot." She gestured inadequately. "I could at least have waited until Katie and Brock were gone."

"I totally blame Brock for this," Tyler said. He looked back at her, his expression warm. "Please, don't be sorry. You Brits and your apologizing for everything. I thought Canadians were bad."

Evie gave a wry smile. "We have a lot to apologize for."

He straightened and reached as though to take her hand, then stopped and rubbed the back of his neck. "If you're going to apologize, then I should too. Because I wasn't exactly honest yesterday, and I'm sorry about that."

Evie's phone buzzed. She ignored it because Tyler was smiling at her and that was too important to miss. This was promising, right?

He indicated the café with his head. "Let me tell you about it over sandwiches?"

Tyler sat down and watched as Evie placed her shopping bag and backpack on the chair next to her. A massive Canadian flag and the words *BEARLY BELIEVABLE SOUVENIRS EH* were emblazoned across the bag. His stomach sank—souvenir shopping already?

Around them, people sat and chatted easily. The air was warm, and light streamed through the windows, catching on Evie's face and hair, and on her fingers as they danced lightly over the menu. Somehow all of these details, from the smell of toasted bread to the curve of her cheek, were infinitely precious because next week she would no longer be there to catch the light.

After ordering, an awkward silence filled the air between them. Tyler had been practising what he wanted to say since yesterday, but the words were threatening to fly out of his head now.

Time to bite the bullet. "Uh, about yesterday . . ." His mouth dried up again. She fixed him with a calm blue stare, waiting. "I'm sorry. I just . . . The last time I had a good connection with a dance partner, it turned out to be a . . ." *Monstrous, toxic shell of a relationship and breakup.* He couldn't say that. He found himself unable to say anything at all. How did anyone even begin to tell someone about the shitty ex? How did people do this?

"It was what?" she asked.

Their drinks arrived, and he gratefully took a gulp of water. "Messy. Like, really messy."

"Oh." Her eyebrows raised, and she rested her chin on one hand, clearly waiting for him to go on.

Okay, however other people did it, *he* wasn't doing this well. It had seemed so straightforward in his head. "She was a dancer too," he explained, "and she and I clicked a lot on a physical level." He found himself fidgeting with his napkin and made himself put it down. "Not so much emotionally. I didn't realize that at the time. I thought . . . I got mixed up. The physical side of stuff can mask a lot of problems, you know?"

Lucette had had the strong, lithe dancer's body, but in a petite frame. He could remember the muscles of her stomach, the sleekness of her thighs, the way her nose turned up, the way her brows drew together when she was angry, and how almost angelic she'd looked. Yes, he'd loved to look, but he'd loved touching her more. He'd loved running a thumb over the delicate features: the cheekbones, the small jaw, the small, perfect mouth. The memory made his stomach knot.

Her mouth twisted wryly. "I can't say I relate, actually, but I understand what you mean."

"Oh, right." *Keep it moving, Ty.* "Basically, I thought I'd found someone who really got me and who liked me for me. We were both dancers, same sort of background and repertoire, great chemistry, similar career goals, all that stuff. She said she didn't mind me being trans." *Didn't* mind *it.* Jesus. How had he not seen that red flag? A lump filled his throat, and he forced it down. "I was really happy, because that's rare. A lot of straight girls, they think it's a fun experience for a one-off, or they don't take the trans man thing well when they find out. She did. So I was all in."

Evie nodded.

"Only, she wasn't that okay with it. Or she was, but it had to be on her terms." Tyler sipped his water again, trying to ease that lump. It wasn't really working. "So, um. Lots of rules. Not all at once, but one after another. And judgment. And tests. Which I kept failing."

Things like dressing and walking in a "manly" way. Taking the "right" kind of dance work. Demanding he not talk to Carmen or Eddie or any of the other female dancers he was friends with. No jobs involving partnerships with other girls. No jobs that involved partnerships with guys either, because that would have been "gay" and no way in hell was someone she dated allowed to be anything other than devoted entirely to her. Saying he'd said something horrible about her to someone, when he hadn't. Checking his phone. Checking his browser history. Checking he was where he'd say he would be. Watching him work in the café, simmering when a female customer had the temerity to talk to him. Yelling at him about how he'd handled all of the above, no matter how he handled it.

He felt positively nauseous now. The familiar feelings of suffocation and being trapped returned.

Evie was frowning. *Don't get carried away. It's in the past.* Tyler took a look around to ground himself in the here and now, to help him push back the awful memories. "She was . . . She wasn't good for me. In the end." *Say it.* "Turns out you don't need to hit people to abuse them."

Evie looked shocked. "Ty—"

"It happens. Happened." Tyler took a deep breath. When Evie didn't interrupt him, he took another. "I liked her and, as it turned out, she liked having a punching bag for her insecurities. All the stuff we talked about, all the things she shared with me, I thought it was trust and love, you know? It looked a lot like trust until one day it wasn't." He exhaled sharply. "I broke up with her last year. She's in Vancouver now. I've moved on. Put my head into dancing, reconnected with people, all that stuff. So it's fine now."

He fidgeted with the cutlery, working to gather more of the right words. Evie stayed quiet across the table

"Only, I haven't danced with a partner or dated since," he confessed. "It's been . . . difficult to do this competition. More difficult than I thought it would be. Nothing to do with you," he added swiftly. "You're awesome. It's just . . . doing this again, this partnering thing again, it's . . ." He struggled to articulate it.

"Dredging up old feelings?"

"Yeah. It is." His throat closed up again.

"Is it scary?" she asked.

"Yeah."

Her hand came across the table, palm up. He blinked in surprise, then took it, looking at her. Evie's mouth had gone tight. "You can tell me if I say or do something that's triggering. The last thing I want is—"

"Evie, no." Her hand was so steady. His was clammy and sweaty. Oh God, that had to feel gross. He needed to finish this, if only so he could relieve her of having to hold his hand. "No, you've been fine. Really. It's not you. You're *nothing* like her." He squeezed her hand to emphasize that, gazed right into her eyes. "It's me and my fucked-up expectations. It's me being, I dunno, defensive. Lucette and I got together because we were partnered for a piece and we clicked. This situation now, it's similar. But not just because we're partnered and learning a new piece and working well together. Because our connection? It is amazing, Evie. It *is*." His gaze flicked down to their hands, then back up to her eyes. Could he do this? He could do this. "I lied. It's not just friendship for me."

Her eyes widened. Then her face set, and she frowned at the table. He could see the wheels turning, processing what he'd said.

And daaamn, if he thought he was nervous before telling her all that, it was nothing compared to waiting for her reaction now. Was she going to flip out? Was she pitying him? Was she trying to find an excuse to leave? Not that he'd blame her. *It's been ever so nice, Mr. Davis, but this is rather a lot of baggage that I'm too British to have time for, and I have a cup of tea to make in a place where you are not physically present.* Oh God. He'd gauged this wrongly. He'd totally—

"Tyler." She reached out for his other hand, and he gave it to her. "I like you." The noises of the café faded, and he was tongue-tied again. Evie was gazing straight at him. No fucking around. "I really like you, and I like what we're doing here. I can be friends. I'd *like* to be friends. If there's more on the table, then yes, that would be wonderful." Her face softened. "Really, that would be . . . amazing.

But you need to understand that if this is too much right now, that's okay, and I mean that. I'm happy to simply be here, with you, in whatever capacity you'll have me." She squeezed his hands. "Take some time to think about it and let me know, all right?"

Tyler wasn't sure he'd heard that right. It had to be some kind of mistake. Oh shit, something was gathering in his eyes and threatening to spill over.

He blinked furiously. She was still there, smiling sadly at him. Still holding his hand.

Still kind.

And somehow still into him.

That *killed* him.

"Uh," he managed.

"Thank you for telling me," she said. "I had no idea you were struggling with something like that."

"It's not . . . I'm dealing with it," he said. "Trying to, anyway." He felt lighter. He'd been honest and somehow it was okay. And she was still sitting there. Granted, she had a chicken bagel coming, but he appreciated it nonetheless.

Not only was she still there, but she *wanted* to be. "How the hell are you single?" he wondered aloud.

She gave him a wry look. "I might say the same about you. But if you really want an answer: it's usually because people hear the word 'asexual,' think I don't like shagging, and fly for the hills."

"Shagging?"

"Sex."

The hell? "Do people honestly say that over there?"

"What, 'shag'?"

"Yeah."

"Yes. We honestly say that."

He shook his head. "British slang is weird."

She stirred her iced tea delicately with her straw. "Is that usual for you, to focus on the word rather than the act? Because for most people it's the other way around."

"Words are important." His brain caught up with what she'd said. "So, wait—you *do* like sex?"

She raised her eyebrows. "Under the right circumstances, with the right person, I like what I like."

Oh, really. Everything south of his belt was suddenly *very* interested. He grinned. "Am I allowed to know what you like?"

"I need something harder than iced tea to share that information." Her mouth twitched as she repressed a smile. Tyler wanted the table gone, wanted to lean right over and kiss that wicked mouth, to push his fingers into her hair and down her back, to pull her tight against him—

The waiter arrived and placed their food. Amid the bustle of that, their hands separated, and the moment was over.

Evie bit into her bagel with a look of bliss. Tyler stared, caught by her expression as his mind lingered on the image of kissing her, then realized he was staring and turned to his own food.

"Take some time to think about it." Ha. As if. He was a goner. He wanted all of her—her expressions, her eyes, her feelings, her thighs, all of it. If she wasn't leaving next week, he'd be crapping himself at just how much he wanted her. He'd been sunk the moment she first spoke to him.

That fucking audition.

"What are you smiling at?" she asked him through a mouthful of bagel. "Do I have mayo on my nose or something?"

He shook his head. "Nope. Just remembering the first thing you ever said to me."

She frowned, then almost choked. He grinned as she laugh-coughed for a moment. "Oh God," she gasped. "I was so *angry*. You'd shown up out of nowhere, and I was wondering who the hell you thought you were." She scowled. "'She'll do it,'" she mimicked with a scowl.

He laughed. "It was a pretty dick move."

"Yeah, it was." Her eyes glittered at him. "I had you down as this gorgeous, entitled jerk."

She thinks I'm gorgeous. "And I thought you were magnificent."

She blushed and found something very interesting outside the window to look at. Tyler glanced outside too, then at his phone. They had twenty minutes until the start of practice. Whatever this was—a date? A beginning? Therapy?—he didn't want it to end. He wanted to sit here for the rest of the afternoon and talk with her, not return to that stuffy practice room and pretend he cared about a stupid routine.

"Did Brock speak with you last night?" she asked him.

"Yeah."

"He caught me on the way out." She smiled softly. "He's not a bad guy. I think he could be very good for Gigi."

He wanted to believe it. "If he's legit changed, *maybe*. Gigi's done with closet cases."

"I can't wait to see what happens tomorrow night." She rested her chin in her hand, eyes twinkling. "I expect nothing less than sheer entertainment, especially from Gigi."

He reached across the table and took her hand again. Eyebrows raised, she sat up a little. "Is this okay?" he asked.

"Of course. Just . . ." She shook her head at whatever she'd been about to say. "Yes."

Her hand tightened around his, warm and secure. He ran his thumb along her knuckles. "I wish," he said quietly, "we didn't have to go back to the school and interrupt this."

"We need to practise the routine."

Fuck the routine.

Wait, I'm being paid for the routine.

"I know," he said.

Maybe the routine wasn't the problem. After all, he'd be dancing with her—that was an awesome thing. Nah, maybe the problem was the freaking *camera* that would be waiting at the school.

"But we don't have to do it at the school."

He looked up.

She inclined her head at the window. "It's a lovely day. Is there a park nearby? We could practise there."

Outside? In front of people? "You sure? We'll be watched."

She leaned in. "I'm into it if you are."

"Hey—"

"And it won't be the strangest thing I've done in a park."

He sputtered.

"Well?"

"I don't know . . ."

"We'll avoid Katie and Brock."

He sat up. "Sold."

Twenty-five minutes later, they were in the nearest park and ignoring their phones. Tyler only had the Jet track on his MP3 player, so he listened to it a couple of times to get the beat down in his head, before handing it to Evie. They ran through the routine like that: her listening and him keeping the pace up internally. Not ideal, but fun—Evie would lose the rhythm or mistime a step, causing them to bump together in hilarious ways. Occasionally, he'd misstep and find himself waiting for her or rushing her.

The electric energy from the previous day surged through them, pushing them to get things right so they could move together in sync. Tyler saw Evie's concentration hold through iteration after iteration of the same steps. He pulled her close and pushed her away; she pulled him close and would shove him back with a wink. They attracted a few curious glances, but no one lingered.

Eventually, sweaty and giggling from another collision, Evie backed off and requested a break. He dug into his bag for his Gatorade. When he heard her clear her throat behind him, he turned to see her standing with Godzilla and her camera.

"When I packed him," she said quietly, "I wasn't sure how today was going to go. But seeing how we're here and we're okay, I think a picture with you two is well overdue."

He grinned. Damn right, Vaughn wasn't the only guy who'd feature in her holiday pics. "Would it be better in the dance studio?"

She waved her hand dismissively. "Yes, and I'll get one there too. But playing truant in the park is fun, and I want to remember it." She thrust Godzilla into his hands and held up the camera. "Smile."

He immediately pulled a scowl and made a faux gang sign. "How's this?"

Her mouth curved under the camera. "Well wicked, bruv, innit." She took the picture. "How about a *smile*, smart-arse?"

Their phones started ringing, and Tyler raised his eyebrows at her. "I won't answer it if you won—" She took another picture. "Hey!" He reached for the camera, and she snapped another, cackling. She darted away.

Oh. It was *on*.

He dropped Godzilla to chase her. Evie ran in a small circuit, jumping around their bags and doubling back around the trees, continually twisting out of reach. Eventually, he caught up and managed to tackle her to the ground, making her squirm deliciously under him.

"Camera," he panted.

"Never!"

They wrestled for the camera until Tyler wrenched it from her. He rolled to his knees and held it above him. "Come on, Evie," he taunted. "It's right here."

She arched an eyebrow and stood. He quickly stood too, keeping the camera out of reach. Evie muttered murderously and tried to jump for it, stretching over him on tiptoes, her face inches from his.

"Not fair," she said as he bent backwards away from her, lending him greater distance from her grasping fingers.

"I know." His free arm wound around her waist and her eyes widened. He kissed her, a sweet brush of lips, as he pulled her close. When he opened his eyes, she gazed back at him in total delight. "Was that okay?" he asked.

"Fuck yes." Her hands took his face and brought him forward into a deeper kiss, one that had him winding both his arms tightly around her so he could feel her warm body against his. Her mouth sent shocks to the soles of his feet. *Yes.* They held each other, their phones chirruping and the camera forgotten in his fist and their clothes covered in grass. She tasted of salt and the lightest dregs of lingering sweetness from the iced tea. Her fingers threaded through his hair, and he moaned, one arm snaking up her back to her neck.

The kiss ended, and he leaned back slightly to drink her in. Her lips were slightly reddened and her hair was falling out of its customary braid. He swept a few strands from her face, not trusting himself to speak.

"That," she breathed, "was stupendous."

Hearing that in an English accent somehow made it truer. He kissed her lightly. "Good."

Her thumb ran along his jaw and her eyelids lowered. "I take it this means you're done thinking about it."

"Nothing to think about."

She rolled her eyes and gently shoved at his shoulder. Tyler knew he was grinning like an idiot, but he couldn't seem to stop.

"I've wanted to do that for a while," she admitted, her palms warm on his shoulders. His brain stuttered over that for a few seconds. "But there is one problem."

Ice shot through his stomach. She looked really serious. What did that—

"How are we going to finish this routine *now*?" Her fingers trailed the side of his jaw, coming to a rest on his lips. "I want to spend this time making out with you."

He kissed her fingers. "I hear that, believe me. But you're right." His arms loosened around her. "We have work to do."

"So much work. I keep messing up my solo." She pressed her mouth to his, then kissed a line from his mouth to the spot below his ear. A lingering press of lips that had him shivering and tightening his grip around her once more.

Their phones rang again, and they reluctantly let go to retrieve them.

"I've got seven messages and a few missed calls from Brock on WhatsApp," Evie reported.

"Ten missed calls and three texts from Katie, five calls and two texts from Brock, and one text from Gigi." Unbelievable. Tyler stopped scanning the call log and checked the texts.

Katie: *Where are you?*

Katie: *Srsly. Where are you two?*

Katie: *Please tell us where you are. You signed a release form and agreed to us filming you. This is highly unprofessional and I expected better from you.*

Brock: *Dude, you guys okay? Are you together? Text back that you're okay.*

Brock: *Omg Katie is so pissed*

Gigi: *Just tell me you and Evie are alive and somewhere close by I want CERTAIN PEOPLE to leave me the fuck alone*

Evie must have received similar messages. "They seem a tad put out." She didn't sound particularly upset about it.

Tyler shared the sentiment. "I'll call Gigi."

Gigi picked up on the second ring. "Holy motherfucking shit."

Tyler could hear piano music in the background. "Are you in class?"

"Yeah, asshole, I'm in class. I have Brock eyeing me through the fucking door every ten minutes because he wants to know where you and Evie are." Gigi didn't sound happy. "Like, fuck if I know. Or care."

"Good. Tell him we called, and we're just . . ." he glanced at Evie, who blinked back innocently ". . . practising elsewhere today."

"Jesus. Katie's going to shove her gum in my eyeball."

"Your problem. And talk to Brock already."

"Fuck you, man. I gotta go; I need to nail these fouettés."

"Bye."

He hung up. They gazed at their phones in collective awe and disbelief for a few moments, then Evie tossed hers into her bag. She sashayed up to him, blue gaze fixing him in place. "Let's make the drama worth it."

While he had plenty of ideas about just how to do that—mostly involving her against a tree or pinned beneath him—he settled for the one that wouldn't get them kicked out of the park for indecency. Tyler put his phone away and took her hands in his, counted out the beat, and they fell back into the dance. To his relief, Tyler found he could separate the two. He could still be the teacher with her, correcting and analysing both of them as they practised, without any worry about criticism affecting the chemistry. Besides, the moves were way too quick to consider fooling around beyond the odd poke and wink.

Despite what she'd said about making out, Evie didn't seem focused on flirting with him either. She was concentrating too much on getting the moves right and up to speed. Yup, business remained business, so Tyler let himself relax.

Even so, their connection still resonated with each touch and step. They snapped together perfectly, their energy flowing and sizzling in the spaces between them. And their character acting was laced with smiles and the odd flicker of fingers against wrist and arm. It was like the edges between him and his character blurred, and he really didn't mind.

When evening stretched over the park, and people hurried through rather than strolling, they slowed down. The partnered section turned into a slow, intimate dance. Evie rested her cheek on his shoulder as they turned in gentle circles. His arm wrapped her waist loosely and he held her hand against his chest. Against one of his scars, not that she could see it through his shirt. He felt her warm breath against his neck.

"I'm enjoying this," she said.

"Me too."

"Can I, um, break the mood a little?" she asked softly.

His stomach somersaulted.

"What *is* this?"

"You're leaving soon," he said.

She sighed against his neck. "Yes, that's true."

"So we could call this—" he played with the ends of her braid "—short but sweet?"

"Mmm. Fast and loose?"

"Fun?"

"Star-crossed, but without the cancer or gang warfare."

He huffed in amusement. "Intense."

"It's definitely that." She raised her head to look at him. "Remember, whatever capacity you'll have me."

He swallowed. "Casual?"

"Casual?" Her brow furrowed, then cleared. "Yes. That works."

He relaxed. He hadn't realized he'd been tense.

"As long as that doesn't extend to nights."

He met her gaze. She was serious. "Nights?" *Sex, Tyler. She means sex.* The thought of sleeping with her caused a pleasant, achy rush.

"I like what I like," and now *she* was the one getting all tense, "but that doesn't include casual sex."

She didn't like casual hookups. So she wasn't interested in sleeping with him. Wait, was that what she was saying? That didn't feel like what she was saying. Shit, he was taking too long to figure this out—she looked nervous.

"I mean," she added when he didn't reply, "it's not about you, because you're clearly gorgeous and attractive, and I definitely *see* that. It's just that for me, the way I am, sex isn't that big a deal unless the *person* I have it with is a big deal." She closed her eyes, clearly mortified. "That's not— What I mean is . . . What I'm trying and failing to say is that *for me*, it doesn't make sense to sleep with someone unless there are mutual serious feelings there.

Because I . . . Well, sex isn't a priority for me. At all. So I don't sleep with anyone unless they're really important to me, and I'm important to them, and they need sex to happen to show that. And we just said this is casual."

Ah. Tyler was back on board.

"If we took this any further," she started fidgeting, "it wouldn't be . . . good. Or fun. For me. That's not to say I think casual sex is bad," she went on in a rush, backing away from him slightly. "Not at all, really; it just doesn't work *for me*, and God will you please say—"

"That's cool." He gathered her back in close to him.

"R-really?"

"Yes."

She sagged against him as Tyler's mind raced. The idea of not taking this further was disappointing, yeah, but surprisingly freeing too. The line was there, clear and defined.

And if he was honest with himself, sex wasn't exactly a top priority for him either. It hadn't been for a while. Getting his head together, going back into the dating scene, feeling okay to flirt and trust again; that was more important. Maybe keeping things simple with Evie was the ideal way to ease himself back into dating. She was leaving in six days. Why complicate things? Especially when he had no idea how she'd handle him sexually anyway. Her leaving soon like this, it wasn't even a concern. Lucette had never exactly . . .

Get Lucette out of your head now.

"Thank you," she said. "Sometimes people aren't okay with that."

And that just made him angry. Because clearly someone in her past hadn't been all right with her wanting to essentially take things slowly. He knew exactly what it felt like when someone refused to respect a boundary. Honestly, "thank you"? For something like that? *Please.*

He pulled her hand to his mouth and kissed her fingers. "I'm happy to make out with you, touch you, dance with you, flirt with you, eat lunch with you, and talk with you. Spending time with you is one of the nicest things I've done in a long time."

"I'm sure you say that to all the girls." Her voice caught a little.

He grinned. "Only the ones who buy me lunch."

"We're okay with this for the next few days?" Her free hand ran lightly along his shoulder blade. "Really?"

If she kept touching him like that, they'd be good for a lot longer than the next few days. "Yeah. We are. Really." He turned his head so he could kiss her again, revelling in how easy and sweet it was.

Phones rang, signalling other responsibilities and people who needed them, and they pulled apart reluctantly.

Evie sighed. "I'm meeting Sarah for drinks."

"I have a class to teach."

Her fingers ran along his hairline. "You work so hard."

He shrugged. "Gotta hustle."

Her phone chimed again. She grunted in frustration, kissed him fiercely, then let him go to pick up her bag. He collected his gear, and they walked to the park entrance holding hands. He'd shoved his phone into his pocket but didn't check it, not just yet. Reality could wait a little longer.

The route back to the subway was slightly different coming from the park, so Tyler led her there and said good-bye. She hugged him tightly, kissed him hard, then ran into the subway station. Tyler spun around, ecstatic—because god*damn*, it had been *so* long since he'd felt this happy—and found himself facing a surprised Jean and Derek.

"Oh." He cut the spin short. "Hey."

"Well *hey* there, Tyler." A massive grin split Derek's face. "How're you doing?"

Never you *mind, Derek.* "Fine."

"How's Evie?"

Tyler could feel himself blushing. "Also fine."

Derek nodded. "Sure looked like she was fine." Jean smacked him lightly in the arm. "I mean, uh, how's practice?"

"We're getting there." Man, this was embarrassing. What were they even doing here? Seeing them outside the school at this time of the evening was unusual; at least one of them tended to hang around until closing time. "Uh, going home early?"

"Date night," Jean said.

"Plus, we're getting away from Katie," Derek said in a stage whisper. "Something seriously jerked her crank today."

You don't say. "She's still there?"

"Carmen and Claude are practising late tonight."

"If you have class," Jean said, "I'd go now while they're busy."

"Got it." Loud and clear. He began moving around them. "Have a good night."

"You too." Derek waggled his eyebrows, earning him another light smack.

On the way to the school, Tyler received a call from Gigi. Hoping he wasn't still mad, Tyler sent up a prayer to the friendship gods and swiped to accept.

"Hey, Gi."

"You asshole."

Apparently the gods weren't listening. Tyler shifted his bag to his other shoulder. "I have a class in like five minutes."

"No. You have a class when I'm done talking to you." He could just picture Gigi doing his angry queen finger waggle. "I am *trying* to keep the hell away from Brock, and you're not helping. It's like you don't even care that he's trying to talk to me. Running off with your English crumpet for an afternoon—what were you thinking?"

Tyler blinked. "Don't call her that."

"Show up tomorrow and distract the bastard, okay? I can't keep shoving Mark between me and the camera. I think he's starting to suspect something. He's not as stupid as he looks, you know? Plus, his girlfriend showed up at practice today and they were *cooing* at each other. I can't deal with that."

"With other people being happy?"

The pause implied either a death glare or hair-tugging. "No. Other people being vomit-inducingly happy. I need to shower off the hetero love vibes. Practise at school tomorrow or I swear to God, I'm going to steal your Gatorade for a week. He kept *talking* to me, and I didn't sign up for my stupid high school mistake to *talk* to me about things I can't brush off."

"Jesus, Gigi, calm down." He was at the door now. "How about *not* brushing him off at all and fucking talking to him? All of this is unnecessary."

"You know what's unnecessary? Increasing *my* stress by playing hooky!" A loud sigh in his ear made Tyler jerk the phone away. "Not that I don't get it. Don't worry, man, she hasn't mentioned Vaughn once. Like, she uploaded some pictures of him on Facebook, and they're Facebook friends now, but I don't think it's more than that because *his* relationship status is set to 'it's complicated' with someone called 'Baroque,' which could mean anything frankly but sort of seems gay to me. You're in the clear, so don't mess it up."

Tyler's head reeled. "You're *Facebook* friends with her?"

"*Focus.* You gotta remember the bigger picture. I got your back. Because us, Ty? We're friends. Friends *help* each other out."

"Not by threatening Gatorade supplies, they don't. And this has nothing to do with Vaughn."

"Sure. Be a friend and practise in school. Okay, good talk. Go teach." He hung up. Tyler stared at his phone in confusion. Since when was Gigi so concerned about him and Evie? And since *when* had Gigi and Evie been Facebook friends? What the hell was going on? Why hadn't she added *him* on Facebook?

He strode into the school and ran through the corridors to his class. Just before he arrived, he closed his eyes and reminded himself of Evie's face as she said, point-blank and with complete openness, *"I like you."* Then the feel of her hands on him, the taste of her mouth, the flash of her eyes as she teased him.

Facebook be damned, he had the real thing.

And Evie definitely wasn't into Vaughn.

He walked into the practice room with a grin on his face.

CHAPTER EIGHT

Evie eyed the spread of food before her. Oh sweet delicious bounties from heaven, if this was a Canadian brunch, then yes, her country was doing it wrong. She took a picture of Godzilla next to the pancakes, then pulled him off the table. Sarah waited until he was safely stowed before digging into her bacon. As well as the pancakes, there was a jug of maple syrup, eggs, bacon, fried potatoes, and French toast. Coffee and orange juice perched on her right. Evie was glad her dance session was in the afternoon, because the rest of the morning would have to be spent lying down digesting all this. She didn't know how Sarah was going to function at her job this afternoon.

"Amazing," she moaned, taking a mouthful of the French toast.

"I know, right?" Sarah snapped a picture on her phone and tapped at her screen. "Not a lumberjack breakfast, but close enough, eh."

Evie's phone buzzed. She checked it to see Gigi had messaged her on Facebook. "You sent that picture to Gigi? He's mad we left him out."

Sarah's eyes widened. "Wow, that was quick."

"He added me on Facebook."

"What?" Sarah put her fork down. "*I* haven't added you on Facebook."

They stared at each other in disbelief, then picked up their phones, added each other, and fell to eating their breakfast. Maple syrup and bacon, she discovered, was a revelation. As were pancakes, maple syrup, and bacon. Pretty much anything with maple syrup and bacon. This was last-meal kind of stuff. "Good God. How are Canadians not fat?"

"Oh, we're getting there."

Evie wouldn't be able to appreciate a fry-up in quite the same way ever again. "We'll have to dance this off tonight when we're out with Gigi."

Sarah's face lit up. Evie had told her about the plan to have Brock meet them and confront Gigi, and Sarah, naturally, was completely on board. Evie wasn't sure how everything was going to play out, but she hoped this was the right step to take.

"It's just a pity that Tyler is working," Evie said.

Sarah waved her hand dismissively. "Don't worry about that. We have you covered."

Evie frowned, but before she could ask what that meant, her phone buzzed again multiple times. She picked it up to see several likes of her breakfast on Facebook, a friend request from Tyler, and another email from her mother.

Evelyn, darling, I know you're having a wonderful time, but remember what I told you about holiday eating and how it doesn't digest differently just because you're somewhere new. Doug is at home for a week and has only checked work emails four times. He sends his love. The vicar popped by today to try my kumquat tart and said he could see why it won the WI competition. Wimbledon is starting soon and I, for one, cannot wait for our annual strawberry cream tea while watching the ladies' final. The vet is still sitting on those test results for Shep, and I'm wondering what our pet insurance really pays for. Shep seems to like being sick on my hydrangeas, and they're starting to wilt. I'm really quite put out. Richard hasn't contacted me—did you speak to him? Also I saw Mel in the village the other day. You remember your primary school friend, Mel? She was with her little daughters, and I have to say she was looking wonderfully well despite the second divorce and all that drama with HMRC. Why did you two fall out again? Yes, please bring back maple syrup for us. Missing you!

Evie groaned and dropped her head back against her chair.

"Gigi?" Sarah asked sympathetically.

"Worse. My mother. And our dog is sick."

Sarah winced. "That sucks. You know, she kinda emails you a lot."

"We're close." Evie frowned at her phone. "Sort of. Is that unusual?"

"You're on vacation, so yeah, I think so. But don't get me started on moms without boundaries."

Evie smiled and let it go. Sarah didn't speak to her family for various good reasons, and Evie wasn't about to compare her mother's minor personality faults with Sarah's mother's not-so-minor drinking problem.

Evie's phone buzzed yet again, and she hesitated before checking it. Couldn't she have a meal without being interrupted? But it was a message from Tyler: *Bringing Godzilla today?*

She responded, *Indeed.*

When she looked back up, Sarah had her chin propped on one hand, a knowing smile curving her mouth. Evie raised an eyebrow. "Gaybeard?"

"Who was that?" Sarah asked. "Because it sure as hell wasn't your mother."

Uh-huh. "It's Tyler."

"*Tyler*, eh." Sarah sat back, coffee in hand and eyes gleaming. "You don't say."

Evie hadn't mentioned their trip to the park or the development in their relationship, such as it was. Things were still so new. She had to remind herself of just how new, actually, because when they'd kissed yesterday, it had been like falling into the arms of someone she'd known forever but had forgotten about until that very moment. Maybe it was the close proximity of dancing for the four days beforehand, but she felt like nothing about him was new, yet everything was. It was a strange feeling.

She'd spent a great deal of the previous evening mulling over Tyler's confession about his ex. Part of her wanted to track Lucette down and slap the shit out of her, part of her wanted to wrap Tyler up and never let anyone hurt him again, and another part of her was shaken. He'd seemed so haunted. He'd also seemed a little uncertain, like he couldn't trust this situation to work out well. He was fighting demons, she understood that, and he'd had to fight in order to tell her he liked her. The way his hand had shaken slightly, the way he'd tripped over his words—it was a big contrast to the smooth way he'd kissed her in the park. Like speaking was hard, but physical stuff was easy.

Well, he *was* a dancer. Physicality was who he was. Yes, that part probably came easier. But he'd almost seemed relieved at sex being taken off the table.

That wasn't usual, in her experience, so she wasn't sure how to read him. In Evie's past relationships, she'd been the one to confess something unusual, to put on the brakes, to negotiate space and time. People seemed to expect relationship events to happen in a certain order, and delaying sex was apparently weird (and for some, a total deal breaker), even though she'd argue it really wasn't. Tyler didn't behave like those people. Which, hey, wonderful, but it was odd to feel like *she* was the one slowing down to *his* speed this time.

It was a nice feeling.

And not one she could think about too much, because Sarah now looked suspiciously gleeful. "Whatever you're thinking, Sarah, it's wrong."

"I'm not thinking anything," Sarah said innocently.

"You're always thinking something."

"Just thinking you look happy." She sipped her coffee. "In fact, you're practically *glowing.*"

Evie groaned. "Give it a rest."

"No." Sarah put her coffee down, her face serious. "Evazilla, for real? Since you've been here, Tyler has been so different. You have no idea how much I've tried to get that guy out of his shell and back into the dating scene. Then you come here with your badass accent and fancy footwork, and suddenly he's cheered up and *chatty*. He's almost back to the guy I knew before his shit-stain of an ex."

Ah yes, the ex. Sarah and Bailey had mentioned the ex before, and now Evie understood why they'd been reluctant to go into detail about her. "He's spoken about her. She sounded less than . . . pleasant."

Sarah's mouth flattened. "I never liked her. She was so sweet it had to be fake, and *such* a drama queen, and nothing was ever good enough. I don't know why Ty liked her. She kept tabs on him, you know? Always calling or texting him, or asking why he hadn't called or texted her. The last six months of their relationship, I didn't see Ty once. *Once.* She wouldn't let him meet with anyone. I heard rumours that she cheated too."

Sarah's whole body was leaning forward, hands gesturing angrily. "And when he left her and I saw him again, I was shocked at the difference in him. Shocked. It was like his *soul* had been drained out of him." Sarah pushed her now-empty plate away a little rougher than was warranted. "He's better now, way better, but she twisted shit in his head, and if I ever see her in Toronto again, I will personally gut her like a fish."

Evie had never, ever seen Sarah like this. "Jesus Christ, Sarah."

Sarah exhaled sharply. "It was *bad*. So you two? I am *so* happy you two are doing this competition. You're good for him. Believe me, you are. I haven't seen him happy like this in a long time. And I know you like him, so stop telling me you don't."

Evie pushed her plate away too. "Fine," she admitted. "I do. But I'm leaving in a week. So even if something *did* happen and even if we make each other happy, there are no guarantees that it'll get serious. Don't get too invested in an idea of him and me."

Sarah rolled her eyes. "Oh gosh, three months of separation; such an insurmountable hardship. Come on, Evie. The expression on your face when you checked your phone wasn't *holiday fling*. No way."

"Seriously, don't make this bigger than it is. Plus, think of Tyler. He's got worse issues than me around relationships."

Sarah slapped the table. "See? You care. *That's* what I'm talking about."

Evie shrugged and eyed her coffee. She was so full, she wasn't sure she could drink another drop. "We shall see how things play out."

"Jesus. Stop being so *practical*."

Evie smiled. "I'm English. Practicality is the order of the day."

She was doubting that statement a few hours later when she arrived at the school twenty minutes ahead of schedule because she was so eager to see Tyler. Yup, *super* "practical." She found the practice room empty and dumped her things at the wall, deciding to take her time warming up. Putting her earbuds in, she turned on her Cure album and started moving.

Evie closed her eyes and reacted to the music, choosing to let memories of the previous day's park session drift through her head.

The blinding hope and disbelief when he'd kissed her. The sheer joy and sense of *rightness* when he'd wrapped his arms around her. His lips, his hands, the feel of his skin under hers, and his solid body beside her own. His lips especially: she loved kissing. She could have kissed him all night. She *wanted* to. Would be happy to kiss him, and more, in spite of her limit on sex.

Which, she noted wryly, was why she'd set that limit in the first place. They liked each other, which was beyond wonderful, but as much as he did like her, she was fairly sure that "casual" remark meant her feelings were stronger than his. She didn't want to handle those feelings if this turned sexual, because she'd been through that before, with people who could separate sex and feelings, and it had *hurt*.

She opened her eyes and gazed at herself in the practice room mirror. She'd lost a little weight and gained some definition after all the dancing, even though it had only been five days. Her face and shoulders were turning brown from being in the sun, her body seemed more poised and controlled, her posture had improved. She *did* glow. Sunshine and good food and great company were having an effect.

Or perhaps she was just happy.

Either way, she looked different. Evie had long given up trying to see herself in a sexual way—she just couldn't see what was "sexy," whatever the hell that meant—but looking at her reflection now, she thought she seemed way healthier and just generally *better* than she had in quite a while. She lifted her leg and arms in a controlled sweep around her body, liking how she looked like a dancer.

She closed her eyes and spun around, taking the space she wanted. It felt wonderful to move like this. She wanted to move and sway to the music, so she did, letting it carry her around the room. If nothing else, this trip had brought her a new connection to herself. Tyler had shown her this, how to channel music and feelings through her arms and legs and face and hips. She made a promise to herself never to forget it.

The door opened and Tyler came in, a shy smile on his face. Evie smiled back, but kept moving. The Cure's "Friday I'm in Love" beat into her ears as Tyler approached her from behind. She watched as he slid into step with her, entwining one arm around her and kissing her neck.

"What are you listening to?" he murmured.

"The Cure." She pulled out an earbud, wiped it, and handed it to him.

He chuckled at the song as they listened and swayed to the music. "It's only Thursday."

"Hush, I'm watching the walls."

That earned her a full-on hug from behind and a nuzzle at her throat. He sighed appreciatively and shivers ran through her. She pulled out the other earbud and turned off her phone, then spun around to hug him fully.

"Hi."

His warm brown eyes met hers. "Hey, Godzilla."

How on earth had she ever found him mean looking?

She breathed him in, loving the mix of cologne and sweat. "I never told you why Sarah calls me Evazilla, did I?"

"Nah, you didn't."

"It's my Tumblr name." She took his hands and stepped back. He spun her around, and when she was facing him again, she added, "The full thing is *queen-evazilla*."

He grinned. "Suits you."

"Sarah calls me that because we called each other by our Tumblr names for ages." She tried not to laugh. "I still have trouble not calling her Gaybeard in company."

He fumbled a step. "*What?*"

"Her Tumblr name is *gaybeard-the-great*."

He laughed. "Oh, that's *rich*. I'm going to have a field day with that." He ran his hands up and down her back lightly. "Queen Evie, how are you doing today?"

Evie put on a posh accent. "Her Royal Evieness is majestic. How are you, loyal subject?" They swayed together, then by unspoken signal moved into a few steps from the routine.

"I'm great." His hands spread on her lower back and pulled her closer, his smile lighting up his face. "So, so great."

The door opened and they pulled apart. Katie marched in, Brock behind her. Evie and Tyler paused as Katie stormed up to them, her red hair awry around her face.

"You two are in *deep shit*," she spat. "I spent hours, *hours*, looking for you yesterday. Do you think this is a joke? That I'm doing this for *fun*? You signed documentation agreeing to being filmed and interviewed and to participate in this, and I am considering you two professionals and holding you to that, and I am *not okay* with you two ducking out of this."

Whoa. Talk about apples and trees. Evie glanced at Tyler, who looked just as taken aback as she felt.

"It might just be a stupid university project to you, but I need this grade," Katie continued, "and I'm not getting a lot of help making it work."

Brock looked up from tinkering with the camera, a hurt expression on his face. "Hey—"

"Therefore, after today's practice, we are going to go wherever you two disappeared to yesterday"—Katie's eyes drilled holes into both of them—"and we're going to shoot twenty stupid minutes of footage of you two dancing and answering my stupid questions, and we're going to pretend yesterday didn't happen. Because I am *not fucking around* here. Is that understood?"

"Oh yeah," Tyler said.

Evie nodded. "Yes. I'm sorry."

"Me too. *We're* sorry."

"Terribly sorry. Won't happen again." Not if she reacted like this. Good God.

Katie sighed and pulled gum out of her pocket. "Christ, the people in this competition," she muttered, unwrapping it and turning around. "I'm going to have an aneurysm at the age of twenty-one, Jesus *fuck* . . ."

Evie turned back to Tyler. "You heard her," she said quietly so Katie wouldn't hear. "No more messing around, *Tyler*."

Tyler rolled his eyes. "Yeah, yeah. I had no idea she was this invested." He nudged her. "Totally worth it. And as long as we do today's interviews with Godzilla, I'll be happy."

"And *you*," Katie was saying to Brock. "If I see you so much as give a thumbs-up to them, I will have the professor dock your grade so low you'll need another semester to graduate."

Brock's face was a study in puppy eyes. "I told you I was sorry about the other day."

Katie held up her hand. "I could *not* be any less interested right now. Now turn the camera on, and let's get this shit-show on the road." With that, she turned and slumped onto the floor, chewing fiercely.

Tyler's mood had lifted substantially the closer he got to the practice session. When he'd shown up and seen Evie already in the room, swaying in a world of her own, his chest had threatened to burst. He could hardly believe it was okay for him to go up to her and touch her the way he had. Standing here now, even with Katie shouting at them, he couldn't remember the last time he'd felt this happy.

Or this nervous. He was glad she'd taken his history so well, but what if he continued to freak out on her? What if he accidentally hurt her again? He didn't want to keep imagining Lucette in his head every time something happened.

Evie took her starting position, and he put his MP3 player into the stereo. He pressed Play, and practice began.

That electricity manifested itself again. So did the footwork. He watched in delight as Evie kept up with the music, and when he joined in, everything came together. She only fumbled a few times near the end of the song, and while the routine wasn't as slick as he'd envisaged, he knew they were almost ready for Saturday.

At the end of it, Evie went to him, her face alight. "Oh my God, Tyler, I *can* do this!"

He took her hands, smiling back at her. Her whole body seemed lifted with joy. Infectious. Sexy. Not that she seemed aware of how attractive she was, especially when she was all lit up like this. "Of course you can. I'm your teacher." She huffed and swiped at him. He dodged her easily, then spun her around and went back to the stereo to start the song over. "Now do it again."

By the time Tyler called a break, they were just about making it through the routine without messing up at all. They were tiring from the pace though, and Tyler knew the more tired they got, the more mistakes they'd make. He didn't want Evie to be discouraged, not when she was doing so well.

She flopped on the floor like she always did. "Bloody hell," she muttered. "I shouldn't have had that brunch this morning."

"Brunch?"

"With Sarah." Evie started listing off the food. "Pancakes, bacon, eggs, French toast, orange juice, so much coffee, maple syrup—"

"Stop," he begged. "You're making *me* feel sick."

"How are you able to dance like that after all that food?" Katie asked.

Evie glanced into the camera. "I'm British and I live in the north; fried food is a cuisine unto itself."

The interviews went on as usual, until things started getting silly. Evie pulled Godzilla out and answered questions holding him. Tyler took his turn, with Godzilla on his head. Evie found it hilarious to "accidentally" poke Tyler as he answered a question, and he made faces behind the camera as she answered hers. After a particularly furious glare from Katie, they both settled and returned to the routine.

Tyler was very aware that this was their second to last session together. Tomorrow would be the last practice before the actual performance on Saturday. They'd have to meet up before she left. Do *something* together that wasn't dancing or eating. He was free on Sunday; it was his first entirely free day in weeks. He'd ask her after the session and make sure they did something as memorable for her as Niagara Falls.

At the end of the session, Katie fixed them with her evil eye. "Take us to where you were yesterday."

Tyler didn't think it wise to refuse and neither did Evie. As if by unspoken consensus, they didn't return to the spot they'd actually used, choosing instead to set up at a spot closer to the entrance of the park. Evie changed out of her usual gear into a skirt she had ready for the evening, and he changed tops. Katie adjusted Evie's hair, her hands gentle despite the hard look on her face.

When she finished, she positioned them in front of Brock. "Now," she glared at them, "do whatever you did yesterday."

Evie immediately turned away from the camera to face him, and he watched her blush furiously. He gave her a wry smile, then held out his hand with a flourish. "Well? Shall we show them?" She rolled her eyes at him and spun away.

They fumbled the routine intentionally, pretending to be a day earlier in progress, and Katie seemed satisfied with that. Evie brought out Godzilla again and introduced him to the camera for the interview. Tyler picked her up in the middle of her answering a question and pulled her away, spinning her around and making her shriek.

Katie and Brock followed them to where he deposited a laughing Evie. She immediately had Godzilla launch a full-scale air attack at him.

"Is this seriously what you two did?" Katie asked incredulously. "Messed around?"

"Yeah." He swiped Godzilla from Evie and waved him out of reach. Evie flashed him a knowing look, then abruptly jumped on his back to get the toy. He relinquished it in order to catch her in a piggyback hold and groan. "Jeez, Godzilla, give a guy a break."

"You two seem to be getting along much better than yesterday," Katie said. "What happened?"

"Well," Tyler said, "we talked things out."

"Yes." Evie rested her chin on his head. "We decided that, well, whatever people interpret about our behaviour is up for them to decide."

He nodded. "Right. We're just having fun here."

"Indubitably," Evie said.

He grinned. "You're so British."

Godzilla mashed into the side of his face. "What else would I be?"

"You could try being older than nine," Katie muttered. She turned to Brock. "That's a cut for today. I'm past done here. See you tomorrow." And with that, she turned and walked away.

Brock nodded, packed the camera up, saluted Evie and Tyler, then hurried after her.

"I don't think she's a fan of ours," Evie said thoughtfully.

"You don't say."

She was warm on his back. The smell of her skin and sweat surrounded him, and it bordered on intoxicating. Almost as good as the feeling of her thighs in his hands where he gripped them. He wanted to slide his hands along her legs, but instead he let her down gently. She came around to face him, Godzilla tucked under one arm. "This documentary had better be brilliant."

He snorted. "I have my doubts. Not because of *her* but because of who she's filming."

"I wonder how the Cherry Studios lot is doing," Evie mused.

"I don't care." Tyler pulled her towards him. "All my attention is here."

She grinned up at him. "Charmer." They kissed, and Tyler revelled in how the world faded away and everything in him surged towards her. Her tongue flickered into his mouth, teasing him. He responded by winding his fingers into her hair and pulling her tighter against him. So soft, so sweet in his arms. He let himself get lost in the taste of her, the feel of her—

His phone buzzed. They ignored it.

Evie started making soft little noises that went straight to Tyler's crotch. He'd missed this, missed touching and feeling another person. Mouth and skin and hands. It was heady and intense, and he swam in the sensations of her.

Then *her* phone rang.

Annoyance broke the mood. They parted, breathless. Evie rested her forehead against his. "One day," she murmured, "we'll have to turn those bloody things off."

"Are you free on Sunday?"

"After the parade, yes."

"Come out with me and turn your phone off."

She smiled. "All right."

"I have to go soon. I have work."

"Can you stay a little longer?"

Warmth filled his chest at that request. *She wants me to stay.* "Yeah." He closed his eyes and took a moment to appreciate this too. How amazing it was that she was happy just to spend time with him like this. He knew this was basic stuff, but not everyone was content with hugging in silence.

Her lips pressed against his neck and her fingers trailed languidly up and down his back. Slow and sweet. Infinitely sweet.

There was only so much time, however, and he soon kissed her good-bye.

His work tonight was a one-off job as a backup dancer at the Cave on Church Street. It was a gay bar as well as a performance venue, and he'd performed at gigs there a few times before. He generally liked the place, but he always had reservations doing work like this. (Lucette had hated this kind of job, but that didn't matter anymore.)

The job itself wasn't the problem, and even mixing amongst the usual clientele afterward generally didn't give him issues. It was the nonqueer guests who could be problematic, the ones who came to see the artist and weren't used to the variety of people in queer spaces. The ones who inspired a constant thrum of fear someone would grope him, realize he wasn't exactly filling out the same way as the other boys, and turn nasty.

He packed for occasions like this, or tried to, but he wasn't used to dancing with a packer. A dance belt, yes, but a packer in a dance belt was just acutely uncomfortable and unnecessary. The close changing quarters meant swapping a dance belt for a packer was a washroom job, and after a performance he was often too tired to care. Normally he left the dance belt on and tried to squeeze a rolled-up sock or something down there to fill it out. Less than ideal.

He wouldn't bother at all if he didn't need the money and if he didn't get better feedback (and bookings) when he did have something meaty-looking filling out his pants.

On the way there, he checked his phone and found a text from Gigi.

Gigi: *Really wish you could come out tonight*
Tyler: *Yeah, me too. Shame.*
Gigi: *What's the job again?*
Tyler: *Backup dancer at the Cave. I think it's an Aqua tribute band.*
Gigi: *JFC. NO WAY ughhh enjoy and remember to wash your pants when you get home*
Tyler: *That would be *your* standard night out, Gigi, not mine.*
Gigi: *:3*

He put his phone away and got out of the subway at Bloor-Yonge, ducking through the crowds towards Church. He walked quickly, wanting as much time to prepare and rehearse as possible. He'd had to practise the routine in whatever free time was left between class, training, and the Pride sessions with Evie, and it looked like he would only have about half an hour to get it down with the other dancers.

When he arrived at the stage door, he was ushered inside and given a pair of leather pants by the stage manager. He stared at them, aghast. "You can't be serious."

"I am. The other dancers have them on already," she said. "Go."

He made his way to the changing room. Three half-naked men turned towards him as he entered, all of them wearing the same pants.

"What the hell are these?" he asked, holding the pants up.

"Well *hello* to you too, gorgeous," a twink with curly brown hair said. He was applying eyeliner with a very steady hand.

"The uniform," another guy growled, looking uncomfortable. He was bulky, and the pants looked ready to burst on him.

"How are we supposed to move in them?" Tyler demanded.

"With difficulty," the final guy, a bearded hipster with snake hips, said. Tyler stared at him as he tried to swing his leg to the side and couldn't.

"I'm not gonna move." The twink gazed over his shoulder at his reflection in the only mirror. "Just stand and let them admire." His ass, neatly showcased in the pants, visibly bounced as he contracted his glutes.

"Please tell me you're wearing underwear," Tyler said as the door opened behind him and the stage manager looked in.

"Two minutes to rehearsal," she snapped before closing the door again.

Fuck. Tyler rushed to the side of the room and quickly changed. He pulled a tight tank on and was still struggling to button the pants over his dance belt as he walked out of the dressing room. He was lucky the pants fit over his thighs and butt. Barely. And he was ecstatic for once that he only had a sock in his dance belt, because anything larger would ensure he'd never be able to get the pants on, let alone off again. Much as he sometimes wished he had the real thing, moments like these made him very glad he didn't. The other guys, excepting the twink, looked like they were ready to cry.

On the stage, the curtain separated them from the main bar and the early birds already there. The stage manager handed a set list to the lead dancer—Beardy Snake Hips—and walked out.

"You've all practised the moves?" Beardy asked them. They all nodded. "Good. Let's run through them. If you mess up, just touch yourself until you can join back in again."

The run-through went without any major hiccups, beyond being unable to do the long reach steps some of the moves demanded. Tyler found the more he moved in them, the more the pants stretched and allowed room. *Okay. This is gonna be okay.* He let himself relax a little.

By the time the band had set up and were in position, Tyler could even do up the top button. He left it undone to add to the sex appeal, and managed to quickly apply eyeliner and basic makeup to match the other guys. He grinned at himself in the mirror—Lucette would have flipped.

The dancers took their places, the curtain went up and it was showtime. Sweaty, grim, constricted showtime. Which actually went well enough until the twink "accidentally" partnered with him during "Barbie Girl" and ground his ass up against him, and Tyler had to improvise. Tyler was pretty sure the guy just wanted to show off— and hey, he could roll with that. So he let loose and danced with him, even managing a slap or two on that bouncing ass—all in the name of nineties-inspired fun. After all, what were gigs like this meant for except fun (and money), right? Okay, the money was awesome, but being free to do this, to be sexual and show his body off without worrying about people judging his technique, felt wonderful.

Even with an overenthusiastic twink helping him, by the time the curtain went down, Tyler was more than ready to rip the pants off and go home. He made for the changing room, the pants sticking tighter to him with sweat. The twink patted him on the shoulder as he hobbled past. "Good job, honey."

Back in the changing room, he joined the other guys in removing his pants with great sighs of appreciation—all of them except the twink, who kept his on.

"*I* am getting laid tonight," he declared.

"Was there ever any doubt?" Bulked asked.

"Ooh, I don't know." He made eyes at Tyler. "It depends." Tyler gave the tiniest shake of his head, and the twink pouted, then turned his attention to Bulked. "You gonna buy me a drink?"

Tyler dumped his stuff in the cloakroom, then worked his way through the crowd to the bar. A few patrons, male and female, recognized him from the set and eyed him lingeringly, but he ignored them. At the bar, the bartender nodded at him and passed him a glass of water. Tyler felt his phone vibrate in his pocket as he drank it.

Gigi: *Were those pants spray-painted on?*

Gigi: *Also, introduce me to that twink who practically fucked you on stage.*

A chill went through him. All the sounds of the bar and people faded. He looked up and cast around. There, near a small table a few feet away from him, was Gigi, and with him was Sarah and *Evie*. She looked amazing, her hair down and eyes made up and a cute dress and—was that *glitter* across her chest and face?

Wait. She'd *seen* him? Seen him grinding against guys on stage to a fucking Aqua tribute band? Lucette had always given him grief about taking jobs like that, and oh man, he didn't want another lecture ever, ever again—

His stomach dropped and his lungs tightened. He struggled for breath. The bar around him seemed even farther away now, and suddenly the noise was sucked out of it. All he could hear was his heart pounding. His vision narrowed to focus entirely on his friends' faces. Shit, what was wrong with him? His entire body was poised to fly away, or to drop to the floor, and that made no sense. These were his friends.

Evie turned and saw him. Her eyes lit up and she gave him a big grin, cutting the anxious chatter in his head like a switch.

Okay. Okay. That was a good sign. She'd seen it and was happy.

Relief flowed through his system like cool water. Suddenly his lungs remembered how to do their job, and he took in a big, shaky breath. *Jeeesus. Keep it together.* Head clear and chest loose, he grabbed his water and walked over to them.

Gigi gave him a massive hug. "You were on fire!" he yelled above the noise. "How the fuck did you move in those pants?"

Trust Gigi to focus on the important things, rather than on Tyler's seconds-long mini-freakout. Tyler was sure Gigi had found his expression hilarious, the asshole. "With great difficulty," he replied.

Gigi waggled his eyebrows. "You filled them out sooo well."

Tyler choked on his water.

"That was *amazing*," Sarah squealed, hugging him too. "Every time I see you dance, I just get blown away."

"Me too." Evie pulled him close and kissed his cheek. He could smell beer on her breath. "You're so gorgeous in leather. And with those guys." She gestured floppily. "You know? The other cute guys also in leather."

"Yeah?" he asked nervously. She nodded emphatically. Good. That was good. But seriously, this was *Evie*, the girl who was so chill it was unreal. He had to start remembering that. "I didn't think you swung that way," he teased.

"I'm a fujoshi," she replied, as if that answered him.

He turned to Gigi. That traitor. "I take it coming here was your idea?"

Gigi grinned. "Oh yeah." He threw an arm around Tyler and yanked him away from the women. "Jesus Christ those two can drink. I knew Sarah could, but God, they breed them different in England."

Tyler frowned. "How much has she had?"

"More than me, and she's barely tipsy. Fucking hard-core. Get her on the dance floor and show her what you've got already."

"Not sure you noticed, man, but we've been dancing together all week? She's seen what I've got." *Dance-wise, at least.*

"Yeah, but you're competing against a guy who curates art."

"No, I'm not, Gigi." Tyler held him steady, making sure to drive home his point. "We're not rivals."

Gigi patted his shoulder happily. "That's the right attitude. He's not even in the same league as you. And look, she actually screamed with me when you fondled that twink's ass. She loved it. She's down no matter what you do. Now go get her."

Tyler was about to say he'd spent over three hours dancing with her that day and was ready to drop from an actual performance, but his hand was taken. He looked over to see Evie with an intent expression on her face. She said something he couldn't hear, and he leaned in closer.

"What?"

"Dance with me." Her eyes sparkled under the lights from the dance floor. "Not the routine."

Screw it. He was too tired to argue. He downed the rest of his water and led her out onto the dance floor. She got up close and held her phone to his face so he could read the screen.

Evie: *At the Cave. Gonna be here awhile.*
Brock: *I'll be there in 20.*

His message had been sent two minutes ago. Tyler blinked, then focused on Evie. She held up a finger to his lips and glanced towards the entrance. They could see it better from the dance floor than Gigi could near the bar.

Hell. "And I thought you actually wanted to dance with me!" Tyler shouted to be heard over the music.

"I do!" she shouted back, putting her phone away into— Wait, were those pockets in her dress? *Damn.* Awesome.

Tyler shook his head. Gripped her waist. Then was shocked when she twisted in his hands and started grinding against him. But why, right? Like, because she was asexual, she couldn't or wouldn't want to do that? Nah, screw that noise. Time to let the music take them wherever they needed to go, bumping along like the rest of the men and women around them. Everyone was packed in tight and close, a sweaty, writhing mass.

Eventually they faced each other again, knees and hands grazing. Seconds passed like eons as he drew Evie closer against him. She put one arm over his shoulder and eased them into a hot kiss, encouraging him to close his eyes and melt against her. She tasted like beer. He wanted to push her against a nearby wall and see how much glitter he could kiss off her skin.

When he opened his eyes, he saw Brock walk in the door. His expression must have changed, because Evie frowned, then turned around. She shot a gleeful look back at Tyler, grabbed his hand, and pulled him towards Brock.

Tyler had to admit, the man cleaned up well. A tight shirt clung to his frame, his jeans had to have been greased in order for him to get them on, his hair was styled, and there was definitely subtle eyeliner happening. The overall effect was fierce and brooding. Absolutely no trace of the cuddly, hoodie-clad student here.

"Hey, guys," he greeted them nervously.

"You made it!" Evie said. She flicked a glance towards Tyler.

He knew instantly what she was thinking. "I'll get Gigi onto the dance floor."

"You have glitter on your face," Brock said to Tyler. He glanced between them. "Wait, both of you—"

"Aaand we'll wait for you here," Evie said, pushing Tyler towards the bar.

Tyler ducked away and went to Gigi and Sarah, rubbing at his face as he went. They met him with huge grins. Gigi lunged forward and hugged him tightly.

"Congrats!" he cried.

"For what?" Tyler asked, thoroughly confused.

"We saw you two out there." Sarah jumped in place, then hugged both of them. "I *knew* you liked her!"

"I knew you wouldn't be able to resist those thighs," Gigi added triumphantly.

Wow. Just wow. With friends like these . . . Tyler didn't want to deal with this right now. "Yeah, yeah, you got me. I like her, she likes me, we all like each other. It's all good. Come dance with us."

"Where is she?" Sarah craned to get a glimpse of Evie.

"Washroom." He coaxed them both onto the dance floor and tried to get them into a spot Evie and Brock could work towards, keeping Gigi facing him as much as possible. Soon Evie's arms entwined themselves around Tyler's middle, and he felt her chin rest on his shoulder. The act sent a weird rush of warmth through him, but before he could think that response through, he saw Brock press up against Gigi's back. Gigi froze, his eyes wide. Tyler held his breath as his friend somehow realized exactly who was behind him.

Gigi spun and took a step away from Brock, scowling. Tyler angled closer so he could see Gigi's face; he didn't want to miss this at all. Brock's expression was intense under the dance floor lights, and he leaned close to Gigi and shouted something to him. Gigi tossed his head as he replied, making Brock half smile. Gigi stared him down as Brock pressed a tentative, quick kiss to Gigi's mouth. Tyler couldn't help grinning, because Gi had this expression on his face that said he wasn't buying what Brock was selling, but his hands had latched on to Brock's shirt apparently without him noticing. When he did notice, Gigi dropped the act, bit his own lip, then yanked Brock towards him. Brock's arms encircled him as they locked faces.

Look at that, Brock got his man.

Sarah tugged Tyler's arm. "Let's give them some privacy."

Hell yeah. Tyler was happy for him, but watching his friend make out was too much. Tyler took Evie's hand in his, and they trailed after Sarah a little way into the crowd, but not so far they lost sight of Gigi and Brock.

Evie faced them both and grinned devilishly. "Perfect!"

Tyler hoped so. That had looked promising, but he didn't like the idea of a morning call from a hungover and regretful Gigi tomorrow. Hopefully Brock wouldn't hurt his friend again.

Sarah pulled the three of them together. "Let's dance!"

And dance they did. It wasn't anything elegant, but bopping along wasn't ever supposed to be. He had to remind himself to just let loose and move, because this wasn't a job and he wasn't being judged, and it was a shame it had been so long he needed the reminder. The crowd around them got progressively more drunk and grabby. Tyler was fairly sure some of the brushes against his ass were intentional. He kept glancing over at Gigi and Brock until they were no longer in the crowd. He checked his phone to see texts.

Gigi: *Gone home.*

Gigi: *Take E home tonight too ;)*

His friend, Gigi Rosenberg: subtle as a brick.

And it was 2 a.m. When had that happened?

He looked up to see Sarah and Evie talking to a guy in tight clothes. Who the heck? The guy looked vaguely familiar— Wait, those were deck shoes. Leather deck shoes. Evie hugged him and Tyler had to throttle the instant pang of jealousy. Sarah caught his eye and raised her eyebrows.

Evie took his hand and pulled him towards the guy. "This is Vaughn," she shouted over the music.

Tyler made himself smile and wave. Vaughn looked like six feet of sex in leather, and Tyler didn't even go for guys. Vaughn smiled cheerily. "I saw you dancing up there. You're very good."

"Thanks."

"Would you do performances in art spaces? I've been trying to get my gallery noticed as a venue for performance-based pieces and perhaps you'd be interested in helping me promote that." Vaughn handed him a business card, which Tyler blinked at. "Interpretive, free-form, that kind of stuff."

"Yeah," he said, surprised. "I do interpretive dance."

"What are you doing here?" Evie asked Vaughn.

He thumbed behind him at a group of people near the bar. "Came with friends. I *love* Aqua."

Was this guy for real? Came here for Aqua and owned leather deck shoes and handed out business cards like it was nothing?

Vaughn patted Evie's shoulder and Tyler's palms itched. "I saw the video of you. The one on YouTube. Nice moves." He glanced at her dress and gasped. "Wait, wait, *wait*. Does your dress have *pockets*?"

Evie beamed and held her dress out. "Yes! Amazing, right?"

And now he felt like an idiot because whatever else Vaughn was into, women wasn't one of them. He was queening like a wealthy version of Gigi. As if to emphasize the point, a shorter guy joined them and planted a kiss on Vaughn's cheek. The shorter one spoke into Vaughn's ear, causing Vaughn to grin, then wind his arm around his boyfriend's waist and kiss his hair.

Yeah. Sweet. Tyler still wanted to rip Evie away from the guy because *strictly* speaking Vaughn wasn't into men either, and come on, *Tyler* was the one who needed to compliment her on good dress choices and make her smile.

Jesus. What was wrong with him? Could he actually kick himself for being jealous? Because he needed to. No, wait, not jealous, he couldn't be jealous of a casual thing. He just *jumped to conclusions*, that's right—

Sarah was gone. He looked around and saw her walking in the direction of the exit. As Vaughn continued to gasp over Evie's dress, Tyler chased after Sarah, catching her arm near the cloakroom.

"Where are you going?" he asked.

She looked back at him, confused. "Home. It's 2 a.m."

"And you're leaving Evie here? Alone?"

She blinked. "Are you serious? *You're* here. The way you were looking at her, I was certain you and Evie would be a sure thing."

Things clicked into place. Why Gigi had brought them here. His and Sarah's behaviour over the last week. Their behaviour tonight.

They'd been set up.

There he and Evie were, thinking they'd set Gigi up with Brock—and they had—but Gigi and Sarah had set *him and Evie* up.

Or were trying to.

He shook his head. "Sarah, it's not like that. We're not like that. Don't leave her stranded at some club."

She frowned. "What do you mean? Have you seen the way she looks at you? Tyler, if you asked her home, she'd go with you in a hot minute."

"No, she wouldn't. Sarah, trust me on this. If you leave her behind, I'm getting her a taxi back to your place and charging you for it."

Her face cleared. "Tyler. Oh my God, Tyler. You *gentleman.*"

He scowled. "Sarah—"

"Are you still the Tyler I met at Queersoc? The one who was the king of casual hookups?"

He waved his hand to dismiss that old version of himself. He didn't do casual hookups like that, not anymore and not in a long time. Even if he did feel up for it, Evie wasn't some curious queer chick wanting a transgender adventure for one night, and he was long over being someone else's interesting sex story. "No, I'm not. And I'm not going to seduce her back to my apartment. She doesn't want that. It's not about that. Think about *her.* She's a visitor staying with you. Don't just leave her with relative strangers in a strange city."

Sarah now looked confused. "You have a point, but, Ty, it's not like—"

"Guys, where are you going?" Evie asked behind them.

They turned to look at her. She blinked at them, beautiful in glitter and tipsy confusion. Even if she *was* looking for a lay like the rest of the crowd in here, Tyler knew he wouldn't pursue that with her. No, she needed to be home and in bed. Safe.

He grabbed her hand and kissed it. "We're deciding when to go home."

"Oh. Now?"

"I have work tomorrow," Sarah said.

Evie checked her phone. "Yikes."

A sly grin unfolded on Sarah's face. "Hey, Tyler, why don't you crash at our place tonight?"

Evie's hand jerked in his. *Hmm.*

"I don't think that's a great idea." He didn't want to get a cab on his own—the fare was always freaking extortionate—but if Evie didn't want him there, he couldn't say yes.

"You can sleep on the spare sofa," Sarah said, turning serious now. "Evie's on the sofa bed, but she can cuddle in with me if you want a proper bed to sleep on."

Evie's hand relaxed a little.

"Would that be a problem?" he asked, hedging his bets.

"No." Sarah yawned. "Plus, I'd rather split a taxi fare three ways than two."

"Evie?"

"That's okay," she said. "Let me grab my stuff."

They all wilted in the taxi home. By the time they pulled up outside of Sarah and Bailey's place, Tyler was ready to crawl into bed and sleep for the next week. They tiptoed in, whispering to avoid waking Bailey. While Sarah made the other sofa up for him, Tyler went to the kitchen and poured out glasses of water for everyone. Evie's was a pint.

She came into the kitchen, freshly showered. Glitter still sparkled in her hair, but she'd washed most of it off her skin. "Oh," she said, as though not expecting to find him here.

He held the pint glass out to her. "Drink."

A sly smile curved her mouth. "I didn't drink *that* much."

"Don't care. Do it."

She took the pint glass and gulped deeply.

"Are you sharing with Sarah tonight?" he asked.

She swallowed. "I . . . don't know."

A thick pause filled the space between them. Tyler picked up a glass of water and stared at it. "I'll crash as soon as I lie down," he said. "In case you're wondering. So you can use the sofa bed like normal. If you want to."

"Do you want privacy?"

"Huh?"

She was looking at her feet, her cheeks red. "You should take the sofa bed. Sleep properly. By yourself, if you want. I don't know how you feel sleeping in the same space as someone else, but if you want privacy for whatever reason, I'll move into Sarah's room for the night."

A lump filled his throat. "That's not . . . No. I don't. Need that. Not that kind of privacy, that is. Not with you and Sarah and Bay. That's—" He took a deep breath. "I'm asking because of what we talked about. You should sleep in your bed. And not worry. I'll stay in mine and you'll be in yours, okay?"

This time, she was the one who had trouble speaking. "Oh. *Oh.* Right."

"Thank you, though." His voice held a slight tremble. He sipped some water. "Thanks for thinking about that."

She gave him a small smile. "Likewise. Thank you."

Sarah breezed into the kitchen. "Sofa's done! No naughty stuff, you two." She picked up the remaining glass of water and drained it. "I'm using the bathroom next. You know where everything is, Ty." She walked out.

"Damn it, I need to shower," Tyler grumbled.

Evie chuckled, then put her empty glass down. "I'm going to bed."

"Wait." He took the glass and refilled it. "Another."

She glared at him. "I went to university in London. I live in York. I've recovered from worse nights on the lash with Lucozade and a bag of Maltesers."

"I don't know what you just said to me, but I do know I really want you to drink this water."

She huffed, downed the pint in one go, then pressed the glass back into his hand. "There you go, *Dad.*"

"Sleep well."

She leaned over and kissed his cheek, then walked out of the kitchen. His chest swelled with emotion. That had been simple. So simple. Was this what it could be like? Asking questions and answering honestly and teasing each other and none of it being a big deal?

Sarah's head ducked around the kitchen door. "Hey. Bathroom's free."

"Thanks. And thanks for letting me stay."

"Never a problem." She winked at him. "I won't say a thing if I find you two cuddled together tomorrow morning."

He rolled his eyes. "Good night, Sarah."

She drifted to bed too, and he showered, tiredness making his limbs heavy. He hit the lights as he stumbled back into the living room, found his way to the sofa past a sleeping Evie, and passed out as soon as his head hit the pillow.

CHAPTER NINE

Evie woke up abruptly. She blinked at the ceiling, gauging the slow creep of light in the room as *very early*. She couldn't have been asleep for more than a few hours. Her bladder was yelling at her. Tyler and his fucking two pints of water.

Wait. Tyler?

The previous evening flashed back to her: the drinks, the dancing, the terrible tribute band, realizing that Tyler was one of the incredible dancers on the stage, realizing Gigi and Sarah had set her up, setting Gigi up, bumping into Vaughn and his boyfriend, kissing Tyler in the middle of the dance floor . . .

She smiled. That had been fun. They'd come home and—

Oh. He was here. He was sleeping on the other sofa. In the same room. She could hear him breathing. She looked over. There he was, curled under a blanket, completely asleep. The awkwardness of the conversation that had led to this was drowned out by the warmth of knowing he was okay with her being here. He felt comfortable. That felt immense.

Her phone vibrated. She turned over carefully and picked it up. There was an old text from Gigi and an email from her mother. The text read: *Gone home.* Yes, with Brock. She'd figured as much.

She turned to the email.

Darling, Richard called and said you hadn't spoken to him. Really, what are you doing over there that you can't spare a few minutes to say hello to your brother? We had a lovely chat and he's bringing Helena for tea today. I'm sorry you can't make it this time around. We'll have to do it again when you're back. I think they're getting serious now, so you should make the effort to know her. The vet finally got back to us about Shep. Turns out the dear old doggy has stomach cancer, and it's too far gone for any treatment to have an effect. We're having him put down on Monday. It's the kindest thing, and we're all terribly upset. Don't worry, darling, it's for the best and he's had a lovely long life. My tart has been devoured by the neighbours. I'll bake another one for your return. When's the return date again? Looking forward to seeing you. Doug sends his love.

Unexpected cold seared through Evie. She reread the message, then put her phone down on the mattress and curled up tightly, bladder be damned. Monday. She was flying back on Tuesday, arriving Wednesday morning. Couldn't they wait a few more days?

She picked her phone back up to respond: *Oh no! Poor Shep. Can you wait until Wednesday? I want to say good-bye to him.*

Ten minutes later, a response arrived. *No, darling, we've already made the appointment and he's in pain. It's a little selfish to prolong that, don't you think? But don't worry, we'll hold a lovely funeral for when you're back. I'll make the tart. Hugs and kisses.*

Evie turned her phone off. She got out of bed and walked to the bathroom as quietly as she could. Once she'd relieved her bladder, she splashed her face with water. That didn't make her feel any better. She didn't feel anything at all. She stared at herself in the mirror. Dark circles in a pale face.

What was she doing here? In an unfamiliar bathroom, in a strange house, in a different country, five time zones away from home? Why was she here instead of in the places she knew? Why was she even *awake* right now?

A soft knock sounded at the door.

She opened it to find a tousled, sleepy Tyler. He leaned against the frame, wearing nothing but boxers, hair curling freely around his head.

"You okay?" he asked in a low voice.

She opened her mouth, but no words came out. She closed it. Looked him over again because she wasn't used to seeing him without clothes on like this. The lean, tight body. The muscles. The scars swooping along his rib cage, only slightly darker than the surrounding skin tone. Her head was fuzzy from the interrupted sleep and news about her childhood pet, and it was somehow easier to just stare at him. He looked good. Much too good for having been disturbed after a late night. A small part of her might have been embarrassed at waking him, but that part was drowned out by what she was realizing was her shock over Shep.

"Evie?"

She swallowed and forced the words out. "I'm sorry I woke you."

He crossed his arms and stifled a yawn. "You didn't wake me. Your phone did."

"I'm sorry my phone woke you."

Now he frowned. "Evie. You look like, I don't know, like someone stole your wallet or something. What happened?"

The words tumbled out of her. "My dog is sick. My parents are putting him down. They're not waiting for me to come back before they do it. I don't know—" She forced herself to stop before she continued the sentence: *I don't know what to do because I want him to live until I get back so I can say good-bye properly and my mother doesn't seem to care.*

Tyler's face softened. "I'm sorry Evie."

She took a deep, shaky breath. "G-go back to bed. It's okay. I'll be okay."

"You trying to convince me or yourself?"

He said it kindly, which was what did it. A wave of hurt and grief finally crashed down on her, completely swamping her. Her stupid family and her stupid pet and her stupid decision to be here right now—all of it hurt so, so much, and she covered her eyes as she started to cry. Strong arms came around her, and she let herself sag against him.

He rocked her gently and didn't say anything except, "It's okay."

It wasn't okay. But the words got through her overloaded head, and eventually she recovered enough to take her hands away and wipe at her tears instead of catching them. Tyler let her go, but stayed close, his hands rubbing her back soothingly.

"I'm sorry," she whispered. "I'm such a mess." She noticed how wet his shoulder was. Wonderful. Just wonderful. Because dowsing your crush's shoulder was completely endearing rather than intensely pathetic. "Oh God, I've cried on you."

"It's all good. Talk to me. When are your parents are putting him down?"

Her throat closed up. "Two days before I arrive. I asked if they could wait so I could say good-bye, and they said no. It's stupid, it's so stupid, because he's in pain and I want him to be out of pain because he's such a good dog, Ty; he's the best, and I should focus on that, not on how selfish I'm being by running around making a new life on the other side of the fucking ocean, away from my family—"

"Shhh. You're not stupid." He reached over and grabbed toilet paper. He started dabbing at her face with a large bundle, making her smile despite herself. "You're upset. It's different."

"I'll be all right in a sec," she managed through paper blots. "It's not the end of the world. He's—he's just a—a . . ."

"Don't say that. If he was 'just a dog,' you wouldn't be crying in your friend's bathroom." He patted his shoulder, drying where she'd wept all over it. "We had a dog when we were younger. Man, we loved that puppy. My parents split up, my dad took off, and money became tight, so my mom gave him up. It was better for him, because we really struggled and couldn't look after him. We all cried the day he left us, even my big brother, Darrell."

That sounded awful. Even though Shep was dying, at least she'd had almost two decades with him. She couldn't imagine having him, then being forced to give him up and live knowing he was being looked after by some other family. "I'm sorry."

He shrugged. "It happened. We were sad. And after some time, we weren't as sad anymore." He threw the paper into the trash can. "So I get it. You feeling better?"

She nodded, even though there was a new hollowness inside her. He took her hand and led her back to the living room. Once there, he urged her back into bed and sat next to her, brushing his fingers through her hair.

"Thank you," she murmured, the movement soothing her.

Tyler's smile was a little pained. "What was I going to do, tell you to get over it?"

"You could have."

"Yeah, well, I'm not a complete asshole."

"No," she agreed. "Not completely."

He nodded sagely. "See, there's the Evie we all know and love."

She managed a laugh. He kept stroking her hair.

"This might be a dumb question," he said quietly, "but why was she messaging you at whatever time this is?"

Evie shrugged. "Time zones. In fairness, I normally would've read it in the morning, not now. I wasn't sleeping well tonight."

"Sure." His fingers felt wonderful against her head. "I still have issues with the timing of this shit though. She knows when you're going back, right? I get that your dog's in pain, but I don't see how one or two days would make a difference. You're really upset now and it's stupid early."

Evie didn't know what to say to that. She felt tears start up again, and she turned her face into the pillow to hide them. "That's just the way she is."

"Can I see what she said?"

Evie dug out her phone, turned it back on, and passed it to him. He didn't say anything as he read their conversation. He passed the phone back to her, then pressed a kiss to her temple.

"I don't know your mom, but if I was going to break news like that to my kid, I'd at least wait a few hours until she was awake."

She shrugged again.

"Plus, you mentioned your arrival date like three times in earlier messages, so I don't know why she's asking that again."

Irritation started overshadowing the hollowness. "She pays attention when she wants to." Evie's voice was a little sharper than she'd intended. "Let's not."

"Not what?"

"Stay up discussing her."

Tyler's fingers stilled in her hair. "Why not?"

Evie struggled to articulate it, finally saying, "She's not worth the lost sleep. Can we go back to bed? I'm fine now."

"You sound mad."

At that, her irritability deflated. "I'm not angry." That wasn't quite the truth. "All right, I am, but not at you. At her. You're right, she could have been more considerate. Here's the thing: my mother is not considerate, and she never has been, and I can't change that, so there's no point in discussing it."

His fingers started moving again. She looked up at him. His face was clouded. "I dunno. I agree you can't change her, but you *can* change what you say in response to her. Because the Evie in those messages isn't the Evie I've been dancing with this past week. Instead of being so nice to her all the time, maybe you could be like, 'Yo, Mom, I was asleep because I'm *in Canada* and couldn't this have waited four hours? And did you read my other messages at all? Also, cancel the appointment and reschedule, because I wanna fucking say good-bye to my dog and this *we already booked it* shit doesn't fly.'"

Evie stared at him. God love him, he was serious. She could just imagine Rowena choking at a response like that. Her mouth quirked in a smile. "'Yo, Mom'?"

Tyler grinned. "It's a work in progress."

"She'd have kittens."

"Well, if a dog's no longer an option . . ."

Unbelievable. The *cheek*. Evie gasped, then started laughing despite her shock. "You're terrible! Too soon!"

After a moment, Tyler joined in. Her eyes went to his torso, to the way his muscles contracted as he tried to laugh quietly. When she looked at his face again, he'd sobered. Apparently he'd noticed where her gaze had gone.

"Do the scars freak you out?"

"No," she said honestly. "I wasn't looking at them. I was watching the way you laughed."

Confusion flickered across his face. "Seriously?"

"Yes."

He pulled his hand away from her and rested it in his lap. Evie didn't like the expression on his face. She reached over and covered his hand with hers. "I see that they're there. They don't bother me. I've seen scars before."

"Scars like these or others?"

"One of my ex-girlfriends had scars. Not like yours," she added, "but they were very much there and part of her. I'm used to seeing scars."

He averted his eyes. "You didn't seem surprised when I said I was trans in that interview with Katie."

Evie frowned and pushed herself into a sitting position. His body had curled in on itself slightly. What was he really saying? "I *was* surprised," she admitted. "But it wasn't a bad surprise. I initially read you as male. Finding out you're transgender didn't and doesn't make you less male."

"How are you so okay with me?" His voice was low and hoarse, and his gaze was fixed on the floor. Evie felt another ache join the one created by her mother and Shep. Had he been worrying about that all this time?

"What do you mean? You're you." She squeezed his hand. "I said I like *you*. I knew you were transgender when I said that. Why wouldn't I be okay with you?"

"That's not usually how these things go," he said thickly.

"Romantically, you mean?"

He nodded.

"I don't know what you've gone through because of being trans," she said carefully, "but I know what it's like for people to hear a label and make snap assumptions."

"Yeah, but . . ." The skin around his eyes was tense with pain. Evie wanted to reach out and smooth it down, soothe him the way he'd soothed her. "I will always be a transgender man. Inside and . . . and outside."

Ah. That old chestnut, of certain parts being certain parts. Evie had never understood what the big deal was about who had what or whether one body part was more attractive than another. She didn't get it because, to her, it just didn't matter. So she shrugged. "I've dated lots of different bodies. I like yours because it's yours."

"Yeah, but this won't ever go away."

She took his hand again. "Why should it? As long as you're okay with you, I'm okay with you. Tyler . . . you're more than your gender, and I'm sure you know that. You're kind and patient, even when you're grumpy or hungover as hell—"

He snorted.

"—and you're smart and disciplined and passionate, and I can't even begin to describe the way you dance." Honestly, where had this come from? Was this from general insecurity or the ex? She was tempted to say the ex, but perhaps it was both. "You let me cry like an idiot at stupid o'clock in the morning over my dog. I think you're amazing." Her voice cracked, already strained from crying earlier.

Why couldn't he see himself like that? Didn't he know what a gift he'd just been? Because he was looking at her with complete disbelief, and she suspected not nearly enough people had told him how totally wonderful he was. She leaned forward and kissed him. "And you're perfect exactly the way you are. *Exactly* as you are."

He scoffed, but it was halfhearted. "Someone's still drunk."

She poked him. "You should thank people when they tell the truth."

A laugh sobbed out of him, and he pulled her onto him so he could kiss her, his lips gentle and sweet despite the strength in his arms.

Fierce protectiveness exploded through Evie, and she held him tightly against her. She wanted to wrap him up and stop anyone from hurting him again. For now, all she could do was kiss him hard, hard enough to press her feelings into his soul.

When the kiss ended, she opened her eyes and looked him straight in his. He smiled at her, his fingers lightly brushing her face. "You're pretty amazing yourself, Godzilla."

Her throat closed up with emotion. Somehow she rather doubted that. "Was this you or your ex talking?"

His mouth twisted. "The worst parts of me and, yeah, her. She thought she was okay with it. And I guess she did try." He sighed. "Luce had all the traditional binary crap in her head. I had to shake out all this toxic stuff about masculinity, but she didn't see any need to do that. She just didn't get why it was a problem. We had a lot of arguments about it."

"Why was she with you, then?" It was something she'd wanted to know ever since he'd first told her about Lucette in the café.

Tyler was quiet for a few minutes, brow furrowed in thought. She could almost see the gears working. He cleared his throat. "When we met, I was missing home and my family. I wasn't doing . . . I mean, romance-wise, people didn't mind hooking up with me, but no one seemed to want more, you know? She and I clicked when we danced, and our chemistry was amazing. It's a tough life, being a dancer. Not everyone gets it, but obviously we did. I guess we thought it was good enough." He shifted in her arms. "I know why I was with her. I still don't know why she stuck with me. But honestly? I think she was lonely too."

Evie ran her hands along his sides, digesting this. She was sure Lucette would have a different story to tell, and probably not one Evie would be interested in hearing. Honestly, how could one person screw with another like this?

"I'm sorry," she said finally. "And just so you know, I had to unlearn a lot of stuff too. I'm still unlearning things." She glanced at him. "I'm trying too. I don't want to ever make you feel bad about yourself, and I hope I haven't. If I have, I'm sor—"

"Hold it there." He kissed her quickly, a kind of no-nonsense kiss. "You haven't asked about my transition, my birth name, or my junk. You've been great, believe me."

Relief trickled through her. "Okay." She leaned forward and rested her chin on his shoulder, relaxing into his warmth. Holding someone like this—being held—was wonderful. She'd missed this, and she wasn't anywhere near ready to stop doing it. "I think you better join me on this sofa bed," she murmured.

"But we agreed that—"

"We did. I'm not changing that." She raised her head so she could read his face and he could see hers. "But I don't want to sleep alone right now, and I don't think you want to either."

His eyes gleamed in the dim dawn light. He lightly kissed her again, then climbed in beside her. Evie lowered herself into his waiting arms and gathered as much of him to her as she could. He kissed her forehead, then her eyes and nose and cheeks and chin before finally brushing her lips. It was as much comfort as romance, and she drank in the sensations as though they were water.

Soon Tyler drifted back to sleep. Evie lay awake, listening to his heartbeat. Now, in the shelter of so much intimacy, the numbness she'd felt receded. Warmth slowly seeped in, and she eventually drowsed too.

A few hours later, a clatter in the kitchen woke her. She blinked, disconcerted, then pleasantly surprised, then embarrassed to find herself facing Tyler, who smiled back at her. Ah, right, she'd practically demanded he sleep with her—*next* to her, not *with* her, goddamn it . . . She hid her face against his chest. Tyler's hand ran up and down her back again, but with more purpose this time.

"Morning," he murmured.

Evie didn't trust herself to look at him. "Good morning."

"I thought I'd dreamed this."

She smiled against his chest. "You're still dreaming."

He laughed, his whole body vibrating against hers. "I hope not." A kiss landed on her hair, then along her neck and down to the edge of her shirt. Okay, all of that was promising. She raised her head to meet his gaze, his dark eyes and skin glowing in the morning light. He looked truly beautiful. *I wouldn't mind seeing this every morning*, crossed her mind before she could help herself. *Stop it right there, Evie. You have* this *morning.*

To distract herself, she moved her fingers warningly against his side, the threat of a tickle, and he huffed in amusement. "Too late."

"Oh *really—*"

He went on the offensive and started tickling her. She laughed and tried to fend him off. The grappling ended up with her trapping his hands on either side of his head, him flat on his back and her kneeling above him, pinning him down.

"Behave."

"Make me," he replied with that devastating smile of his, the one that lit up his entire face. He raised his upper body towards her so he could whisper in her ear, "This is a good start."

His breath against her ear sent a shiver down her spine. It went straight to her groin, which ached in response. That was good to note: everything was working as usual. Her mind, as ever, was crystal clear and focused. She could end this or continue it. Evie was pretty sure this was only flirting. Heavy flirting, but flirting nonetheless. So she decided to play along. Just for now. Because she trusted him to know they were only messing around.

"Is it now?" she teased, wriggling a little. "You like being held down?" His breath drew in sharply. She leaned down, keeping her weight on his hands, so she in turn could whisper to him. "Do you wish I had some rope or cuffs here?" A small moan escaped him.

"Good morning," Bailey called, passing by the living room door.

Startled, Evie looked up, only to be tackled and rolled onto her back, several feet of dancer and muscle pinning *her* now. Tyler grinned down at her, his leg rubbing against her thigh. Evie had to admit that felt damn good.

"Shame we're here," he said, "and that we agreed not to go too far, otherwise I would definitely be exploring that suggestion of yours right now."

She raised her eyebrows, then wriggled once more, wanting to feel his leg against hers again. He lowered down and nuzzled her neck, brushing day-old stubble along her clavicle and up to her jaw. She closed her eyes to really *feel* all that sensation: his stubble, his weight, his hands against hers.

His lips found hers again, and he released her hands in order to cup her face and run his thumb along her neck. She wrapped her arms around him and traced the muscles along his back. The kiss deepened to slow tongue. The feel of his lips against hers, the hard press of his hands along her skin and in her hair, and the smell of his body curling around her—all of it was intense. Hot. Sweet. Hard.

Too soon, Bailey walked back along the corridor and called, "Breakfast's ready."

They finished the kiss, and Tyler rested his forehead against hers with an irritated sigh. "Damn it." She couldn't help agreeing.

"They have coffee," she said.

Tyler's gaze snapped to hers. "They do?"

"Yes."

He looked at the door. "Hmm."

"Thank you for last night. And this morning." Her thumb brushed his jaw. "I could do more with you very easily, Tyler." She hoped he understood what she was saying.

His eyes darkened. His hands fluttered at her waist, edging her shirt. Evie paused, then trailed her fingers down his bare chest—

Both of their stomachs growled at the same time, and they laughed.

Spell broken, they rose and Evie straightened her hair as they joined Bailey in the kitchen. Bailey didn't say a word about anything they must've seen, merely handed Evie her usual cup of tea and a plate of toast.

"Coffee?" they asked Tyler as he dug into his own plate.

"Yeah. Please."

Evie sipped her tea as Bailey poured Tyler a cup of coffee.

"Thanks, Bay," he said.

"My pleasure. Milk?" Bailey shot a glance over their shoulder at Evie and waggled their eyebrows.

Evie blushed. "Stop."

"No way."

Tyler smiled into his cup of coffee. Evie thought he looked just right like that, tousled from sleep, mug in hand, relaxed against the counter—

"*Oh my God, is that the time?*" Sarah screeched from the bedroom.

Steps thumped along the corridor, then she slid into the kitchen, tucking a shirt into her pencil skirt. Bailey nonchalantly handed her a slice of toast and mug of coffee. She chewed a mouthful of it and sipped the coffee, then eyed Evie and Tyler. "You two look well slept," she said sarcastically. Evie wanted to roll her eyes; Sarah's bags were as heavy as theirs.

Oh leave it. "Time, Sarah," Evie said.

"Fuck fuck fuck. I'm so fucking late." Sarah's panic reasserted itself, and she raced out of the kitchen, toast in hand.

"She like this every morning?" Tyler asked.

"Usually." Bailey sipped their coffee. "Only several hours earlier."

"What time *is* it?" Evie asked.

"Nine thirty."

Tyler put down his mug. "Wait, *what*? I have a class in thirty minutes." He strode out, and Evie smiled into her tea. Bailey met her glance and winked.

"Make sure you eat something," she called after him.

Tyler walked back into the kitchen five minutes later, dressed in his gear from yesterday. He kissed Evie quickly, then grabbed a last piece of toast. "I gotta run. I'll see you later."

"Bye."

Tyler strode out, waving at Bailey. "Thanks for having me, Bay."

"No probs. Bye!" Bailey called after him.

The front door closed shut.

"I see the appeal," Bailey remarked, indicating their torso. Evie blushed.

Sarah ran back in, shoes on and hair brushed. Crumbs coated her shirt. She took another sip of coffee, kissed Bailey's cheek, and ran out.

"So what are your plans this morning?" Evie asked Bailey.

They shrugged. "I'm easy. Anywhere you wanna go in particular?"

"AGO, then Timmies?" she suggested.

They nodded.

Good. A nice way to kill time until Evie could see Tyler again.

Tyler reached the school with seconds to spare. He ran into the practice room and found Gigi there, stretching languidly against the barre. The guy looked satisfied and happy. Ah, right, he'd gone home with Brock. Tyler flashed back to his own intense make-out session and immediately pushed the memory away. The last thing he needed was to be turned on for hours. He dumped his stuff and joined Gigi.

"Someone's got a sex glow going," he remarked.

Gigi leered at him in the mirror. "And *you* look like you're wearing the same clothes as yesterday."

Tyler bent over and stretched his hamstrings and calves. His spine cracked pleasantly as he let his head hang down. "So are you."

"Hell yeah." Gigi wiggled his ass happily. "Was it good for you?"

"I crashed at Sarah's." He arched out of the stretch and felt his back pull unusually. He carefully stretched one side, then the other, feeling out the discrepancy, then tried a few exploratory moves. Nope. Something was off. Too tight? Sleep-deprived? *More like, that's what sleeping on a sofa bed does.* Shit. Extra coffee and Gatorade was on the agenda for today.

"So you *didn't* hook up with her?" Gigi sounded like he didn't believe what he was saying.

"We made out." Tyler grabbed the barre and leaned back, stretching his chest and abs.

Gigi came into view, upside down. "Ty, help me out. Did you or did you not get together with our English flower?"

Tyler blinked. "*My* English flower. And yeah I did. But it's nothing serious." A little bell rang in his mind at those words, because that morning's confessions were the definition of serious. He shoved the thought away. "How was your night?"

Gigi preened. "*Well*. Since you asked, Brock and I had a *wonderful* time last night."

Oh God. This was a mistake. "Forget it. I don't want to know."

"We went back to my place—"

"Gigi—"

"—and made out—"

"I really, *really* don't—"

"—and practically tore our clothes off—"

"Oh God—"

"—and you would not *believe* the things he can do with his—"

"*Ahem!*"

Tyler and Gigi snapped face forward. Their friend and resident fouetté master Eddie stood at the head of the class. "Keep it down, boys. Literally."

They murmured apologies and continued with their stretching. Tyler frowned as he moved around. Today wasn't going to be a great day for dancing, he could tell.

"Basically, he's hung like a fucking horse," Gigi whispered dreamily.

Tyler closed his eyes and counted to ten.

"Now that I've shared with the class, you wanna tell me why, after all my efforts, you didn't do anything more than kiss the girl?"

"We're not serious, so sex doesn't feel right."

Gigi's eyes nearly popped out of his face. "Not serious? Sex doesn't *feel* right? What's wrong with you?" he hissed, barely keeping it down.

Tyler glared at him. "Come on! We're not all wired like you. Not every relationship works the way yours has."

"I'm not in a relationship, I'm in a hookup."

Tyler rolled his eyes. Brock had his work cut out for him.

Gigi continued, "She said in her interview that she's had sex. So she does do it. I thought you were in there." He frowned. "Waaait, you're not serious? How are you not serious? Have you *seen* yourselves?"

"This is a competition. She's leaving soon." Not that he wanted her to leave. Not now. He really, really didn't. Shit. Wasn't that a slightly terrifying realization? When had that happened?

Sure, "no harm in asking the girl out." Shana, you liar.

"So? She's coming back. You can't handle three months of long distance? It's not like *Evie* will find someone else she wants to fuck before she comes back." Gigi shook his head, earrings flashing. "I'm not the one who was in a relationship for over a year, and if even *I* can see you two work, then sweetie, your biggest problem is that nasty case of denial on your face."

Tyler was having problems processing what Gigi was saying. *Evie's coming back?* "Three months? She's coming back?"

Gigi quirked an eyebrow. "Uh, yeah? She's doing some super fancy degree in the fall? That's kind of the big main reason she's here? She's scoping the territory."

This was the first Tyler had heard of it. His confusion must've been obvious, because Gigi's jaw dropped. "You didn't know?"

"No."

"How the fuck did you not know? She said it in her interview! Like multiple times! Weren't you there?"

"I was distracted."

Gigi shook his head. "Unbelievable."

Yeah, okay. He got it: he didn't pay attention. So . . . she was *coming back*?

Tyler kicked out a leg behind him and heard his hips click. He remembered conversations over the past week that now made much more sense. Like his hips, things fell into place.

"Oh my God," he said. She was sticking around. Evie was going to be here. In Toronto. Somewhat permanently. They didn't have to end this fledgling thing between them. Delight sang through him . . . Rapidly followed by a hit of nausea. His stomach writhed as though snakes had taken up residence. His hand grew clammy against the barre. His vision narrowed to the floor at his foot. *No. No no no no no.* This was bad. So bad. He couldn't do this.

But why is it bad? asked a small, deeply hidden part of himself. He ignored that voice because it clearly knew nothing.

Oblivious to his panic, Gigi continued to stretch languidly. "I mean, not that it really matters anyway. She comes back, you and her can keep the magic going, and—" He caught sight of Tyler's face and came out of the stretch. "Ty? You okay? You look like shit."

Tyler's head reeled. He straightened abruptly and blinked until his vision returned to normal. *Get a grip, Ty. Focus.* "I can't," fell out of his mouth.

Gigi blinked. "You can't what?"

Tyler sagged against the barre. "I finally did an interview for a magazine. And I have more lined up. And this competition is another opportunity to push myself forward. I'm going to be an uncle. Lots of good things are happening." He rubbed his hands against his clothes, trying to dry them enough to grip the barre. "I can't handle a relationship right now."

Gigi stared at him like he'd said he was giving up dance. "*What?*"

"This thing with Evie, it's a casual thing. One week. That's it. She goes, it's over, we both move on." The nausea faded, leaving behind nervous energy instead. That was better. He could dance off nervous.

Gigi snorted. "Are you listening to yourself?" He crossed his arms and regarded Tyler thoughtfully. "I don't know what shit is going through your head right now, but ignore it and listen to your wise Aunt Gigi: Evie is a *good thing*. This 'casual' bull you just said to me? That isn't what I've been seeing this past week."

"Tough. That's all it is."

"And just what in the hell is wrong with lots of good things happening at once? You don't think you deserve good shit after last year?"

Tyler couldn't answer that, not without the nausea returning. When Gigi realized he wasn't going to get an answer, he scoffed and turned away. "Fine. Do the angsty silent act. See if Aunt Gigi cares."

The class was starting properly now. Tyler turned his back on him and settled into stance. He could still see Gigi in the mirror on the wall opposite him, and his friend looked worried.

After the class, Gigi was thankfully distracted by Brock. Tyler had the time and space to snarf down food while turning over the revelation that Evie was going to be a permanent fixture in Toronto. He knew he should be ecstatic she was staying, and on one level he *was*. He really, truly was. But the potential reality of another relationship, even with Evie, poured ice in his veins whenever he thought about it. Relationships were not okay. This wasn't okay. It was far too soon. Over a year *was* too soon, right? Right. Oh sure, she wouldn't be like Lucette, wouldn't demand the same things from him, but girlfriends always had *expectations*. Tyler knew that intimately.

And the timing was terrible. He felt like he was treading water career-wise; his head was a mess. A girlfriend on top of that? Too much.

Way too much. He couldn't deal with that. He had to break whatever this was off.

Even though she makes you happy? that annoyingly persistent little voice said to him. *Even though she's actually a nice person and everyone you know likes her? Even though she doesn't give a crap about you being transgender? Even though this week with her has been the best you can remember and being with her feels nothing like being with Lucette? Still sure you can't handle a good thing?*

What did any of that matter? She might be nice now, but so was Lucette at first. They'd had fun together like this. Just like this. And what if Evie, brilliant wicked Evie, turned sour like Luce did? Disappointed and angry and entrenched in hurting him? No way. He couldn't run that risk. The sheer idea of it was terrifying.

Numb, he went straight to the practice room after finishing his food.

She wasn't there. He was a little disappointed, and then felt stupid. Why was he disappointed when he was early and he'd seen her all of four hours ago, *and* he'd decided to end this not-so-casual thing between them?

He started stretching and moving around, shaking off the ballet of the earlier class. Memories from the morning flickered in front of him whenever he closed his eyes, so he tried not to do that too often. It was hard though, because he hadn't realized how much he'd missed having someone in bed with him. Having Evie there was beyond words—the way she'd burrowed next to him, like she really needed him; the way she'd gently touched him; the look in her eyes when she had flirted with him: that all had felt amazing. He'd forgotten just how sweet it was to lie with another person. Not to mention the feel of her body under his, the soft warmth of her mouth, the small noises she made when he touched somewhere sensitive, the smell of her hair and skin, and that hint at a little kink . . . *Goddamn.*

Nope, thinking about this morning definitely wasn't helping him. *Okay, Tyler, yes, it felt good, but you* know *physical means nothing.*

The door opened and he looked up eagerly—to see Mark stop short in the doorway.

"Oh, hey, Tyler." Mark blinked. "Guess I got the wrong room, huh?"

"Guess you did."

"Uh-oh. Gigi is going to whup my ass." He smiled. "You good, man?"

Mark didn't seem too upset at the idea of Gigi going postal. "Mostly. You?"

"Apart from an oncoming ass-kicking, yeah man, I'm fucking sweet. Check this out." He pulled out a massive mess of keys and key rings from his pocket. "Jean gave me this righteous key ring." Tyler could see the distinctive rainbow letters peeking out of the clutter.

"Oh, wow." Was Mark seriously lingering here to talk about the freaking merchandise?

Mark nodded. "Right, right? I got one for my little brother too. Have I told you about him? He's—" Startled by something, he looked down the corridor. "Yo, Evie!" he called, and Tyler's heart jumped. Mark turned back to him. "Heard you two were getting close, bro," he whispered approvingly. "I owe you a high five."

"Bye, Mark." Tyler couldn't help admiring Mark's sheer enthusiasm and cheerfulness. He was dancing with *Gigi* for fuck's sake—and enjoying it, apparently. It was like the *Odd Couple* with tap shoes. How did he do it?

Because Mark is good people. So's Evie. If Mark the Hetero Jock can be chill about dancing with a gay man, surely cisgender Evie will be cool with— He squashed that stupid persistent little voice because he'd made his decision already, damn it.

He got to his feet just as Evie stepped in. She closed the door with one hand, tossed her bag to the floor with the other, and without breaking stride, walked up to him and kissed him hard. Tyler's eyes rolled back into his head, and he gathered her closer to him, almost lifting her off her feet. She felt indescribably good.

She ended the kiss and smiled at him. "I missed you."

Such a dork. "Me too." They could both be dorks. He kissed her again. Shit. *Shit.* She was so happy she practically glowed.

"I've been looking forward to this since you left." Her fingers traced his jaw. "I can't believe it's the last practice session."

"Me either." His heart sank. He was going to miss doing this with her. "This has been a lot of fun."

She nodded, her face sombre.

The last session. Not even the cowering, anxious snake pit in his stomach wanted to ruin that. At least let him—let *them*—have this last session together. He put his hand over hers and brought it to his lips, stomach roiling. "Come on," he said. "Let's make it count."

Evie smiled sadly and spun away from him. He set up the MP3 player and hit Play.

It passed all too quickly. They blasted through the routine, executing it almost exactly the way he'd pictured it that first night in his apartment. Only, Evie was flesh and blood and making faces at him, rather than an imaginary partner who crackled in his arms, then evaporated when she was done. He really pushed her, realizing they finally had a slick performance. They actually had a chance of winning the stupid dance-off (if Cherry didn't school all of their asses). And he was thinking of wrecking this dynamic the day before the performance? The professional part of Tyler was screaming at him to reconsider.

So was the personal side, the part that wasn't quaking at the prospect of being emotionally tied down again.

Evie called a break, flopping down without waiting for him to agree. He crouched next to her, smiling at her sweaty red face. He'd miss this too, the way she sprawled out unapologetically when she was tired.

"You all right?" she asked him.

"Yeah. Why?"

"You look a little sad."

He reached and mussed her hair, earning a screech and a successfully distracted Evie.

"Do you two ever practise when we're not filming you?" Katie asked, freezing them in place.

Tyler held back a sigh. Another silent entrance by the Coen wannabes.

"Yo." Brock waved. He looked happy. Bastard.

"We do." Evie pulled her hair free and retied it with a sidelong glare at Tyler. He blinked innocently back at her, waiting for her to finish so he could tease it out again.

Katie crouched in front of them, Brock joining her and aiming the camera at their faces. The microphone was thrust in front of them. "How are you two feeling about the performance tomorrow?"

"Good but sad," Tyler said.

"Me too," Evie agreed.

"Sad? Why?"

Tyler glanced at Evie.

She blushed and said, "Because I've had a lot of fun doing this. I've met some wonderful people and learnt some new moves. But mostly," she poked him, "I won't ever have as good an excuse to spend this much time with a gorgeous dancer again."

He decided her hair could stay as it was.

"And what about you, Tyler?" Katie asked.

"I'm sad because tomorrow will be the last time I dance with Evie." He turned to her. "It's been a pleasure to teach you, Godzilla."

"It's been a pleasure to learn," she replied softly.

"Will you two keep in touch?" Katie asked.

"Yes," Evie said.

A lump formed in his throat.

Katie smiled. "What's been the worst thing about this experience?"

"Falling out of love with a really good song," Evie said darkly. "I used to like Jet."

Tyler forced the lump down. "Told you so," he said, voice only slightly raspy.

Evie raised an eyebrow. "Can I change my answer to 'Dealing with this guy's snark'?"

Oh. So that's how it's gonna be? Tyler grinned and tickled her. She tried to tackle him. They wrestled until they spotted Katie glaring at them, prompting them to sit up and straighten their clothes. Brock's grin threatened to split his face. Ass. He had too much to smile about.

"As I was saying," Katie said icily, "what was the best thing about this?"

Tyler felt himself go red. He glanced at Evie. She was blushing too.

"Meeting her," he said just as she blurted out, "Meeting him." They looked at each other in surprise, then turned away, embarrassed.

The side of Katie's mouth jumped upwards. She suppressed it with visible effort and asked a few more questions. Evie took his hand and he held it tight, not quite able to make himself let go.

Finally, Katie sat back. "That's it for today. We're going to watch you practise some more, then we'll be on-site tomorrow. We'll just be in the background, filming you and your interactions with the other couples. I might ask a few questions, but we'll play it by ear."

She and Brock retreated to the side of the room, and Tyler was left sitting next to Evie, hands clasped together and more than a little nervous.

"Bollocks," she said suddenly.

He jumped. "What?"

"I should have said that I enjoyed getting to know you." She'd gone fully red and wasn't meeting his eye.

He squeezed her hand. "Me too, Evie."

She leaned against him. "I don't want this to stop," she whispered.

Oh *God*. Tyler stood with a heavy heart. "Let's get back to it, Godzilla."

She stood reluctantly and moved to the centre of the room. Tyler watched her go, imprinting her figure into his brain. He didn't want to ever forget the image of her taking her space in the practice room, reflections of her poised and centred in the mirrors.

He sighed and pressed Play.

The end of the session came too quickly. Katie and Brock left soon after the interviews, so Tyler and Evie were alone for almost two hours. Two hours that were spent moving together and apart like clockwork. The steps were down, they could do it to the music, and Tyler couldn't be happier with how it had come together.

Then why did he feel so fucking *heavy*? And why, when he noticed the clock inching closer to the hour, did he slow down? It was like he couldn't separate his professional side from his personal one, not for this. He watched himself come to a stop during a run-through, causing Evie to pause in the middle of the quick footwork and frown at him.

"Okay, seriously, what's wrong?" she asked.

I can't do this.

"It's hard to think about this ending." Air wasn't reaching his lungs. He forced a deep breath.

She gave him a small smile. "I know, it sucks. I'll miss dancing with you. But it's not for forever. I'll be back in the autumn."

Seriously, how had he missed that? "I know."

Her eyes lit up. "I took Jean's membership offer. I thought it would be good to continue dancing when I get back."

Tyler froze. Shit. Right. Jean had made her that offer. He'd forgotten. And she'd be hanging around here.

This is my space. And you weren't supposed to be here in a year's time.
Evie frowned at him and reached for his hand. "Ty?"

"You know, I didn't fully catch that part at first," he confessed.
"That you were coming back this fall."

Evie scoffed. "Really?" She shook her head. "You didn't miss too
much. Only that I'm, you know, moving here and doing a master's
and starting my life afresh. Nothing major." She bumped his shoulder
playfully. "So I'll be bumming around, pretending to study. Lots of
free time to dance here. I'll be able to see you. We could maybe, if
you're interested, keep doing this. Sound all right?"

No. Yes? But what if what if what if . . . No. He couldn't. Words
fluttered in his head, trapped and useless. Evie's teasing smile faded the
longer he didn't respond.

"Oh," she said softly. "Not all right." She took his hands in hers.
"Tyler, what's wrong?"

"Casual," came out. He cleared his throat. "We were supposed to
keep this casual."

Evie frowned. "I know we agreed on that, but after the last few
days and this morning, I thought . . . Didn't things change?"

His gut clenched. *I should never have checked on her in the
bathroom.* "Yes. No. Shit." He dropped her hands and crossed his
arms. "This is too much. This wasn't what I was expecting."

Evie stared at him, hurt and surprise crossing her face. "You
weren't saying that this morning."

"This morning I thought you were leaving for good next week."

"Oh. *Oh.* So this—" she gestured between them, heat building
in her voice "—was only okay because it was short-term? 'Whatever,
she's only around for a week, what's the harm'?" She was angry now.
"This isn't a shitty holiday rom-com, Tyler. I know we said casual, but
my feelings for you are definitely not casual." Her eyes bored into his.
"And I think you feel the same way."

Of course he did. That wasn't the problem. "It doesn't matter."

"It does matter!" Those hands fluttered in the suddenly wide
space between them. "Why would you say something like that? Tyler,
where is this coming from? What happened between breakfast and
now?" Her hands stopped in midair. "Have you felt like this all this
time? Through Katie's questions today? What the hell?"

So much anger. And too many questions. Too hard to even attempt to answer them. And she'd still be mad, so what was the point?

He shrugged.

Evie made a choking noise. "I don't understand. This thing that's happened with us, it *does* matter. This is important."

Tyler couldn't feel his body. "And what about when this thing fades? When it ends?"

Evie looked confused now. "When it ends? What does . . . Are you saying you don't think we can do a relationship?"

"Basically, I'm saying it's better if we don't. It's too much and I can't. I just can't do it again. Not now, and not with you."

The moment the words slipped out, he wished he could take them back. The horrible look he remembered from the bathroom froze her face—the same hollow, kicked expression. "But . . . this morning . . ." She trailed off, sucking in a sharp breath.

"That came out wrong."

Who knew blue eyes could blaze as fierce as the sun? "I think that came out exactly the way it was meant to," she snapped. "'Not with me.' Let me guess, the sex thing? I don't give a shit about putting out, so that's not doable long-term? I got it, Tyler. Loud and clear." She turned away and picked up her bag.

Words escaped him. His stomach felt like it was about to drop out of his body. He opened his mouth to say something, anything, to stop her, to explain, but nothing came out. Evie paused and looked at him, her posture slumped. "I'll see you tomorrow for the performance. Don't worry, I'll show up and do it, but don't expect me to be happy to see you."

And she left.

Tyler stood in the middle of the room, his head spinning. He'd done it. He'd saved himself from the possibility of Lucette version 2.0. He was free to pursue his career on his terms, free to help Shana, free to do whatever he wanted.

Why wasn't he relieved, then? Why did he feel like crying?

His phone buzzed, and he almost threw it across the room.

Evie sat on her sofa bed, wrapped up in a blanket. Bailey pressed a glass of wine into her hand, and she took a grateful gulp. Sarah sat on the rug, sorting through DVDs.

She'd never considered herself a particularly violent person, but the moment Tyler had said he couldn't keep this going, she'd wanted to throttle him. After the sweetness of the past week, it was like receiving a bucket of ice water in the face. The worst part was that she didn't get it. He'd done a complete one eighty in a few hours. That morning he'd been kind and close and almost lov— *Stop* right *there, madam.*

But he had been wonderful. Evie cringed to remember how she'd cried and the things she'd said, and how he'd taken all that upset and made it okay. What had happened since then? Where had that considerate, sweet person gone?

"Men are faithless," she said morosely.

"Damn right," Sarah replied, holding up two DVDs: *Mulan* and *The Room.* "Well?"

"*Mulan*? Really?"

"I take my Disney feminist representation where I can."

"Let's watch *The Room*." Evie eyed her glass. "I'll drink every time a man says something stupid."

Sarah waggled her finger at her. "Nooo you don't. You still have a dance to perform tomorrow. You're allowed another glass, on account of Tyler being a jerk, but no more." She turned and inserted the DVD.

Evie eyed the wine. "Was it bad of me to expect more from him?" she asked quietly.

"Judging from what you've told me?" Sarah settled next to her. "No. Things changed."

"But I'm not good at judging these things."

"Who told you that?" Sarah narrowed her eyes. "Is that coming from your mom?"

Evie pursed her mouth. "No, life. I've misinterpreted feelings and intentions in other relationships and friendships before. I get things wrong. I can't help thinking I read too much into what we said this morning."

Sarah took her hand. "Oh, honey, you really liked him, didn't you?"

Evie nodded.

"And you two seriously clicked. We all saw that. So you acted on your feelings. And he . . . God, he ran away from his. Like he *always does*." She turned to Bailey, who sat on the other sofa. "You remember how he totally shut down for like a month after breaking up with Lucette, but kept saying he was fine?"

"Yup."

"He was never good with feelings. Idiot." Sarah turned back to her. "He freaked out. That's what happened here. He freaked out and said shit he'll regret, and tomorrow you're going to dance with him and make him realize just how crappy he's been, and he's going to regret it some more. And probably freak out more. Jesus. I love the guy, seriously, but if this is how he's going to be, you're better off just backing away." Sarah seemed sad to say that about her friend, but Evie appreciated her honesty.

Gigi had said as much too. She'd run into him on her way out after practice. One look at her face and he'd marched her into the canteen, bought her a drink, and forced her to tell him what was wrong. Gigi, as it turned out, could be a very good listener when he wanted to be.

He'd also said it wasn't personal. Evie wasn't inclined to believe that, given Tyler had said he couldn't do anything more with *her* specifically. Big surprise. She took a large gulp of wine. People who knew about her asexuality (those she hadn't dated) had said explicitly she couldn't expect anything romantic if she didn't have sex out the gate. An ex had once told her she was wonderful, but her limits around sex weren't viable for anything long-term. That had *hurt*. Not least because it was wrong. Tyler hadn't even given her a chance. He'd just said his piece and shut down.

Remembering the argument sucked. How quiet he'd been, how solid and mute. Completely unmoving. Like he'd just shut down. *I can't do this. It doesn't matter.* Weird, defeated words.

Which was kind of at odds with the other time he'd had problems talking to her. When he'd told her over lunch about his ex and the way she'd messed with him, he'd had problems shaping sentences and being clear about what he needed to say. So, Evie could understand that part. But at lunch he hadn't let that stop him. He'd powered through. There'd been hope in his face.

So what had happened today? Why had he shut down like that? Granted, she probably could have helped by letting him take his time to speak, but God, she'd been so upset. And he'd just *stood* there.

If this was some leftover psychological mess from Lucette, Evie was going to buy a ticket to Vancouver and snap all her bones into tiny little fragments, then return to Toronto and shake sense into Tyler until he got over whatever the problem was. Because she wanted to be with *him*, not him and the aftermath of his ex-girlfriend.

Though that didn't look likely right now. If at all.

And fuck if that didn't hurt almost as much as having all of *her* bones snapped into pieces.

On the screen, stock footage of San Francisco rolled to brooding, tinny intro music. In her pocket, her phone buzzed. Evie pulled it out and saw another email from her mother. Oh, wonderful. *Just* what she needed.

"Tyler?" Bailey asked.

"My mum."

"What, two shitty messages in a day weren't enough?" Sarah muttered.

Evie ignored her. There was a photo of Richard, Helena, and Doug at the table with scones and cakes around them. Shep was visible in the background. Her stomach clenched at the sight of him.

This is everyone at tea! I redid the kumquat tart for Helena, and she loved it. Richard says his work is hiring, perhaps you could join it instead of doing that course? Think about it. I also tried out a new cake recipe: ginger and saffron cake, and it went down a treat. I want to win next month's WI competition. I know you're not much of a baker, but do send any recipes you come across, will you? Your father says—

Evie abruptly closed her eyes. The intro music of the movie faded into the first scene and people started talking. She didn't want to keep reading this email. She was meant to be drowning her sorrows in wine.

And damn it, she was going to do that. Drown in this glass and the next one, then she'd sniffle herself to sleep, and she'd wake up in the morning and do the stupid performance. She'd be polite to Tyler, but only because there was nothing else she could be right now.

Then she was going to enjoy her last days in Toronto with her friends. Reading daily messages about her mother's baking adventures wasn't conducive to any of that.

She opened her eyes and began typing.

Mum, I can't tell you how much I'm looking forward to studying here in Toronto. The people are welcoming and the city is exciting and I've already seen the university. The course director gave me a tour. I CANNOT wait to be here. Also: I've been having dance lessons. Not ballroom, modern dance. That YouTube video you showed me? That was me. I'm doing a performance tomorrow and once I'm back, I'll send you a video of it. It'll be at Pride, so be prepared for rainbows. Hug Shep for me, as I won't get a chance to say good-bye in person due to your appointment scheduling. Please check your email for the multiple copies of my flight itinerary I sent you before I left. I don't have time to hunt recipes for you. My phone will be off until I'm home. I'll see you when I get back.

She pressed Send and put her phone down. Sarah cast her an inquisitive look. Evie only smiled and picked up her wineglass. She settled back to watch the worst movie she'd ever seen, tossing everything else out of her mind.

Tyler sat in his living room and eyed his phone. Gigi had sent demanding texts while Sarah had left a voice message asking if he was okay and if he needed to talk. Ignoring them all, he'd staggered home, showered, and eaten. Now he stared at the luminescent square of his laptop screen, totally ignoring whatever show he'd put on, and debated with himself.

As the day had edged into evening, he'd felt more and more conflicted about what he'd done. Now that his panic had faded, Tyler could step back and say that *maybe* he'd acted somewhat hastily. He could have handled confronting Evie better. The hurt on her face haunted him, as did the way he'd stood there without explaining himself properly. Especially about her last remark on sex; he hadn't considered that *at all*. Hadn't considered that maybe she had damage of her own to deal with.

The worst part was that the expected sense of relief had never arrived. Sorrow and guilt and anger swam around, but no relief and none of the release he'd felt when he walked away from Lucette. *So what the hell was all that for, Ty?*

Facing the music seemed easier than facing that question. He paused the video and picked up his phone.

Gigi: *Sooo, Evie's upset and I bet you're upset too. Meet me in the canteen.*

Gigi: *Dude, seriously, where are you??!?*

Gigi: *Fine, you're busy, w/e. I'm not seeing Brock tonight. CALL ME.*

Gigi: *Hey, Ty. How are you? Before you ask, I'm just sitting here, at home, all alone, thinking of the cock I've sacrificed for you and wondering why. CALL ME.*

Gigi: *CALL*

Gigi: *ME*

Gigi: *Fine. Don't call me. Just don't back off like after the Bitch-Who-Shall-Not-Be-Named. Evie is nothing like Überbitch and if she was, you'd have noticed because I'd have told you. You've been happy and I like seeing that. Get with the girl.*

Gigi: *And I'M the one telling you that. Jfc, take the fucking hint already. Suck it up (>:D) and apologize because you deserve someone nice. You're being fucking stupid.*

Gigi: *Btw I'm meeting Mark for pre-performance coffee tomorrow, so you're on your own for the coffee run, which frankly is the least you deserve after upsetting Evie like that.*

A lump rose in Tyler's throat. Gigi was wasted on him. More remarkably, Gigi was right.

His fingers hovered over the phone. Instead of selecting Gigi's name, he scrolled down to Shana's number and pressed that. As it was officially past 11 p.m., he braced himself and held his phone to his ear.

"'Llo?" She sounded tired. "Everything okay, bro?"

She wasn't mad at being woken up. Good start. "Sorry if I woke you. I have to ask you something." He took a deep breath. "You know the girl? Evie."

Silence.

"Evie? You know? My temporary dance partner. That girl."

"Oh my God. *Oh my God.*"

He was almost scared to ask. "What?"

"My little brother is calling me up *again* for girl advice. Jesus. I'm glad I'm already lying down."

"Shana . . ."

Rustling noises indicated she was getting comfy. "Okay, kid. Come at me. Big sister, ready."

Uuuggghhh. Why were older sisters allowed to exist? "Listen. Would you say my judgment in women sucks?"

"How would I know? You've never told me about the girls you've dated before."

Not until he was with Lucette. Then she'd certainly heard about her. Surely Luce was evidence enough his judgment was terrible. He closed his eyes. "I'm asking because I broke it off with Evie, and I'm not so sure it was the right thing to do anymore."

Shana gave a soft sigh. "Why was it the right thing to do in the first place?"

Tyler's head sagged against the sofa cushion. "I found out she's coming back in the fall. She's moving here to do a master's. She mentioned maybe continuing things, and I . . . I mean, what if she's another Luce?"

"*Is* she another Luce?"

He slumped low on the sofa. "If I didn't notice it with Lucette, how would I notice it with Evie?"

"Pretty sure you'd notice that shit again. *Do* you think she's another Lucette?"

"No," he admitted. "Probably not."

"Does Gigi like her?"

"Yeah."

"Wow. Ty, that's a sign." More rustling down the line. "How did she react when you broke this thing off?"

Guilt curdled his insides. "She got confused and upset. Mad. She told me she didn't understand why. When I said something I shouldn't have, she just left." He cringed at the memory. "I said I didn't want to be in a relationship again and not with her."

Pause. "Tyler, I love you dearly, but that would upset me too."

"I didn't mean it! It came out all wrong." He slumped lower, miserable. "I meant that—that, she's so fun and sweet and great, right? And if things turned toxic, I wouldn't be able to handle that. Seeing her turn all . . . hateful. I don't want her hating me. And I don't want to hate her."

"Oh, Ty." There was a wobble in Shana's voice. "Baby, relationships aren't meant to be like that, you know? Lucette's the example of how things shouldn't be, not how they actually are. Remind me again, how did Lucette react when you broke up with her?"

He scowled and slid onto the floor. "She laughed at me. Then she said I was"—*a total pussy*, but he hadn't told anyone that because those words were poison on so many levels he wasn't sure he could even begin to process them—"nothing without her. That I wouldn't last a week, and I'd be back in no time." He'd walked out shaking with fear and adrenaline, a death grip on his suitcase and his laptop bag. Slamming a door had never felt so good.

"And Evie did what, again?"

He gave in to a heavy sigh. "Okay, I get it."

"Do you? Because here's the thing about people: they don't change. They reveal themselves. So maybe you didn't see the manipulative, life-sucking succubus that was Lucette's inner self at first. So what? Now you would. And all right, you've known this woman a week. But the way Evie reacted sounds like someone who was honestly pissed at you, let you know it, then did what you wanted by walking away, so I think you're safe there. Relatively speaking."

He shifted so he was more comfortable on the floor. "You think being with Evie would be different."

"That's a no-brainer. Yeah. I think Lucette has warped what love looks like to you." She paused. "As far as I can tell, Ty, this issue you're having isn't even about Evie. It's about you."

Tyler had just realized the same thing. "Yeah, I got that." He took a deep breath. "I'm scared." His voice cracked.

"No shit. It's understandable, bro. You went through some nasty times."

"And I was better." He stared up at the blotches on the ceiling. "I was feeling okay and getting my life back. Then Evie stepped on a freaking dance machine and kind of blew me away. I wasn't expecting something *real*, you know?"

"Yeah, Ty. I know. So what do you do now?"

It was a leading question. They both knew what he had to do. Lying there on the floor, letting his body sink into the hard boards, Ty swallowed. "I have to apologize. Then tell her everything I just told you."

"That's my little brother." She sounded proud.

"And maybe get a therapist."

Amusement curled her voice. "Might help, yeah."

Imagining the next day, explaining to Evie just how extensive the network of crap in his head was, sent a heady rush of hope through him. Hope and sheer nerves. "I'm not good with words, Shan. It's not going to be easy telling her this stuff." Maybe he had some cue cards lying around.

"This stuff isn't easy to figure out or to talk about. You're doing great, bro. And you'll do great tomorrow."

"Do you think she'll take me back?"

"I don't know. It's up to her. But," she still sounded proud, "you can be irresistible when you want to be."

"Thanks."

"Can I share something with you? I'm a little envious." Her voice turned sad. "I think you two have your shit more together than Ray and I ever did. And you're not even a couple."

Ty sat up, instantly defensive. "Ray being a total dick-bag is not your fault, Shana."

"Yeah, well. I know that. I just wanted what he was offering even though I knew better."

He could relate to that so hard it wasn't funny. "I hear that."

"You feeling better, baby?"

"Yeah. Thank you."

"Good. Go get her. Catch me up tomorrow."

They hung up. Tyler sat on the floor, almost vibrating with restrained energy. He wanted to call Evie right away. He wanted to run out and get the streetcar to Sarah and Bailey's place and clear things up in person, so he could see her and touch her. But it was close to midnight and neither of those gestures would be appreciated.

How could he sleep now?

Gigi's and Shana's words echoed through his head: *"This is about you. Lucette has warped what love looks like to you. You've been happy. Evie is a good thing. You're being fucking stupid."*

Evie's betrayed expression flashed into his head. *"I'm not good at judging situations like this. I thought you liked me. This morning was anything but casual."*

"You're perfect exactly the way you are."

Tears threatened. She'd said that completely unprompted. Like she'd read his mind and said what he'd needed to hear. Like she was that good a person she really believed it. Perhaps he'd waited so long to hear someone say it to him, hearing it had sent him into shock. Perhaps he thought he really didn't deserve that kind of unconditional love. She hadn't misgendered him or made him feel unsafe or like he was worthless because he dared to live the way he wanted to. She hadn't belittled him or thrown gendered slurs at him or made him feel like shit at all, not even when he'd upset her. Hadn't he told himself after Lucette to find someone who said what she thought? Evie was honest and sweet and magnificent. Wasn't *she* perfect as she was? Didn't she deserve someone who saw her for *her* instead of the labels too?

He'd made a huge mistake.

Tomorrow. Tomorrow he would talk to her before the performance. Hopefully he'd be able to claw back some of their fledgling happiness and promise. Hopefully he'd be able to make this right.

CHAPTER TEN

Evie eyed the stage on Church Street twenty minutes before the advertized performance time. The sun was strong on her hair, the air was extra hot with cooking from nearby stalls, and everyone was smiling. People streamed around her, enjoying the street festival. Sarah, Bailey, Vaughn, and his boyfriend, Jonah, flanked her, sporting beads and Pride flags and glitter. It felt good to have supporters.

She had debated on the best way to handle this, and could feel herself falling back on the British method: ignore the awkwardness and sheer embarrassment of yesterday by being unfailingly polite and aloof. She'd say hello, dance with him, say good-bye, and never speak to him again. She was also going to ignore how upset the idea of never speaking to him again made her, because she was going to be *just fine* without him.

It helped that she hadn't seen Tyler yet, so she could still hope it would work.

Seeing how the crowd was swelling around the stage suddenly put their romantic drama out of mind. There were a *lot* of people here. Was she really going to dance on that stage? At Pride? In another country? With a man for whom she definitely had *no* feelings *whatsoever*?

Why had she agreed to do this again?

"You ready?" Sarah asked her.

"No."

Bailey's phone buzzed. They glanced at it, nudged Sarah, and tilted their head at Evie.

"Um," Sarah said.

"Tyler?" Evie asked.

"Yeah." Bailey frowned down at their phone.

"No."

Sarah exhaled. "I really think you should turn your cell on and at least read the messages he's sent you. He wanted to meet you before the show."

"Doesn't matter." She had kept her phone off since messaging her mum. Evie didn't want to deal with her or Tyler. As she had no choice about one of them, she was determined to avoid the other until she went home. She refused to think about what Tyler could want to say to her.

Vaughn squeezed her shoulder. "Nervous?"

"No."

He laughed, and rightly so because who was she kidding? She steeled herself. "I'm going in."

"Good luck," Vaughn said. "Not that you'll need it." Beside him, Jonah gave her a thumbs-up.

Evie took a deep breath and walked to the side of the stage. She gave her name to the official, who let her into the backstage area. It was a pavilion with lots of quirky people running around doing important-looking things. She spotted Brock and Katie filming the general scene. Derek and Jean stood with Justine Cherry and a Pride staff member. Gigi was nearby with Mark, and she walked over to them.

Gigi stood and gave her a slow once-over. "Killer," was the verdict.

She'd decided to wear something revealing yet comfortable, and that turned out to be high-waisted shorts, a low-cut top currently hidden by an off-the-shoulder jumper, and sneakers. Her character was meant to be powerful and active and desirable, so she thought she'd work the look.

"You don't scrub up half bad yourself," she said.

Gigi preened. He and Mark were dressed in black tie. The pair of them struck a suave image, but Evie had no idea if their dance would live up to their costumes.

"Frannie said I looked sharp," Mark said happily.

"Oh, honey," Gigi said, straightening Mark's lapels. "Take it from a gay man, you do."

"Thanks, bro!"

Evie raised her eyebrows. Gigi had almost been *affectionate* there. "Where is your girlfriend?" she asked him.

"Out front with a camera and my little bro," Mark said. "She's going to tape it so I can show my mom."

Oh bloody hell, *bless* the boy. Evie almost pinched his cheeks but stopped herself.

Gigi's attention had been caught by someone behind Evie. "Oh my God. We look sharp, you look hot, and Carmen looks . . ."

Evie turned. Carmen and her partner, Claude, walked past in heels and dresses, looking more like models than dancers.

"Wow," Evie breathed.

Mark grinned, his gaze following them. "I know, right?"

Gigi's lip curled. "I can dance in higher heels than those."

"We're good, man. We got the game in the bag." Mark turned back to Evie. "Where's Tyler?"

Evie shrugged, making sure it was casual. "Not sure."

Gigi's eyes narrowed. "One sec, Mark." He beckoned Evie over to the side of the tent and leaned in. "He was waiting for you outside. Didn't he message you?"

"I haven't turned my phone on today," she admitted.

"Cold but fair." Gigi studied her closely. "You doing okay, sugarplum?"

She couldn't help smiling. "I'll be fine, Gigi. I'll do this dance with him and that will be that."

"We'll see."

Evie noticed a gaggle of fit-looking people on the other side of the pavilion. Judging by how they were dressed and stretching, she figured they were the Cherry Studios lot. They glanced over at Evie and Gigi like sharks eyeing potential prey. Two women were dressed in sequinned ball gowns, two men in street clothes like her, and another male pair were dressed in heels and leather. She felt like she'd fallen into a dance movie.

"Assholes," Gigi muttered, following her gaze. "Stuck up rich kids whose parents can afford their tuition and bills."

"Gigi, sportsmanship is a virtue," Evie said. One of the women eyed her outfit and openly sneered. Evie bristled. "That said, this *is* a competition."

"Gigi?"

They turned. Mark stood there looking a little forlorn. "Man, I know we've gone over it lots of times, but I'm super bugging out and, like, can we practise one more time?"

Gigi rolled his eyes and nodded. They walked out of the pavilion for some privacy. Evie looked around for Ty— No, someone else to talk to. Jean caught her eye, but before she could talk to her, a Pride organizer stepped into the tent. "Dancers on in ten minutes! Directors to the stage!"

Evie's skin prickled. Awkwardness would be better than standing in line alone. She walked to the entrance, intending to look for Tyler, when he rushed in and almost collided with her.

Seeing him sent a shock through her, and she stepped back. He looked good, as always—hair back, clothes fitting close to his lean body, those gorgeous brown eyes . . . *You know what he looks like, Evie.* Yes, she knew, but it didn't explain why he took her breath away.

He stared at her, eyes wide, chest heaving. Neither of them seemed able to speak.

"We're on in ten minutes," she managed at the same time that he said, "Have you warmed up yet?"

Abashed, they both looked away.

"*There* you two are!"

Their heads snapped to the side. Jean smiled tightly at them. "They're lining the dancers up. Derek and Justine are on stage. Go on. What's with those faces? I hear you've got this down. You'll do great."

Evie couldn't look at Tyler. He moved stiffly past her, and she followed. As she passed Jean, she could've sworn she heard her mutter, "Cheer up. Half an hour and this farce will be over." When she looked back, Jean was walking towards a side exit of the pavilion, face inscrutable.

The dancers gathered together near the stairs to the stage. It was set up facing Church Street, and their pavilion was hidden at the back. Another organizer told them their time slot was short, so the acts would run one directly after the other. He lined them up in order of billed appearance: the Cherry Studios women wearing ballroom outfits, Gigi and Mark, the leather heel-wearers, Evie and

Tyler, the male couple who were dressed like Evie and Tyler, and finally Carmen and Claude.

Gigi glanced back and gave them a thumbs-up. Evie waved, then glanced at Tyler. He looked nervous. They stood directly next to each other, but the space seemed insurmountable. Evie took it back: standing alone in line was *definitely* better than this awkwardness.

On the stage, Derek and Justine were talking about their studios, the privilege of showcasing their dancers, and the joys of including queer people amongst their staff and students. Justine in particular was expounding at great length about the qualities of her school. In line, the dancers were stretching.

Tyler cleared his throat. "We need to warm up."

Evie nodded, throat thick, and started moving mechanically. God, this was going to be terrible. They couldn't dance like this. Not if they couldn't at least speak to each other. But having that conversation *here*? Standing in line between leather-bound muscles and street cool?

Derek interrupted Justine and started waxing lyrical about QS Dance.

Now or never. She straightened from a hamstring stretch and turned to him.

He was already looking at her. "Evie," he said softly. "I'm sorry."

"What for?" she asked. "You can't help the way you feel."

He shook his head, then glanced around. "Can we step out for a bit?"

Goodlordthankfuck yes. They took three steps away from the line before being ushered back into it by an organizer. "Stay here," he said. "We have to be *really* quick because we're officially running over time now."

Onstage, the MC had tactfully taken the microphones from Derek and Justine. The crowd clapped as Derek and Justine descended from the stage, stiff-backed and barely looking at each other.

"I didn't know you cared," Evie overhead Derek say to Justine.

"And I didn't know your vocabulary was that extensive," Justine replied sweetly.

The opening bars of the first couple's song struck up, and the ballroom dancers took the stage in a whirl of sequins. Evie's stomach churned. "We better make this quick," she hissed at Tyler.

He grabbed her hand. Surprised, she gaped at their hands, then at him.

"I'm sorry," he said again. "I'm sorry about what I said yesterday. Knowing you were coming back took me by surprise because it meant this thing between us could become *real*, and I got scared."

Evie was suddenly all ears. "Scared?"

"Yeah. You know my last relationship messed me up. That was me being messed up."

Hope fluttered in her, fiery and raw. "Why didn't you *tell* me that? All you said was you couldn't do this anymore and you didn't want me."

On the edges of her peripheral vision, she saw the street dancers nudge each other. Gigi kept glancing back. Tyler kept his eyes on her, however.

"That was fear talking."

Evie closed her eyes for a second. She'd heard that before. "You know, that's the second time you've said one thing to me, then told me the next day you didn't mean it."

He huffed in frustration. "I know, but it's something I'm going to work on."

She pulled her hand out of his. "Yes, well, you don't need me around for that."

The organizer was monitoring his watch. Onstage, the dancers did their routine, a quickstep with lots of flourishes and longing looks. Their song ended, and Evie turned around just as the organizer waved Gigi and Mark on. "Good luck," Evie hissed down the line.

Gigi glanced back and winked at her. "You too." Then he sashayed onto the stage past the ballroom dancers leaving it. He held his hand out to Mark as a heavily dubstepped remix of Frank Sinatra's "I Won't Dance" started.

"Evie."

Evie swallowed and tried to focus on Gigi and Mark. They were surprisingly good. She'd worried what Gigi would make Mark do; she'd imagined heels and hooker eye shadow at one point. But no, Gigi had choreographed a clever, slick routine straight out of a fifties movie. He'd clearly drawn a lot of moves from the Rat Pack era, and the two of them danced circles around each other.

"Evie!"

"*What?*" she snapped, looking at him.

Tyler glared at her. "I *do* need you around. And I'm not finished. I was scared you'd come to hate me the way Luce did. I was scared I wasn't enough for you. I was scared of being hurt again. I was scared and I pushed you away and I'm sorry."

One of the dancers behind her murmured, "Dude, this is better than TV."

Fucking Lucette. "You know, your ex is really starting to piss me off." Evie barely managed to keep herself from snarling at him. "Considering how smart you are, I'm having trouble understanding why you stayed with her."

"Because I wanted someone to love me for me and she said she did." His voice was hoarse. "I believed her because I didn't know better. Because I wanted to believe her. But it wasn't real and it fucked me over. You're real. *This* is real."

Oh God. *Oh God.* She was *not* going to cry here.

Onstage, Gigi pulled Mark into a hold and waltzed him around the stage, dipping him at the finale. The audience cheered and clapped enthusiastically, then gasped and screamed in appreciation as the Cherry Studios leather hunks took the stage. Evie and Tyler were now at the front of the line. Gigi and Mark stumbled down the stairs, grinning widely and high-fiving everyone.

Once they were past, Evie dredged up her courage to say, "How funny. I was starting to think I was in love with you. Look how that turned out." She couldn't quite meet his eyes after saying that.

One of the dancers behind her sucked in a breath. In front of them, the organizer's eyes flickered up from his watch.

"Really?" Tyler sounded like he couldn't believe it. "Evie, look at me. Please."

She somehow made herself do that. He seemed ready to cry.

"I'm not good at this, figuring this stuff out. Words, that is. I froze up and I didn't explain myself and I hurt you. *I'm sorry.* Here's what I should have said: this past week with you has been the best week I can remember in a long fucking time. You're kind and funny and beautiful and so fucking intelligent and you blew me away the first time I saw you. You were right—this isn't casual. This is so much more. You're amazing and I can't imagine you being here in Toronto and not being with me. I'm definitely falling in love with you. I want this to continue. I want *us*."

He swallowed. "But I'm scared too. I'm scared it will all go to shit and leave me wrecked again, and I don't think I could handle that. But I want to try because being without you would be worse." He looked around, then leaned in and whispered, "I don't know why you think I care about sex. I don't. We can figure that out later, but it doesn't matter to me. I just want you. In whatever way you'll have me."

Was this real? Evie was dimly aware that her mouth had dropped open. She closed it and swallowed, uncertain of what to say.

"Omigod," the Cherry Studios guy whispered behind her.

"Whoo, Tyler!" Carmen crowed from behind the Cherry Studios guys.

"Wow, this is actually like super ridiculously cute," the organizer said.

"And if you don't want to try again," Tyler's cheeks were dark with a blush, "I'll understand. But I really hope you do."

Relief and delight bubbled up. He was serious. He was *so* serious. Not one stutter or misplaced word. "How many times did you practise that speech?"

"You don't want to know." He searched her face anxiously. "Evie? Do you still want to—"

"Sorry to interrupt, but you're, like, on." The organizer waved at them.

"Are you fucking kidding me?" Tyler said before Carmen reached forward and shoved him towards the stairs.

Evie was suddenly lighter than she'd been all week. He still wanted her. It was just a stupid argument and misunderstanding. He was insecure too. Was it silly that she felt infinitely better now? She sprang onto the stage ahead of Tyler, passing between the leather guys as they bowed. Realization after realization churned in her head. Tyler was there. He'd figured his shit out and shown up.

Pure joy and energy thrummed through her as she strode towards the audience. *She could do this.* For possibly the first time ever, she understood what it felt like to be powerful and in control and completely on form. She blew kisses at the leather guys as they left the stage, ignored the dirty looks they shot her in return, and soaked in the applause from the crowd.

Tyler took his position. Glancing at him, she could instantly tell he wasn't happy. He was still waiting for her answer.

And she knew how to tell him without waiting for the end of the performance.

The opening bars started and she kicked into motion, the moves second nature now. The adrenaline from the crowd lent extra sway and power to her hips and legs, surging through her as she met Tyler in the middle of the stage. He took her hand with a hopeful expression that burned into her memory. They started moving together.

They tore through the routine, lifting and kicking and shoving at each other. Tyler's movements were tinged with desperation and Evie relished the knowledge that he moved so emotively because of her, *for her*. And he was there, ready, just as he had been in every rehearsal, lifting her, leading her, retreating from her, moving with her, partnering her. Gazing at her as though she was the only thing that mattered.

And this routine was seamless, as was her feeling of reconnecting physically with him in that electric way they had. Slowly, she bled off her character's aloofness. She gentled, softened towards him, expressing herself in the way he'd taught her.

He noticed.

Slipping out of a hold, she came to a stop opposite him in time with a gap in the music. Tyler reached out and hooked a finger in the belt loops of her shorts, eyes dark. The music began to drawl the second chorus, and she yanked her sweater off to reveal her top, which read *ASEXUAL PRIDE* in the flag colours, earning her a cheer from the audience. Tyler grinned and pulled her into the next segment. Blindingly quick footwork took them to the end of the tune and to her character sending Tyler's to his knees. Only, she wasn't sure they were acting anymore.

They stared at each other, wide-eyed and panting. Instead of walking away like the routine dictated, Evie put a finger under his chin to lift his face, leaned down, and kissed him. Hard. Then she marched off as the two street guys jumped on stage, high-fiving her as she exited.

Evie had never felt this alive in her life.

Tyler stood, electrified by the kiss, then raced after her. He barely noticed the two Cherry Studios guys in his haste to follow her down the stairs. *That dance.* The way she'd moved, the way she'd looked at him, the way she'd led and followed, equally and trustingly; it could only mean one thing right? One simple thing: *she said yes she said yes she said* yes.

He caught up with her at the bottom of the stairs and grabbed her around her middle, swinging her around. She shrieked, and when he set her down, she turned and poked him hard in the shoulder, glaring playfully at him. "I haven't totally forgiven you, you know."

He grinned at her. "Just so we're clear: that *was* a yes, right?"

She nodded. "Yes, Tyler. I want to be with you." Her eyes abruptly grew shiny. "I really do."

The organizer near the stairs let out an audible "Awww." Tyler started pulling her back to the pavilion, wanting space and some attempt at privacy. He could see Carmen and Claude eyeing them gleefully.

"But," Evie said as they walked, "you seriously need to tell me what you're feeling. Please don't freak out and break up with me every time something difficult happens."

That was legit. "I can do that. I meant it about working on that."

"All right." Her mouth twisted wryly. "And I'll make sure to give you time to speak. I don't think that happened yesterday."

His heart swelled. "For real. Therapy. I'll be all over this sharing shit by the time you're back in the fall."

Her mouth shook as if hiding a smile. "I still can't believe you didn't know I was coming back. You idiot."

"Yeah, but I'm your idiot now." He pulled her close and kissed her, revelling in his freedom to do so. The fear was still there, but it flickered at the back of his mind, noticed but not fed. This felt good.

This felt *really* good. She was slightly sweaty, and wearing clingy clothing that emphasized how gorgeous she was, and she smelled amazing. Dizzy, he held on tighter.

She took a deep breath. "You know, we were bloody excellent up there."

He leaned back so he could look at her face. "We were fucking fantastic. All that practice—"

"Well, isn't this cozy," Gigi said behind them.

Tyler's eye twitched. God, couldn't they be left alone for five minutes? He turned around to see Gigi and Mark wearing matching tuxes. He'd been too occupied earlier to notice just how coordinated they were. "Oh hey," he said. "Monkeys in monkey suits."

Gigi snorted. "Cute. C'mere." He grabbed Tyler's arm and dragged him a short distance away. Evie and Mark eyed them in bemusement. Tyler braced himself. Gigi drew himself up. "One: that was a sick routine."

Tyler grinned. Yup, it totally had been. "Thanks."

"Was the shirt your idea?"

"Nah, hers." That had surprised him. It had surprised the crowd too. He noticed the organizer handing Evie her sweater; apparently he'd retrieved it for her.

"I figured. Two: thanks for sharing all that drama with the class." Gigi grinned. "I will be milking that story for *years*."

Oh *crap*. Tyler looked around to see organizers and Cherry dancers alike pretending not to watch him. "I don't think you'll be the only one."

"Three: congrats." Tyler was yanked into a tight hug. He blinked, then hugged his friend back.

"I should say the same for you and Brock," he realized.

Gigi made a garbled noise. "Shut up. I'm just happy you're with someone who's not another Überbitch."

"Likewise."

"Guys, watch this," Evie called.

They turned. Evie, Mark, and the other dancers were entranced by the dancers on the stage. He followed their gaze to see Carmen and Claude taking up dramatic, emotive poses. All long lines and serious expressions, and combined with the heels and dresses, they looked amazing. But something about the poses niggled at Tyler. He got it just as the music kicked in.

"No," Gigi gasped, realizing it at the same time.

"I know," Tyler said.

"What?" Evie asked.

"They're doing the Argentine tango," Tyler replied.

Evie's eyes went wide, and she looked back at the stage. They watched as Carmen and Claude stalked and wound themselves around each other, fierce and strong. Carmen blocked Claude with a parada, which Claude turned into a bone-melting pasada.

"How the fuck did they learn an Argentine tango routine in *one week*?" Tyler asked, not expecting an answer.

"It's unbelievable," one of the leather guys said.

"It's genius," Gigi breathed.

"It's hot," Evie said.

They all looked at her, surprised.

"I'm asexual, not blind," she pointed out blithely.

"Yeah," Mark agreed. "What she said."

Gigi glowered at the couple as they marched, dipped, and caressed each other's legs. Carmen stroked Claude's cheek with the back of her hand. "This is making me confused," he complained.

Tyler craned his head to check the audience and was fairly sure the crowd had doubled in size. Evie was right: the routine was fucking hot. It was also complicated, almost expert dancing, and if this didn't win it for QS, he wasn't sure what would. He went to Evie and wrapped his arms around her waist from behind. They watched Carmen and Claude finish to thunderous applause.

"Jesus Christ." One of the Cherry ballroom dancers whistled. "That's the competition in the bag. Nice one, guys."

The leather guys muttered darkly, one of them adjusting a delicately positioned strap while the other took his heels off with a sigh of relief.

Carmen and Claude curtseyed, then beckoned at them. The dancers crowded back onstage and jostled for a position in view of the crowd. Tyler held Evie's hand tightly, happy she stood in front of him. Performing in front of crowds wasn't a problem, but simply standing and being a focus of attention was a whole other issue.

The MC for the stage came up and blabbed on and on about Pride and the arts. Derek and Justine stood next to her, faces forced into big smiles. Tyler noticed Jean at the front of the crowd, distributing key rings. Dead centre in the crowd were Sarah, Bailey, Vaughn, and Jonah, waving and beaming.

"Even though every performance was absolutely stellar," the MC was saying, "we still have to judge the best dancers in this dance-off. Judges?"

Judges? Tyler had been so distracted he hadn't noticed the small stand near the stage. Several people he didn't recognize sat in there, drinking and looking mildly entertained. One of them walked onstage and delivered an envelope to the MC.

"Who are those people?" he asked Evie quietly.

"Didn't you read the paperwork?" she whispered back. "They're LGBTQ activists and journalists."

"The winners are Carmen and Claude, from QS Dance!" the MC announced. The crowd went ballistic as Carmen and Claude stepped forward and bowed. Derek's grin threatened to split his face in half as the MC handed them a plastic trophy. Tyler knew that trophy was going into the awards case near Derek's office and that Derek wouldn't shut up about it for the rest of the year.

"Oh, what a surprise," a nearby Cherry dancer griped.

Evie's hand tightened on his. "What do you say we get out of here?"

Best plan he'd heard in days.

They were delayed by the other dancers, who were shaking hands and commenting on each other's routines. They left the stage in one massive group, chatting and demonstrating moves. Somewhere along the way, he was separated from her, and Tyler found himself hugging Claude and Carmen at the same time. When he managed to get rid of them, he found Evie talking with the Cherry Studios street dancers near the exit of the pavilion.

Gigi intercepted him. "Hold your fire," he said. "You got any plans for this afternoon?"

"Yeah." Tyler itched to get past Gigi. "Take my girlfriend home and make up for being a jerk."

Gigi's eyebrow arched. "*Girlfriend*, eh?"

"Fucking A." Tyler noticed he'd changed out of the suit. "What are you going to do?"

"Brock said to hang around," Gigi pouted, "but I really, really want a cocktail right now."

Mark ran up to them excitedly. "Gigi, my little bro is here! Come say hi!"

Gigi's face *softened*. Tyler blinked, wondering if he was seeing things. Gigi kind of looked . . . maternal. And he wasn't even in drag.

"Oh. My. God. The time has come. Mark, honey," Gigi flung out his arm for Mark to take, "bring me to him."

Mark pulled Gigi to the fence separating the pedestrians from the stage area, to a teenager who shook Gigi's hand. Tyler had to pinch himself to make sure he wasn't dreaming. Gigi was being civil. To *Mark*. To Mark's family. What the hell? When had that happened?

It seemed this week had changed things for other people too.

"There you are," Evie said beside him.

He turned to her. "Ready to go?"

She nodded and clasped his hand. They grinned at each other and took four steps into the street before being mobbed by Sarah, Bailey, Vaughn, and Jonah.

"You were *awesome*!" Sarah shrieked, hugging Evie, then him.

"Wonderful," Vaughn added, beaming at Evie. "That was incredible. You learned that in one week?"

She grinned back at him. "Yeah! I can't believe it myself."

Jonah nodded beside Vaughn. "That was awesome."

Vaughn held up a camera. "I filmed you. Can I upload it to YouTube?"

Bailey was suddenly in front of Tyler. "You guys were totally boss," they said, fist at the ready. They bumped.

"I take it you two made up?" Sarah asked him, one eyebrow arched.

"Yeah." They had, but Tyler thought they probably had a bit more to do. "I got my head out my ass and apologized. We're good." And he was very abruptly done with all this socializing. *Done*. He and Evie needed to talk, they needed privacy, and they needed it yesterday. Definitely while he was on a roll with articulating his feelings.

Mostly, he needed to kiss her before he burst with all the feelings swarming inside him.

"Evie, we have to go," he said.

She patted Vaughn's arm. "Let's do coffee before I leave, okay? I'll be in touch."

"You're going?" Bailey asked. "Where?"

Evie took his hand, and Tyler grinned at them. "We'll see you tomorrow for the Pride march."

Sarah's jaw dropped. "Hey, what the—"

He pulled her away before any of them could stop him. Behind them, he heard Vaughn remark, "I'd say they more than made up."

"No shit, babe," Jonah replied.

Damn right, buddy.

Evie walked alongside him, eyebrows raised. "Not that I mind being alone with you, but where are we going?"

"If you agree," he said, "we're going to my place, where we will talk and eat and watch movies and hopefully make out a lot."

"*Oh.*"

"If you want to. The alternative is, I don't know, a park? A coffee shop? Wherever." He glanced at her, taking in her happy expression. He'd put that there. Why had he ever doubted this? "As long as we can talk without interruption."

She squeezed his hand. "I'd like to see your place." Her gaze turned wicked. "So, *just* making out?"

He felt himself blushing. "Um. Yeah. No pressure for more. Because that's something we need to talk about."

"You're right, but for the record, I think I'd be amenable to more."

Heat pooled in his stomach and his groin ached. She *did* like him. "Oh yeah? You said you were good with your hands."

A slow smile spread across her face. "I did indeed say that."

"I'm good with mine too."

Her hand squeezed his, and his heart soared.

They stopped at a junction, and while they waited for the lights to change, Tyler's phone buzzed. He took it out and turned it off.

EPILOGUE

Evie stared up at the baggage reclaim status board, wondering what the holdup was this time. She'd been sitting on the floor with her backpack for ten minutes already. The flight had been delayed too. Her fingers played with her pen instead of finishing the doodle she'd worked on throughout the flight. Cheap airline tea had her wired beyond belief, and she could already tell that four cups had been a bad idea. She was tired and excited and ready to cry from the anticipation.

She was finally back.

The last three months in England had been crazy. She hadn't thought they would pass as quickly or, at times, as slowly as they had. She'd broken her lease in York, cried over Shep, received the settlement from her old job, sorted her visa, met her parents' new dog, temped for her brother for a month, then packed up the things she needed for her course and new life in Toronto. Said good-bye to her friends. Made promises for visits home soon.

She'd spoken to Tyler almost every day. Quick, rushed chats as well as hours-long conversations about anything and everything, from the minutiae of their lives as they lived them on opposite sides of the Atlantic to what they wanted to do when she was back in Canada. Some days, all she'd wanted was to reach through the screen and hug him, but mostly they were great. Better than great. She was so lucky.

Queen-evazilla and *gaybeard-the-great* had reblogged photos from Toronto Pride, no doubt baffling those of their followers used to manga posts. Sarah had even sent her a dance magazine that had published a feature on Tyler, complete with the most gorgeous photos she'd ever seen. Tyler gazed out into the world, his focus sharp and his body stunning in its raw physicality. She'd stared at the pictures of him in awe, then in misery whenever she missed him. Part of her could barely believe that this powerful, fierce man was her boyfriend, and that he was waiting for her across the Atlantic.

It had been a dull, grey day when she'd arrived at Heathrow ten hours earlier with Rowena and Doug. She'd hugged her mother tightly, knowing she was going to miss her, even if she was insufferable at times. Rowena had sniffled into her shoulder and made her promise to call often and to stay off YouTube this time. Doug had hugged her stiffly and wished her luck.

Her backpack held her laptop and converter plug and a few other homey bits and pieces. Her massive suitcase contained clothes and important documents and British souvenirs. She was coming to a new country carrying everything on her. Another new experience, but one so welcome and freeing that her chest felt ready to burst.

The carousel started turning. She bounced to her feet. When her suitcase finally showed, she pulled it off with all her strength, then turned to the exit. It took serious effort not to run to the arrivals gate, but finally she was through.

She saw the signs first: a huge Godzilla poster drawn in green glitter attacking a massive *WELCOME BACK EVIE* sign, and an inflatable Godzilla with a sign around its neck saying, *THE QUEEN RETURNS*. Then she saw the heads of the people carrying those things.

The next thing she saw was Tyler Davis, sprinting towards her. He caught her up in a bear hug, and she clutched him close. His familiar scent, his hard body, his strong arms, his curly hair, *him*. She breathed him in. Real. Hers. Finally.

"Godzilla, what took you so long?" he said tightly.

A strangled sob escaped her, and she kissed him hard. "I missed you so much."

He smiled softly. "Me too."

"This is disgusting," Bailey said behind him.

"Oh my God, this is *too cute*." Sarah hugged both of them at once.

Tyler rolled his eyes. "I told them not to come, but they wouldn't listen to me."

Evie laughed and twisted her head to see a few more familiar people standing behind Bailey.

"Evie, it's great to see you." Brock waved. "But can you keep it moving?"

Ah. They were blocking the flow of people from Arrivals.

"Oh my fucking God," Gigi exclaimed, swatting at Brock with the inflated Godzilla. "She just got off a fucking plane, you animal." He handed the balloon over, then swanned to her and hugged her tightly. "Welcome back, babe."

She hugged him with genuine pleasure. "Hi, gorgeous."

He returned to Brock's side, practically glowing.

Vaughn came forward next, tucking the *WELCOME BACK* sign behind him. "Evie, it's wonderful to see you again." He smelt expensive and looked polished as usual. Evie had talked with him too, and occasionally his boyfriend, arranging field trips and gallery visits.

She managed to hide a grin at Tyler's annoyed expression, then was suddenly very close to crying. All these people had come to meet her at the airport. Sunlight streamed through the windows. Her course waited for her. The airport was familiar. There was glitter again.

Tyler cleared his throat as Sarah took Evie's suitcase. Evie looked at him as the group turned towards the doors. He held out the stuffed Godzilla to her.

"I kept him safe," he said shyly.

A lump rose in her throat. She'd given him the toy at the airport when she'd left. She'd tried to blot out the memory, but she was fairly certain she'd said something embarrassing like, "At least one Godzilla should get to hug you over the next three months."

"That you did," she managed, taking the toy and giving it a squeeze.

Tyler put an arm around her. "Of course I did. I'm glad the real one is back." He kissed her gently. "You ready for some new experiences?"

She leaned into him, looked at the faces of her friends as they bickered amongst themselves, and blinked back tears. The future beckoned, bright and exciting. Her face hurt from smiling. "Let's do this."

Explore more of the *Toronto Connections* at:
riptidepublishing.com/titles/universe/toronto-connections

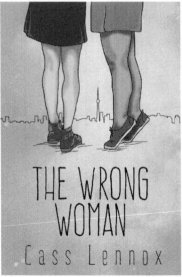

Dear Reader,

Thank you for reading Cass Lennox's *Finding Your Feet*!

We know your time is precious and you have many, many entertainment options, so it means a lot that you've chosen to spend your time reading. We really hope you enjoyed it.

We'd be honored if you'd consider posting a review—good or bad—on sites like **Amazon, Barnes & Noble, Kobo, Goodreads, Twitter, Facebook, Tumblr,** and your blog or website. We'd also be honored if you told your friends and family about this book. Word of mouth is a book's lifeblood!

For more information on upcoming releases, author interviews, blog tours, contests, giveaways, and more, please sign up for our weekly, spam-free newsletter and visit us around the web:

Newsletter: tinyurl.com/RiptideSignup
Twitter: twitter.com/RiptideBooks
Facebook: facebook.com/RiptidePublishing
Goodreads: tinyurl.com/RiptideOnGoodreads
Tumblr: riptidepublishing.tumblr.com

Thank you so much for Reading the Rainbow!

RiptidePublishing.com

ACKNOWLEDGEMENTS

I am endlessly grateful to my eagle-eyed editor, Chris Muldoon, for her insights and her support of this particular book.

Thanks to Riptide's staff for liking this book so much (even in its first, atrocious form).

I must also thank my housemates, R.M., A.D.G., and W.M., who put up with me failing to do chores because I'm editing; my Canadian friends, who remain my friends despite my many questions; and P.K. and A.B., whose understanding and patience is truly that of the divine.

ALSO BY CASS LENNOX

Toronto Connections
Blank Spaces
Growing Pains (coming soon)
The Wrong Woman (coming soon)

ABOUT THE AUTHOR

Cass Lennox is a permanent expat who has lived in more countries than she cares to admit to and suffers from a chronic case of wanderlust as a result. She started writing stories at the tender age of eleven, but would be the first to say that the early years are best left forgotten and unread. A great believer in happy endings, she arrived at queer romance via fantasy, science fiction, literary fiction, and manga, and she can't believe it took her that long. She likes diverse characters who have gooey happy ever afters, and brownies. She's currently sequestered in a valley in southeast England.

Blog: casslennox.wordpress.com

Facebook: facebook.com/Cass-Lennox-1704635609768647

Twitter: twitter.com/CassLennox

Enjoy more stories like
Finding Your Feet
at RiptidePublishing.com!

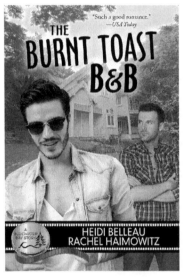

Made in the USA
Middletown, DE
05 February 2021

33127555R00151